"I WANT TO TOUCH YOU, KISS YOU . . . ALL OVER . . ."

Kit was waging an internal battle. Her brain commanded her to resist, to deny the longing in her heart, but her body refused to obey, wanting more . . . Never had she felt so drawn to a man.

He devoured her with his eyes and lips and fingers, and despite her turmoil, Kit's hands began to caress him, exploring the wonders of his magnificent body. His tongue moved down her throat as he nimbly unbuttoned her shirt, and her breasts became vulnerable to the hungry warmth of his mouth. She moaned deep in her throat and clutched him tightly against her.

He raised his head to gaze down at her, hunger evident in his eyes. "I want you, Kit, more than I've ever wanted a woman before . . . But I want more than your body, Kit . . ."

Avon Books are available at special quantity discounts for bulk purchases for sales promotions, premiums, fund raising or educational use. Special books, or book excerpts, can also be created to fit specific needs.

For details write or telephone the office of the Director of Special Markets, Avon Books, Dept. FP, 105 Madison Avenue, New York, New York 10016, 212-481-5653.

LOVE AND HONOR

PATRICIA HAGAN

AVON BOOKS NEW YORK

AVON BOOKS
A division of
The Hearst Corporation
105 Madison Avenue
New York, New York 10016

Copyright © 1989 by Patricia Hagan
Cover illustration by Robert McGinnis
Published by arrangement with the author
Library of Congress Catalog Card Number: 88-92979
ISBN: 0-380-75557-2

First Avon Books Printing: September 1989

AVON TRADEMARK REG. U.S. PAT. OFF. AND IN OTHER COUNTRIES, MARCA REGISTRADA, HECHO EN U.S.A.

Printed in the U.S.A.

K-R 10 9 8 7 6 5 4 3 2 1

For Helen P.
and eighteen years of zany and treasured friendship

LOVE and HONOR

Prologue

Paris
1895

A SOFT breeze wafted through the window, over-powering the medicinal smell of the hospital room with the sweet breath of spring.

Jade O'Bannon Coltrane lay quietly on the iron poster bed. Her eyes were closed, her long dark lashes feathering her pale cheeks. Even in her state of exhaustion, her rare and delicate Irish-Russian beauty was breathtaking to behold. She was royal, a Romanov by blood, and everyone who knew her agreed that she was as lovely in nature as she was in looks.

Jade was having her first child. She placed her hands on her swollen stomach as another contraction caused her to moan suddenly.

Colt Coltrane stared down at his wife. God, he loved her. To think that he had lost her once . . .

He shook his head, as if to cast away painful memories. That was a lifetime ago. Those turbulent times didn't matter anymore, because they were together now, and they always would be. Until a few hours ago, Colt had been eagerly looking forward to having their first baby, but something was wrong. It was too early—the baby wasn't due for another six weeks or so.

Colt tore his gaze from Jade and looked across the bed at his mother. Kitty Wright Coltrane was as magnificently lovely in her maturity as she had been in her youth. Her startlingly beautiful lavender eyes still sparkled with glints of gold, and her red hair still glowed like the fiery embers of sunset.

Kitty met her son's pleading eyes and solemnly shook her head. She could not give him the reassurance she knew he desperately wanted . . . and needed. The baby would be premature, tiny, and weak. The odds that it would survive were not strong. She did not, however, speak her negative thoughts. Instead she said, "I told you before, labor for the first baby always takes longer."

Colt nodded in resignation, looking down at his wife once more. Her eyes remained closed, and she was biting her lower lip to stifle a scream as the pain bore down. He reached out to hold her hands, whispering words of love and encouragement until the contraction subsided.

Jade began to breathe evenly once more, She looked up at him and whispered hoarsely, "She's right. It's going to take a long time. Please go and get some rest, something to eat."

Colt shook his head adamantly. "I won't leave you."

Kitty told him that he had no choice. "I'm surprised the nurses have let you stay this long. Having a baby is a very personal, private time for a woman.

"Now . . ." She walked around the bed and placed a firm hand on his shoulder. "You go home and see how your father is doing. No doubt he's pacing the floor. Get something to eat and rest for a while. When you come back you'll probably still have some time to wait . . . outside," she emphasized,

Just then the door opened and a nun wearing a nurse's starched white habit walked into the room carrying a cloth-covered tray. With an authoritarian tone, she introduced herself as Sister Fifine, then declared, "There are some things I need to do to prepare Madame Coltrane for the birth. I must ask you to leave." She looked at Colt impatiently.

"You couldn't have come at a better time." Kitty laughed. "I was just running him out."

"Please give me a minute with her . . . alone," Colt said.

The three women looked at him and saw that he was not to be dissuaded. Sister Fifine frowned. "One minute," she snapped, setting the tray down before stiffly walking out. Kitty followed, closing the door behind her.

Colt knelt beside the bed, clasping Jade's hands once more. "I love you, Jade. Believe that."

"And I love you, my darling." She lifted her hand feebly to push back a strand of his coal-black hair, smiling at the way he was looking at her with the intense gray eyes she adored. "This is the beginning—for our baby, for us, and for our future together. Nothing else matters."

Colt nodded absently in agreement as that strange feeling began to come over him again . . . the feeling that Jade was not as happy about the baby as she pretended to be. He thought it even stranger that when her labor had begun prematurely, she had actually seemed glad.

Jade licked her parched lips, took a deep breath, and held it against another rising contraction. Even though he heard the door opening, Colt did not move from her side until her latest pain subsided.

"Monsieur . . ." Sister Fifine said, sounding extremely agitated.

"Colt . . ." Kitty coaxed, her voice soft with compassion.

He leaned to kiss Jade one more time, then reluctantly backed toward the door. "I'm not leaving this building. I'll be outside." He winked. "I'm not leaving till John Travis Coltrane, Junior, arrives."

Jade managed a smile. "You mean when *Katherine Wright Coltrane* arrives!"

Kitty gave Colt a gentle push toward the door. "Katherine, or Travis, or whatever you name it, just be gone with you!"

Sister Fifine was not amused by their bantering. With a stern look at Kitty, she jerked her head toward the door and said, "If you please, madame, I should like for you to also leave us."

Kitty stiffened, raising an imperious eyebrow. "I certainly do *not* please! This happens to be my grandchild who is about to be born, and I've no intention of going anywhere until that happens."

Sister Fifine shook her head in resignation. She knew from the way Madame Kitty Coltrane's eyes flashed that she meant what she said. She replied haughtily, "That will be up to the doctor, but for now, I must ask that you wait outside until I finish what I must do."

Kitty blew Jade a kiss. "I'll see you in a little while. I'm going to try to talk this stubborn son of mine into going home for a while." Jade nodded her approval.

The instant the door closed behind them, Colt exploded. "Mother, I'm not going anywhere! Jade's having a rough time. You know as well as I do that it's too early for the baby, and it might not live.''

"I won't lie to you," she replied. "We may lose the baby, but we won't lose Jade. She's young and strong, and there will be other babies. Think that way, Colt—and let's pray it will all soon be over.''

"I won't lose her again. I swear it . . .''

Daylight turned to dusk, then night fell like a velvet drape against the glittering, diamond-studded sky over Paris, the City of Light.

Within the hospital, all was quiet. Around midnight, a trio of heavyset, grim-faced nuns had escorted Colt to a waiting room out of sight and hearing of the maternity ward. He found himself sitting alone in a small, cheerless room, furnished only with rows of wooden benches. There were no windows, and only a large crucifix hung on the wall.

Every so often his mother would come to tell him the same thing—that they still didn't know when the baby would be born. Finally he exploded and told her not to come back until it was all over, because every time he heard the door open, his heart leaped into his throat. It was better, he thought, when a woman gave birth at home, but the elite of Paris no longer believed in home deliveries. And the Coltranes were certainly the cream of the elite, he reflected somewhat wryly.

Colt had never wanted to return to Paris. Born and raised in America, he had come to Europe for the first time a few years ago to visit his parents. His father, Travis Coltrane, wealthy and successful, had only accepted the appointment as emissary to France out of respect for his friend President Harrison. His parents had fallen in love with France, leaving him behind to manage the family ranch and silver mines in Nevada. Colt's visit had resulted in meeting Jade and falling eternally in love. He smiled, lost in the happy memories of his past, thinking of their beautiful, royal wedding in Russia, and their unforgettable honeymoon sailing around the Greek islands in the Czar's magnificent yacht. Then his smile faded as he remembered another voyage . . . a trip to America to begin a new life in New York, ended by a storm at sea. Jade had been washed overboard, and he'd been knocked unconscious by flying debris . . . and stricken with amnesia.

Then a true nightmare had begun for them both.

Jade had been found drifting at sea by Bryan Stevens, a wealthy widower still grieving over the recent deaths of his beloved young wife and son. Mesmerized by Jade's beauty, he doggedly set out to make her his new wife, but she had clung tenaciously to the hope that Colt might somehow be alive. Determined to keep her, Stevens had hired Pinkerton detectives and kept from Jade the most important part of their findings. Oh, he had told her that Colt was alive, gloating over the discovery that he was married to another woman, and they were happily expecting a baby. But Stevens did not tell her that Colt had amnesia. He was not really married, but was, in fact, the victim of a scheme by society matron Triesta Vordane to achieve respectability for her unwed and pregnant daughter, Lorena.

Furious to think Colt could have forgotten her so quickly, Jade fell into Bryan Stevens's trap and married him, only to discover the truth later.

Colt thought about that fateful night only seven months ago, when he'd regained his memory, and shuddered. When Stevens realized that Jade had learned the truth, he had forced her to leave New

York, intending to take her to his private island in the Caribbean and hold her forever his prisoner of love. Colt had gone after them in the midst of a raging storm. He'd been washed overboard, holding on to Jade with all his strength. In that instant, struggling above the snapping jaws of death, it all came rushing back to him. He remembered everything . . . and when he awoke later, the nightmare had mercifully ended. Jade was his, forever and always, and he hoped that Bryan Stevens was burning in hell for the way he had made them suffer . . . hoped that Triesta Vordane would join him one day. Colt held no hatred for Lorena, for she had stood up to her domineering mother in the end. He had even come to care for her son, Andy, and hoped one day to see him again. But he and Jade had decided it best that they leave America for a while to let the wounds heal.

Jade was drifting once more . . . but not in the cold, chopping waters of the ocean. She was swirling within the turbulent sea of her own taunting doubts and fears.

When she had found Colt, she'd been shocked to realize that he did not know who she was, could not remember ever having been married to anyone but Lorena Vordane. However, the passion between them could not, would not, be denied. Colt had not understood why and how he could love her so quickly, so completely; knew only that he could not control his all-consuming desire for her. Jade could not tell him the truth, for she had talked with a doctor who had told her that the shock of reality might take him over the brink to insanity.

With her heart breaking, Jade had decided that she would have to leave him. She could not settle for a tawdry affair, especially after Triesta Vordane had found out and threatened to expose them. She was also going to leave Bryan, the man who had so cruelly manipulated her with his lies of omission. But Bryan had been determined not to let her go, and had taken her against her will, forcing himself upon her that raging, storming night. . . .

Now, floundering helplessly in the sea of pain that rocked her, waves of torment striking her relentlessly, Jade saw Colt's face above her, claiming her for his own. Then he melted away, replaced by Bryan, taunting her, swearing that he would never let her go. . . .

Jade and Colt had never talked about what happened that night, whether Bryan had succeeded in forcing himself upon her then, or at any time during those last frenzied weeks and months when she and Colt had found each other again. Although it had been a mockery, a sham, Bryan had been her husband. Colt had not wanted to know if they'd had relations, and she had certainly not wanted to tell him, so they had avoided the subject altogether. When they learned that she was going to have a baby, it still was not discussed. Jade kept her fears to herself, and suffered her own private hell.

That was the reason she had not been overjoyed to learn that she was pregnant. God forgive her, she had no way of knowing whether Colt or Bryan was the father . . . until now. The baby really wasn't premature, and Colt *had* to be the father!

Kitty's voice called out to her from somewhere beyond the dense fog that engulfed her. "Push, darling, push. It's almost here. . . . Push. . . . It will soon be over. . . ."

Consciousness faded away. Jade was too weak, too

weary from the long, long hours of labor to help in the delivery.

There was a hush, then a gasp, followed by yet another silence, this one reverent, awed. It was broken by the sound of the doctor's hand firmly slapping flesh, followed by an angry, indignant cry.

Kitty was laughing and crying at once as she leaned down to give Jade a joyous hug. "It's a boy, Jade! It's John Travis Coltrane, Junior, and he's beautiful! He looks just like Colt when he was born. . . ."

Jade wept and raised weak arms to clutch Kitty and plead, "Tell me, please. . . . Is he all right?"

But Kitty did not answer, because the doctor had just cried out in surprise. Sister Fifine had handed over the newborn baby to another nurse and was standing beside the doctor, openmouthed and wide-eyed. "I don't believe it," she whispered, then laughed nervously.

Kitty turned and looked, then clapped her hands together in delight. "Twins! Another baby is coming, Jade . . . another baby!"

"A girl!" the doctor proclaimed proudly, holding the red-faced infant by her ankles and soundly smacking her bottom with the palm of his hand. "Healthy, too. They both are. That explains why you delivered early. Twins never go to term, and they're usually good weight. Congratulations, Madame Coltrane!"

Kitty was sobbing happily. She planted a teary kiss on Jade's cheek and ran out to tell Colt that he was the father of twins.

But Jade could not join in their jubilation. The old nightmare had returned with all the fury of a tornado. She had given birth to twins prematurely, and that meant that Bryan could indeed be the father. She shuddered at the memory of how he'd once confided that he himself was a twin, his sister having died at birth. Dear God, didn't twins run in families? She didn't know of any twins in Colt's family. Was Bryan actually the father of her babies?

No, no, no. . . . Jade turned her head from side to side, moaning in denial, her heart breaking.

From somewhere far, far away, beyond the mist that surrounded her, Sister Fifine's voice reached her. "I think hearing she has two babies is too much for her. Can you give her something to make her rest?"

The doctor laughed, a warm, kind sound. "Of course. I imagine it would come as quite a shock to a woman to find that her blessing is double . . . as well as her responsibilities!"

Jade felt herself drifting away. As she reached out for the welcome black void, she made a silent vow that it would not matter, because she would not let it matter.

Colt was alive and he was here with her.

Bryan had died that fateful stormy night.

Colt was her husband, her love, the father of her son and daughter.

That was what she would make herself believe. And so it would be.

Chapter One

Spain
November 1912

J ADE'S impatience was giving way to anger with each glance at her wristwatch. *Where was Kit?* It was time to leave for the depot, and missing the noon train to Madrid meant waiting another day to leave, which also meant missing out on some of the fun. American dignitaries and citizens living and working in Spain were celebrating Thanksgiving, as well as the election of their twenty-eighth president, Woodrow Wilson, back in Washington. Jade had been looking forward to the festivities for months and wanted to be part of the gala celebration.

She paced up and down the pink marble floor of her bedroom, pausing now and then to stare out the wide windows to the balcony and the fields beyond. Surely Kit hadn't left the ranch, but where could she be?

With a sigh, she turned to the mirror, studying her traveling costume—dark silk blouse, blue serge jacket with a short flare above the hip, peg-top skirt, kid pumps. Her dark hair was parted in the middle and plaited in braids that crossed in back. She knew she

11

looked conservative and dignified, the way people expected the wife of an emissary to look.

For maybe the hundredth time, Jade wished she had never given in to Colt's and Kit's pleadings that she buy the ranch near Valencia, although she had to admit that it was one of the most beautiful regions of the Spanish countryside. With its abundance of orange, lemon, almond, and olive trees, pomegranates and palms, she found the area truly breathtaking.

Their home dated back to the era of El Cid, the most famous of all Spanish heroes. The palatial structure was designed with an inner garden laid out in terraces paved with mosaics and bordered with cypress and myrtle trees, fragrant with the scent of jasmine and roses. The house was built to afford a sweeping view of the aquamarine Mediterranean in front, and the land gently sloping to the rear was perfect for raising horses and cattle. Colt, however, had no time for that although he did arrange his schedule in Madrid to allow him time at home to enjoy the peace and tranquillity.

It was truly a paradise, but Jade still harbored reservations about raising Kit here, amid a ruggedness that she'd never know in the cosmopolitan atmosphere of Madrid embassy life. Here Kit sometimes rode with the vaqueros working on the Frazier ranch down the road, even though it was forbidden. And Jade also did not like the way Kit trailed after Doc Frazier, their veterinarian, as he made his rounds. She had nothing against him personally. He was a nice enough man, an American who had decided to make his home in Spain after inheriting land from a distant Spanish relative. Jade just felt that such a free outdoor existence was not proper for a young girl of royal blood—*Romanov* blood. She had pleaded with Colt to send

Kit to a finishing school, but he wouldn't agree because Kit didn't want it. She had a way of wrapping her daddy around her little finger that infuriated Jade. It was also, she mused resentfully, because of Colt's mother. Jade adored and respected Kitty Coltrane, but they sometimes clashed because Kitty was very vocal in her opinion that Kit should be allowed to live her own life the way she chose. More than once Jade had let her mother-in-law know that Kitty was not going to tell her how to raise her daughter. It did no good. Kitty still spoke her mind when she felt like it . . . and *always* took her namesake's side.

Colt laughed when Jade worried, saying that his father had told him that his mother had been the same way when she was younger. Kit was the spitting image of Kitty Wright Coltrane, and that wasn't so bad, was it? Jade would reluctantly agree, thinking all the while that things had no doubt been different when his mother was young and growing up on a small farm in North Carolina. She much preferred her daughter to be more genteel.

Jade had not wanted to leave New York nearly fourteen years ago to move to Spain. She had loved her life there, teaching ballet and dance in her very own, successful studio, enjoying her family, her church and charity work. It was flattering and exciting to be considered one of the city's most respected society matrons. An invitation to a party at the palatial Coltrane mansion on Riverside Drive was almost as coveted as a weekend at their elegant home in the Catskills. In turn, she and Colt had been on the preferred guest list of every social function from New York to the White House.

All things considered however, Colt's being asked to accept the position of emissary to Spain was an

honor too grand to even consider not accepting . . .
even though the offer had come at a very sad time in
all their lives.

After months of smoldering tension, war had been
declared between the United States and Spain. When
President McKinley had persuaded Colt's father,
Travis, to come out of retirement in October of 1898
to serve as a special adviser during peace negotiations
in Paris, the entire family had worried that the stress
might be too much for him. Travis Coltrane had
turned a deaf ear to their protests. He was a man of
honor and dedication, and if he felt that his country
needed him, he would be there to serve, as best he
could. He did, however, request that his only son accompany him, and together the two had proven in-
valuable diplomats.

Sadly, however, the family's fears proved true. On
the tenth day of December, 1898, the day the Treaty
of Paris was signed, formally ending the war, Travis
Coltrane succumbed to a fatal heart attack.

It had been a difficult time for Colt, and Jade had
felt that the assignment in Spain would help him get
on with his life. She'd pushed aside her personal re-
grets over leaving, because she loved him so.

All had gone well. Colt was one of the most respected government emissaries in Spain. Their life
had been pleasant enough, but as Kit grew older, Jade
felt that if she couldn't persuade her to go to finishing
school, then they should consider moving back to New
York for the social and educational advantages there.
Kit disagreed vehemently, arguing that if Kit's twin,
Travis, could live in France with Grandma Kitty, then
she should be able to enjoy Europe, too. Jade knew
that was only an excuse. Kit just preferred riding and

the outdoors to what she considered "boring girl things."

And as for John Travis living with his grandmother, well, Jade had reluctantly given in, with the understanding that he would live at home during the summer. He did, and they were all very close. Kitty was raising her other granddaughter, Marilee, alone. Marilee was actually Kitty's *step*-granddaughter. A long time ago, in a dark part of Kitty and Travis's lives, Travis had thought that Kitty was dead. He'd married a Kentucky lady named Marilee Barbeau who had died giving birth to their first and only child, Dani, Marilee's mother.

Jade swallowed the painful lump that still rose in her throat whenever she thought of Dani . . . dear, sweet, gentle Dani, who had married Jade's close Russian friend Drakar Mikhailonov. Theirs had been a rare and special kind of love, shadowed only by Dani's inability to carry a baby to term. Then, on the day her father had died, Dani had given birth to a beautiful and healthy baby girl . . . and joined her father in death.

Jade had promised Dani that she would raise her child as her own, but Kitty had insisted, and who could deny her in her grief over losing Travis? Despite their clashes over Kit, Jade admitted to having deep affection and respect for her mother-in-law.

As for Drakar, his wounded heart would never heal, for a part of him had died with his wife. He had returned to Russia to aid his lifelong friend, the Czar Nicholas, in troubled times. Though she seldom heard from him, Jade thought of him often, and fondly.

A knock on the door chased away her painful memories. She saw with disappointment, however, that it was the servant girl, Carasia, and not Kit. "Well, did you find her? Have any of the servants seen her?"

Carasia stared at the floor, picking nervously at her long peasant skirt, then admitted, *"Sí,* I have found her, *señora,* but she said to tell you she cannot come now. She said she is sorry you will miss the train, but it cannot be helped, and she begs your forgiveness."

Jade's eyes grew wide with disbelief. "You mean she refuses to come?"

Carasia nodded and whispered, *"Sí."*

"Well, exactly where is she?" Jade exploded.

"In the stable. The mare the *veterinario* loaned to her is foaling . . . having *mucho* difficulty. Dr. Frazier could not be found, and Señorita Kit must deliver the colt herself, or the mare will die."

Jade fumed. "Oh, for heaven's sake! I told her she had to take that horse back, that she had no business having it here."

Carasia's chin lifted in loyalty to her mistress and friend. "Señorita Kit loves horses. She wants one badly for herself."

Jade regarded the girl coldly, not about to discuss personal matters with a servant. She brushed by her and hurried out of the house and down the path leading through a grove of lemon trees to the rustic barns. She recognized Julio, the young son of one of the servants, standing outside the open doors. His eyes were large with fear as he stepped out of her way.

Jade started into the barn but turned at the sound of her name. It was the chauffeur, Muego, coming down the path toward her. He was supposed to be waiting in the front courtyard to drive them to the station in Colt's new pride and joy, a sleek gold and black Alfonso. Built by Hispano Suiza in Barcelona, it was considered one of the finest and fastest cars on the road. But she cared nothing about the fancy car now, only the fact that Muego looked as agitated as she felt.

"I heard about the mare foaling," he said. "I doubt there will be time to make the train, but I'll keep the car ready just the same."

"Do that," Jade snapped, then hurried into the barn. She found Kit in one of the stalls at the rear. Her daughter was kneeling in the hay beside her borrowed mare, Belle. Wearing the denim trousers Jade detested and a worn flannel shirt with the sleeves rolled to the elbows, Kit looked as if Madrid festivities were the farthest thing from her mind.

Jade's hand flew to her mouth at the sight of blood on Kit's hands and shirt. She gasped, her stomach rolling.

Kit turned to look at her, aware of her presence for the first time. "She's foaling," she said quietly, worry apparent on her fine-boned face. "And it's early. She wasn't due for a few weeks yet. I came out to check on her and saw she was acting strangely. Then I saw that her udder had started to swell, and I knew she was going into labor."

With angry resignation, Jade said, "What can you do about it? This is something for Dr. Frazier to tend to, not you. Besides, it's his horse," she added icily.

Kit shook her head stubbornly. "I sent Julio to get him, but nobody knows where he is. I won't leave her. He told me once that when a mare is foaling, and she starts acting nervous and sweating and straining, everything moves fast, and it's usually over in a half hour or so.

"I waited," Kit hurried to explain, "but when nothing happened, I reached up inside her and found that the colt is turned wrong. It's supposed to come out with its nose lying on its forelegs, but this one is lying on its side. I've got to turn it. Maybe you should wait outside,'' she suggested with an apologetic smile before dipping her hands into the bucket of lard Julio had brought earlier.

By now, Julio and Muego had come inside the stall and were also kneeling beside Kit and the mare, ready to assist if needed. Jade, feeling sick to her stomach, backed away into the shadows. She turned aside, unable to watch.

Several moments passed, then suddenly everyone cried out with delight. Jade forced herself to look, watching in awe, as a tiny, fuzzy, wet newborn colt made his way into the world, struggling to stand on wobbly legs.

"He's beautiful." Kit was crying happily. "He's beautiful, and healthy. I can't believe we did it, Belle . . ." She threw her arms around the mare as Belle got to her feet to inspect her new son.

Jade could not deny that she was proud of her daughter, but she found herself suddenly fired with renewed determination to leave the ranch . . . and Spain. Kit needed the cultural and educational advantages of New York if she were to blossom, and grow, and one day marry someone of refinement and wealth. Maybe, after Colt heard about this unladylike performance, and with so much talk of war in Europe, he might be more easily convinced. Jade had a feeling that maybe he, too, was ready to go home.

For the moment, however, they had to get to the depot. There might still be time to catch their train. "You did a nice job, dear," Jade began. "And I'm proud of you, but if you hurry, we can—"

"No." Kit stood, whisking a strand of coppery golden hair back from her damp forehead with the back of her bloodied hand. Her voice was soft, but there was no mistaking the look of determination in the steady gaze of her wide lavender eyes. "I have to wait an hour or so, to make sure Belle passes her afterbirth. Then I've got to make sure he starts suckling, and that's not always easy. I may have to—"

Jade suddenly cried out in complete frustration, "Kit, I'm sorry, but I find all of this disgusting and unladylike! When you father hears about it, you can be sure he'll agree with me that we need to get you back to civilization and teach you how to be a lady. You are young and beautiful, and you should be looking forward to going to Madrid and being the center of attention, having men flock around you, instead of wallowing in blood and straw and filth!"

Kit listened quietly to her mother's ranting and raving. When Jade had calmed down somewhat, she said contritely, "I'm sorry. I really am. And I promise to be ready on time tomorrow."

"You see to it!" Jade cried furiously, storming out of the barn.

Kit stared after her and shook her head sadly. Why, she wondered, couldn't her mother see that she had dreams of her own? It wasn't fair to be expected to *live* a certain way, *think* a certain way, *act* a certain way just because she was a woman. She wanted to be *herself*. She didn't mean to be disrespectful or disobedient, and the last thing she wanted to do was hurt anybody, but that's the way she was—the way she *had* to be.

Chapter Two

JADE was able to reserve a private compartment on the next morning train to Madrid, but Kit refused to leave for the station till Dr. Frazier arrived to check both mare and newborn colt. Jade was furious, but Kit said there was just no way she could go away for a week until she heard the veterinarian say that all was well. So, once again, Jade had paced the floor and wrung her hands, worrying that they would miss the train. Finally they'd left with no time to spare, arriving at the depot just as the conductor was calling his last "All aboard."

Once settled, Jade continued to fume. "It wouldn't even have mattered to you if we hadn't got here in time! All you care about is that horse, and—" She shook her head and sighed. "Oh, why do I even bother? You never listen to anything I say. You were told to give that horse back to Dr. Frazier! Sometimes I wonder if they mixed up the babies seventeen years ago, because you are nothing like me! You don't care anything about the finer things in life—art, theater, fashionable clothes, entertaining, or . . . or anything I care about," Jade sputtered in frustration.

Kit stared out at the passing countryside, loving the tranquillity of the plains, framed by rocky hills in the distance. Now and then the tracks passed through

vineyards and orange and lemon groves. It was a
lovely trip to Madrid, and she had been looking forward to it, but now it was being ruined by the tension
between her mother and herself. Why did it have to
be this way? Why couldn't her mother understand?
Her father didn't like being in the middle and never
took sides, just discreetly made himself scarce when
there was any trouble. When Grandma Kitty was
around, though, it was another story. Once, after several glasses of wine, she'd told Kit that although she
adored her mother, she thought Jade was a bit of a
snob because of her aristocratic background.

As Kit tried to concentrate on the beauty of the passing scenery, her mother fussed on and on. When she
began to say once more that there was nothing left to
do but return to New York and expose Kit to the finer
things in life, Kit could remain silent no longer.

"Mother, have you ever stopped to think that
maybe *you're* the one who's different, and not me?"
she pointed out coldly.

Jade glared at Kit, emerald eyes narrowing. "And
what is that supposed to mean?"

"You're a Romanov, a princess, and the Czar of
Russia is your third cousin. That sets you apart from
other people."

Incredulous, Jade countered, "Well, *my* blood is
your blood! You are also of Romanov lineage, however distant it may be, and the Czar would be *your*
fourth cousin. If I'm different, then so are you, although you certainly inherited none of my royal
traits," she added waspishly. "And besides, royal or
not, a girl your age should be looking forward to
dancing, and parties, and being courted by men."

Kit snickered. "I'm not interested in being courted,

and I'd rather be out riding than prancing around in a fancy dress with men ogling me. Is that so wrong?"

"Frankly, yes."

"Well, can't we just forget about it for now and enjoy the trip?" Kit asked wearily.

Jade looked at her daughter thoughtfully, then leaned back against her seat and closed her eyes in momentary defeat. "We might as well. You never listen, anyway."

Kit felt a wave of relief, and seized the opportunity to change the subject. She began to talk about how nice it would be to visit Madrid again, how much she enjoyed staying in their apartment there because it was near Retiro Park, with over three hundred acres of bridle paths, and how she loved renting a horse and riding there.

"Bridle paths?" Jade's eyes flew open. "That's what I mean, Kit. You have no cultural interests. We're on our way to the most beautiful city in Spain, and all you can think about is horseback riding in the park. Last time we were there, I had to drag you to the Prado, one of the most superb galleries in the world, and all you did was yawn!"

"That's not true! I enjoyed it, but I'd rather have been riding. Is that so wrong?" Here we go again, she groaned inwardly.

Jade silently cursed herself for picking up the argument again, but she couldn't help herself. She wanted only the best for her lovely daughter, and it was driving her crazy to see Kit ignore her beauty and femininity in favor of pursuits that were anything but genteel. Why, she wouldn't even ride a horse with an English saddle, but insisted on straddling like a man! Sadly, Jade conceded that it might have been best if she hadn't insisted Kit come on the holiday. "You'd probably be happier at home with that horse."

Kit mumbled woodenly, "No doubt."

"What do you plan to wear to the embassy ball? I told the seamstress to make anything you wanted, and she had the sketches of the latest Paris designs."

Kit shrugged. "Carasia packed for me. I really don't know."

"Didn't you have a new gown made?"

"Why should I? I've got lots of beautiful dresses, Mother."

Jade was appalled. "But this is an important occasion—the embassy ball to celebrate Thanksgiving, as well as Mr. Wilson's being elected the new President. Every gown you have was designed for some past function at the embassy, which means you'll be wearing a dress you've worn before."

Kit gritted her teeth. She did not want to be insolent, but oh, how she wished she was back at the ranch instead of sitting across from her mother for a two-hundred-mile train ride that suddenly seemed endless. "I'm sorry." She bit out the words. "But I don't care. It seems so silly, anyway . . . and a waste of money as well."

"We're fortunate that we don't have to worry about money, Kit. In case you haven't noticed, we're quite wealthy. Your father works only to keep from being bored. If he didn't work another day in his life, we'd never see any difference in our life-style, without even touching *my* money . . . and you dare to sit there and say we can't afford for you to have a new gown?"

Frustrated, Kit protested, "No, that's not what I meant—"

"You are so beautiful," Jade interrupted her. "Prettier than I was when I was a prima ballerina

with the Imperial Ballet in St. Petersburg. I am proud
that you are my daughter, Kit, and I want to show
you off. I want every eligible young man in Europe
to fall down on his knees and beg you to marry him.
Is that too much for a mother to ask?''

Kit wanted to laugh but didn't. Only her mother
could harbor such a wish, much less admit it. Now
Kit wished she'd just kept her mouth shut. When her
mother was in one of these moods there was no rea-
soning with her. Her father laughingly said that when
the blood of her Irish spirit, her Romanov snobbism,
and her Russian obstinacy all ran together, it was best
to just leave her alone till the flow separated again.

''First thing tomorrow we're going shopping. It
means I'll have to miss a morning tea with the wife
of the ambassador that I'd looked forward to, but I'll
not have my daughter at the ball wearing a dress that
everyone has already seen.''

Kit's mind raced with schemes of rebellious revenge. So her mother wanted her to be the center of
attention, did she? And wanted men to fawn over her?
Well, maybe she should just give her what she wanted!
Let her see that it just might be better to allow her
the innocent pursuit of her own interests instead of
playing the role of a femme fatale.

Her lavender eyes sparkling mischievously, Kit said
sweetly, ''You won't have to miss the tea, Mother. I
can go shopping by myself, and I really want to.''

''Are you sure?'' Jade asked suspiciously.

Kit was quick to reassure her. ''Oh, yes. Don't
worry.''

''And you'll choose a nice gown? Something fashionable?''

Kit nodded again, turning her face to the window
lest her amusement be detected. What she planned

was a harmless prank, but it would make her mother see that it wasn't always desirable to be the center of attention.

When they arrived at the depot in Madrid, Kit was delighted to see her cousin, Marilee, with her father. That meant that her brother and Grandma Kitty had made the trip from Paris for the festivities.

As Kit hugged her father happily, he asked why they'd missed the train the day before, as they'd sent a telegram with no explanation. Her mother was only too glad to tell him, reaffirming her argument that it was time they left Spain if Kit was to be saved from becoming one of the common bourgeois.

Kit turned away to greet Marilee. She was a pretty girl, with friendly brown eyes and thick, naturally curly chestnut hair. She had a heart-shaped face, a sprinkle of freckles across her upturned nose, and dimpled cheeks. Tall and slender, she had already developed curves that turned men's heads even though she was not quite fourteen.

"I want to hear what happened," Marilee protested as Kit drew her away from her mother's impassioned account of the day before.

"Oh, it's just the same old thing." As they walked through the terminal, Kit told Marilee about the birth of the colt. "He's beautiful. I can't wait for you to see him. Doc Frazier said since I delivered him I can keep him and Belle till spring, so I can watch him grow. I wish I could buy them both, because I know he'd sell them to me, but . . ." Her voice trailed away.

"You're in a lot of trouble, aren't you?" Marilee asked worriedly. Looking over her shoulder, she saw that her aunt was still talking angrily about Kit's causing them to arrive a day late.

Kit nodded, then grinned impishly. "But not as much as I'm going to be in. Want to go shopping with me tomorrow morning? I have to buy a dress for the ball tomorrow night."

"You mean you don't have one?" Marilee asked incredulously.

"Mother wants me to have a new dress, Marilee," Kit explained carefully, "and she wants it to be a very special dress. She wants me to be the center of attention, so I'm going to be an obedient daughter and do exactly as she wants."

Marilee wasn't fooled. She'd witnessed too many of her cousin's antics in the past to take her seriously. She warned, "I've got a feeling that you're right— you really *are* going to be in a lot of trouble."

Kit giggled. "I'm just obeying my mother's wishes!"

The lavish Coltrane apartment was situated in a section of Madrid replete with foreign embassies and luxury hotels. They occupied three floors of a tall, narrow stone building on the Paseo de la Castaellana boulevard.

When their car pulled to the curb in front, a doorman waited to assist them. He stepped back quickly as Kitty Wright Coltrane nearly knocked him down running from the building to hug her namesake.

"Oh, how I've missed you!" Kitty squealed with delight, hugging Kit tightly. She then held her at arm's length to confide, "And I missed you last night, too. Travis and Marilee and I went to the Casa Mingo, your favorite tavern."

"Oh, Kitty, really!" Jade sighed with displeasure, tugging at her gloves as they walked toward the entrance. "I can't believe that with so many splendid restaurants in Madrid, you took the children to a common *tavern!*'' She looked at Colt, hoping that he would voice his agreement, but, as always, he refused to comment and did not meet her gaze.

Kitty responded with a haughty toss of her head. ''It is *not* a common tavern. In fact, it's very popular and happens to be the only place in Madrid where authentic sweet Asturian cider is served.''

Kit chimed in to agree. ''It really is. The waiter holds the glass as low as he can in his left hand, and the bottle of cider as high as he can in his right. Then he pours. It's like a ritual. And you can also get crusty bread and *cabrales*—goat cheese.'' Glancing at her grandmother, she felt a strange, familiar sensation at seeing another pair of lavender eyes, so like her own. It was like looking in a mirror. She did favor Kitty, and she was glad, because she thought her grandmother was beautiful. ''Would you mind going again tonight?''

Kitty started to say that of course they could, but Jade declared sharply that was out of the question. ''We're all invited to a dinner party being hosted by Don Jose Yubero and his wife. She sent me a personal invitation in Valencia, and I accepted.''

Kit groaned, following her mother into the foyer, with its black marble floors and ceiling-high mirrors. ''I don't see why Marilee and Travis and I have to go,'' she moaned. ''I hate eating with the Yuberos.''

Jade turned on her furiously. ''Don Yubero is a very important man, Kit, and he and his wife have always been nice to us. Why don't you want to go?''

Kit's jaw set stubbornly. ''Well, for one thing, I think the food they serve is disgusting—bull testicles!''

Kitty made a face and cried, ''Is that what that

horrible dish was the last time we were there? Now I don't want to go, either.''

Marilee, instinctively moving closer to her grandmother and cousin for support, chimed in meekly, ''They also had eel, Aunt Jade, and it made me sick to look at it. I don't want to go, either. I'd rather go to the tavern.''

Jade gave them all a scathing look while Colt moved toward the stairs, trying to hide his amusement. With hands on her hips, Jade informed them firmly, ''Well, I accepted the invitation, and we are *all* going. And as for the food they serve, young lady . . .'' She pointed a scolding finger at Kit. ''If you had the culture and refinement I've tried, unsuccessfully it seems, to instill in you since birth, you would realize that you never turn your nose up at local cuisine, especially in a person's home. It is the epitome of bad manners.''

Kitty bristled. ''That doesn't mean we want to eat bull testicles, Jade, for heaven's sake. I don't think I'll go.''

Jade murmured under her breath that Colt had to do something about his mother's interference. As she stomped up the stairs, she called back that Kitty could do as she pleased, but the children were going.

''*Children,* she calls us.'' Kit shook her head and sighed. ''That's all we'll ever be to her.''

Kitty gave her an encouraging hug. ''Don't worry. One day you'll grow up and leave the nest, and then your mother will have to acknowledge that you do, indeed, have wings, my dear.''

''She's going to realize that sooner than she thinks,'' Kit mumbled, heading doggedly up the stairs.

Baffled, Kitty asked Marilee what Kit meant. Since

Kit had not sworn her to secrecy, Marilee obligingly told her grandmother about her cousin's plans.

As Marilee spoke, a slow grin spread over Kitty's face. Kit's scheme sounded exactly like something she would have done in her day. And, she thought wickedly, she was going to lend a hand!

Chapter Three

"KIT, wake up, darling."

Kit blinked against the sudden flood of light as her grandmother opened the drapes. She sat up and sleepily rubbed her eyes. It had been late when they got home last night, nearly two A.M., but not because *she* had wanted it that way. She had been bored silly, especially when the Yuberos' son, Esteban, had had a few too many glasses of sangria and had reached under the table to give her thigh a suggestive squeeze. Twice she had brushed him away, giving him icy glares. The third time she gave his hand a sharp little prick with her fork. He kept his hands to himself after that, but continued to fawn over her and make a nuisance of himself.

"It's nearly ten," Kitty told her. "Marilee is dressed and waiting for us downstairs, but your mother is still asleep, and we need to be on our way before she wakes up."

Kit was bewildered. "Where are we going?"

"Why, shopping, of course, to buy your gown for tonight."

Kit's eyes narrowed suspiciously. "Who told you I was going shopping for a new gown?"

"Marilee. She didn't think it was a secret."

"Did she also tell you—"

"About your scheme to make your mother stop nagging you to be a 'femme fatale'?" Kitty interrupted with delight. "She did, and I think it's a fine idea. I want to be a part of it."

"Oh, Grandma . . ." Kit scrambled from the bed and ran to give her a big hug. "I should've known you'd be on my side."

"Of course. Did you think I wouldn't be? And," she scolded, "I've told you and Travis and Marilee a million times—don't call me Grandma. Call me Kitty. Grandma makes me feel old, and I don't like that."

"But Mother says it isn't proper."

"Your mother and I disagree on a lot of things, but don't misunderstand," Kitty was quick to add, "I love her like a daughter. We just have different views on life sometimes and, unfortunately, I've never been the kind to keep my opinions to myself."

"But what about Daddy?" Kit asked worriedly. "Do you think he'll be mad?"

"Because his daughter is the belle of the ball?" Kitty asked incredulously, laughing. "He's going to be furious. So furious, in fact, that he'll make your mother see that she's wrong to nag at you as she does. It's fine to expect respect and obedience from your children, but it's very wrong to demand that they think as you do. This is just your way of letting them know that."

"She wants us to leave Spain, you know," Kit told her sadly, "and go back to New York to live."

"I'm not surprised. She's been wanting to go back for some time now. There are lots of things happening there, things she'd like to be involved in. But that's no reason to drag you away from the life you've come to know and love. After all, you're nearly eighteen years old. When I was your age, I was on my own."

"Mother doesn't think that way." Kit sighed. "She's perfectly content for you to raise Travis along with Marilee, but she wants *me* with her every second."

"Well, it's different with a daughter, I suppose. She loves you, and she means well. She just doesn't realize that she's smothering you. Maybe tonight's little display will make her see that she's wrong."

While her grandmother waited, Kit quickly washed and dressed. She was wearing a simple white blouse and a long blue wool skirt. November could be quite cold in Madrid, so she slipped on a short, snug-fitting seal jacket. She hated to wear a hat but she knew her mother would fuss if she didn't, so she chose a small button-type, with a veil only to her nose. Picking up her leather gloves, she announced, "Well, I'm ready, but I haven't got the slightest idea where to go to look for the kind of gown I need on such short notice."

"Well, I do!" Kitty was happy to announce, her lavender eyes bright with anticipation. "I happen to know the perfect place—the Casa del Pasion, a shop that has all the latest and most daring fashions from Paris. The owner is Mademoiselle Denise Delacorte, and her mother is a good friend of mine in France. She has the only shop in Spain that's able to offer the creations of Paul Poiret. You've heard of him, haven't you?" She did not give Kit a chance to admit that she hadn't. "He's considered the most fashionable designer in France, and he's credited for doing away with that unbearable 'kangaroo' corset. I hate those things—hide a woman's curves, make her bend over like she's got a bellyache. Anyway, he's designed one with a natural shape, as well as some new and sophisticated evening gowns, so he's quite famous in the fashion world. I'm sure we'll find exactly what we're looking for.''

When they reached the foyer, Marilee was waiting anxiously, nervous that Kit would be angry. ''Was it all right that I told her?'' she asked. ''I mean, you didn't tell me not to tell.''

''I didn't think I had to,'' Kit told her, ''but it's all right since it's just Grandma you told.''

Marilee breathed a sigh of relief, and they hurried on their way. Kitty had one of the family cars waiting. Once they were settled in the back seat, Marilee declared exuberantly, ''I'm so excited about tonight that I can't wait!''

Kit and Kitty exchanged amused smiles, and Kitty observed, ''Well, bless your heart, child, you really are beside yourself, aren't you? So tell me about this young man who has you all aflutter.''

Marilee blinked in astonishment. Kit laughed at the expression on her face as Kitty said with feigned indignation, ''Well, I was young once myself, and I know all the signs of a young lady being smitten with a young man. But who do you know in Spain?''

''I don't actually know him,'' Marilee admitted reluctantly. ''I mean, I've never met him, but I don't suppose there's a girl in Europe who hasn't heard about him . . . how handsome and exciting he is.''

''Who?'' Kit prodded, trying to hide her amusement. She didn't want her cousin to think she was making fun of her.

Marilee turned on her almost angrily. ''Well, *you* should know,'' she said defensively. ''He lives near Valencia, and it's said he owns one of the largest ranches in all of Spain.''

Kit raised an eyebrow. Surely, she didn't mean . . .

''Yes!'' Marilee's long auburn curls danced about

her face as she confirmed Kit's unspoken question. "Kurt Tanner. He's rich and handsome and exciting, and—"

"And he's legend with women," Kit supplied harshly. "And I said *women,* not *girls.*"

"Oh, what difference does that make? Lots of girls my age are married!"

"You just get those kind of thoughts out of your head, Miss Mikhailonov," Kitty admonished quickly. "Your father would have a fit if he heard you talking like that. He promised your mother he'd send you to that finishing school in Switzerland, and—"

"Well, there's nothing wrong with my just dancing with him tonight," Marilee told her petulantly. Then she added wistfully, "If he asks me."

Kit snorted with unladylike disdain. "Honestly, Marilee, why would you even want to be seen with a man of his reputation?"

"What reputation?" Marilee demanded. "He wouldn't be invited to the embassy ball if he wasn't somebody important."

"I'm talking about his reputation where women are concerned. Don't you have any pride?"

With haughty indignation, Marilee challenged, "How would you know? Have you met him?"

"I wouldn't know him if I saw him," Kit was quick to inform her. "I just know what I've heard."

"Then you really don't know anything about him except gossip, and that's not fair!" Marilee declared, settling back against the seat and folding her arms across her bosom.

Kit said nothing more. She was reflecting on the intimate talks she and Carasia sometimes had, sharing their personal feelings about life and love. It had been Carasia who had told her about the enigmatic

Señor Tanner, and how it was said that he was so
fascinating and exciting that any woman who had ever
known him whispered his name into her pillow with
longing at night . . . and fantasized about him when
other men held her. At the time, she and Carasia had
wickedly and deliciously pondered what it could be
about him that cast such a spell over women, but, of
course, Kit would never admit to such nonsense.

After they had a quick lunch, Kitty led the way
down a narrow, cobblestoned street, away from the
main shopping district. They would have just enough
time to buy everything they needed before the afternoon siesta began and all the stores closed for a few
hours.

The Casa del Pasion was down a flight of steps, its
glass window just visible from the sidewalk. The instant they entered, an elegantly dressed woman rushed
from behind a velvet curtain at the rear to meet them.
"Madame Coltrane! Welcome. And these are your
granddaughters?" She clapped her hands together in
delight. "I don't believe it! My mother was right when
she said you are beautiful. I cannot believe you are
old enough to have grandchildren!"

Kitty smiled indulgently, for she was accustomed
to being flattered and fawned over, as the Coltranes
were known and respected internationally. She introduced Kit and Marilee, explaining to them that she
had called earlier to say they were coming. Then,
patting Kit's shoulder, she instructed Mademoiselle
Delacorte: "Now, make this young lady bewitching,
beguiling, and even more beautiful than she already
is."

"Ah, but you have given me an impossible task,
madame, because how can one improve on perfection? But I shall try, and—" she winked conspirato-

rially—"I think I have just what you might be looking for—a new creation by Paul Poiret that arrived only last week. If," she challenged Kit, "you are daring enough to wear it."

Kit asked to see the gown, fighting the impulse to say that she was willing to wear anything to make her own personal declaration of independence to her mother.

Mademoiselle Delacorte went back behind the curtain and returned a few moments later looking quite pleased as she held up a sensuous creation of black velvet. Poiret had revived the empire style by wrapping a band of gold cording just beneath the bosom, but that was not all. A daring slit went from floor to upper thigh; Kit's leg would be exposed when she walked or danced. She'd heard about these new sheathlike dresses with slits that were declared indecent by bishops and ministers.

Marilee stared at the dress for a moment, then cried, "Oh, Kit, it's gorgeous . . . but do you dare?"

Kit looked at her grandmother. There was no mistaking the approving gleam in her eyes. "I'll try it on," Kit said tonelessly, trying to hide her own excitement.

Moments later she stared with a mixture of emotions at her reflection in the full-length mirror. The cap sleeves were draped off her shoulders, and beneath a sensuous spiderweb of black lace, her full bosom showed above the straight-line bodice. Beneath her bosom, it hung in a straight sheath, curving provocatively to her small, rounded rear. The dress fit perfectly—not a nip or tuck would have to be taken. *Did* she dare? she wondered anxiously as Kitty and Marilee called to her to let them see.

Twisting and turning in front of the mirror, she

experimented with the way her left leg was exposed when she moved. If, by chance, she encountered someone at the ball who could dance the tango as she had learned it from Carasia, there was no doubt that she would be the center of attention—and would be talked about for a long time to come. Carasia knew a different version from the ordinary dance that was currently all the rage in Europe. She knew the steps that had evolved from the Argentine milonga—fast, sensual, and in some circles considered indecent. Incorporating steps of the flamenco, the Spanish tango could be deliciously wicked. But Kit doubted there would be any really experienced dancers among the men at the ball.

Kit took off the dress without modeling it. Stepping from behind the curtain she said to the anxious trio, "You'll have to wait till tonight. I want everyone to be surprised." Then, as Mademoiselle Delacorte happily rang up the sale, Kit said worriedly to Kitty, "If Mother sees me in that dress, she'll never let me out of the house!"

Kitty said that she had already thought about that. "She'll want to see what you bought, so let's just pick out one she'd approve of. You can put that on and make her think it's what you're wearing, but just as everyone is getting ready to leave, I'll have some kind of emergency that will make me late. You can say that you'll wait and come with me, and then you can change after the others have gone on ahead."

"Perfect," Kit agreed. "Now I know where I inherited my devious nature."

Kitty winked. "Was there ever any doubt?"

* * *

Only Travis was at the apartment when they got home. Colt was at an embassy smoker being held for out-of-town dignitaries, and Jade had gone to a tea for the wives.

Travis started teasing Kit about Esteban Yubero. "Why did you stab him?" he asked. "I didn't know my little sister was capable of such violence!"

"Little sister!" Kit hooted. She turned to Kitty and demanded, "By how many seconds? You were there."

She gave them an indulgent smile, accustomed to their playful bickering. "It was less than a minute, and you both know it. Now, I don't have time for your nonsense. I'm going up to take a nice, long bath and have a glass of sherry so I'll be in the proper mood for tonight."

Following her, Marilee paused midway up the steps and grinned impishly at Travis, teasing, "If you don't leave Kit alone, I'll tell her about you and that demimonde you're sneaking off to see."

Kitty froze, and as Marilee approached her on the stairs she coolly asked, "And what do *you* know about demimondes, young lady?"

"Nothing." Marilee ran on up the steps. "I was just teasing!"

But Kitty knew that she wasn't teasing, just as she knew all too well that women found her grandson as handsome and desirable as they'd found his father, and his father's father. Well, she wasn't going to worry about it. He'd learn, as they had, how to deal with it. He probably already had, she thought to herself, smiling.

When they were alone, Travis and Kit went into the first floor parlor and helped themselves to a glass of cognac before sitting down on the divan.

"Okay," Travis said when they were settled. "I've

heard Mother's side of the story, *several* times. Let's hear yours.''

Kit shrugged. "It's as she said. Belle was foaling, having trouble, and I helped her. We missed the train. It couldn't be helped."

Travis shook his head. "I don't know, Kit. Parents are always stricter with girls, I guess, but she seems extra hard on you. I think it's because she wants you to pick up where she left off and be famous, so she can live her life over again through you. It's sad, and I'm sorry it's like that for you."

"It's too late for her," Kit said somewhat harshly. "I love to dance, but I never cared for ballet, and she's always been a little hurt about that. No, I think she just wants to see me properly married. She's worried that I've got a wild streak and will ruin the good name of Coltrane."

"You'd never do that, and she knows it. I also think that Mother is bored with Spain. If it hadn't been for her constant traveling around Europe, she wouldn't have been able to stand it for as long she has. But now there's so much going on back in the States that she can't stand being away any longer. She wants to go home, but you don't, do you?"

"Home?" Kit echoed. "Spain is the only home I've ever really known, Travis. I was just a little girl when we came here. I've grown up feeling that *this* is home, and the times we went to New York for a visit, I couldn't wait to get back here. I love everything about it, and I don't want to leave. And I'll tell you something else, too. . . ." She leaned forward and met the steady gaze of his steel-gray eyes, so like their father's and grandfather's. "I've never told anyone this, not even Grandma, but if they move back to New York, I swear to you I'll find a way to come back here.''

Travis looked at her as though he thought she'd lost her mind. ''Come back to what? They'll sell the ranch. You'll have nothing left to come back to. And even though you don't like to be reminded of the fact, Kit, you *are* a woman, and women just don't go to foreign countries to live by themselves. Father wouldn't stand for it. You know that.''

Kit pursed her lips thoughtfully. She could confide anything to her twin, so she plunged on. ''What about Grandma and Marilee?''

''What about them? Marilee is going to finishing school in Switzerland next year, remember? And what makes you think Grandma would want to live in Spain?''

''She might. With me.''

''Probably,'' he conceded. ''It's no secret that you're her favorite.''

Kit made no attempt to deny it, since everyone knew it was so. ''Besides, she'll be lonesome in Paris when you go to West Point.''

''*If* I go to West Point,'' Travis solemnly corrected.

''If? Ha! You're certain to get an appointment from the President himself, and you know it. That should be the least of your worries, and I'm proud and happy for you. I read the papers, Travis,'' she reminded him with a frown, ''and I know there are a lot of problems between America and Mexico. I'll be just as happy as our parents to see you in West Point for the next four years instead of in Europe . . . trying to stay out of war, if it comes, and away from demimondes,'' she finished with a giggle, leaping from the divan as he reached to give her hair a playful yank.

"Mother is right," he yelled after her, pretending to be mad. "You're incorrigible!"

Kit ran from the room, warmed by the cognac . . . and thoughts of the exciting evening ahead.

Chapter Four

EVERYTHING went according to plan. Kit dressed in a green satin gown, the epitome of quiet elegance, and made her appearance in the foyer. Her mother, lovely in blue velvet, was fretting about Kitty's being so slow. Her father, was as handsome and striking as her brother. They both wore formal tuxedoes with tails, pleated white shirts, white vests, bold red ties, and shining black patent slippers. They could almost have passed for twins, Kit mused, were it not for her father's close-clipped mustache and the distinguished gray at his temples.

Marilee was adorable in her pink and white ruffled gown but she fumed, "I look like a birthday cake! I'm nearly fourteen! Why do I have to dress like a little girl?"

"You look like what you are," Colt tried to comfort his niece. "A fairy princess."

"I don't want to look like a fairy princess," she protested petulantly. "I want to be able to dress up like Kit."

Only Kit caught her meaning, and she gave Marilee a scathing look, silently warning her not to say anything else. Marilee looked apologetic, and was grateful that Kitty called down the stairs at that precise moment. "You're going to have to go on without me.

I'm all thumbs tonight. Kit, would you come up here and help me with my hair?''

Jade groaned, ''Oh, for heaven's sake! I believe in being fashionably late, but this is a bit too much.'' She told Kit to go up, motioning the others toward the door and the waiting car outside.

Kit was halfway up the stairs, a rush of excitement washing over her. Then she heard Marilee wailing again and froze where she stood, bristling with anger she dared not express.

''Why can't I wait and go with Kit? Why do I have to look even more like a little girl by walking in with all of you?''

Jade had reached the point where she did not care what anybody did as long as she and Colt got to the ball before the hour grew any later. ''Do what you want, Marilee,'' she said irritably, gathering her mink cape and walking out.

The front door closed after them, and Kitty appeared on the landing to wave Kit up the stairs. ''Hurry! We don't have long. What are you going to do with your hair? That style just doesn't go with your dress, and . . .''

Kit wasn't listening. Dizzy with excitement, she hurried to her room to take off the dress she was wearing. Then she took the box containing the black velvet sheath from its hiding place beneath the bed.

A sudden thought made her stiffen. She looked from the dress to the white lawn knickers she was wearing, open between the legs front and back and joined only at waist and knees. She could not wear anything so bulky beneath the clinging sheath! In her excitement, she had neglected to buy a dancing corset!

Kitty knocked on the door. "You really must hurry, dear. Can I help?"

"No. I'm almost ready. I'll be right down."

What difference did it make, she asked herself recklessly as she yanked off the knickers, tossing them aside. Who would know, anyway? She stepped gingerly into the sheath and began to pull it up over her naked body, relishing the way the soft velvet felt against her bare flesh. It clung like a second skin across her hips, flowing smoothly to the floor from beneath her firm, round breasts.

Whirling in front of the mirror, Kit admitted to herself, with a delicious wave of wickedness, that she liked what she saw . . . except for her hair. With a few yanks, the pins were out of the sophisticated pouf. With a wild toss, her thick, golden-red hair fell to her bare shoulders.

Stepping into black beaded slippers, Kit was ready to make her debut . . . in her own unforgettable way.

Kitty and Marilee were waiting in the foyer. When they saw her, Kitty actually swayed, so impressed was she with her granddaughter's stunning beauty. Marilee just stood there, her eyes wide with shocked admiration.

"Do I dare?" Kit grinned.

"You dare!" Kitty confirmed, then she challenged, "Are you sure you don't enjoy looking like a *femme fatale?*"

"Of course I do," Kit admitted, "but most of all I enjoy being *me* . . . which means presenting whatever side of me I wish to present . . . when *I* wish it . . . not my mother!"

Marilee was unimpressed by her cousin's personal declaration of independence. "Aunt Jade is going to send you to that convent in Nice where my mother once lived,'' she predicted. ''And not to be a nun, either. Just you wait and see.''

Kitty quickly rejected that notion. ''That's when I'd turn into the busybody she already thinks I am. No granddaughter of mine will ever be sent to a convent because she's got a mind of her own. Now let's be on our way. You and I, freckle-face,''—she gave Marilee an affectionate hug, lest her feelings be hurt by her brusqueness—''will go in first. We want Kit to make a very, very grand entrance.''

When they arrived at the embassy, they could hear the gay sound of music. The party had already begun. ''Wait a few minutes before you enter,'' Kitty whispered conspiratorially.

Kit nodded, trembling with excitement. She looked lovely and she knew it. If her parents were furious, so be it. She was going to show them, once and for all, that it would be much, much better if they would just let her be herself. If that meant riding and roping cattle, so be it. She gave her grandmother a kiss, fondly patted her cousin's cheek, then stepped into the shadows to wait until the right moment for her entrance.

After perhaps five minutes, she moved to the huge double doors, ignoring the doorman's wide-eyed stare. She stepped into the marble foyer overlooking the huge ballroom. It was like entering another world—a world of crystal and light, gold and silver, against a background of soft music and laughter.

Then, just as she had anticipated, a hush fell over the ballroom. Every guest looked up to stare as Kit allowed the white ermine cape she was wearing to fall into the waiting arms of a servant.

She stood regally at the top of the stairway leading down to the circular room, her chin held high as soft whispers began to creep out of the silence. What would happen next? she wondered frantically. Was her mother going to faint? Would her father furiously escort her out?

Through the blur of faces staring up at her as she began to descend the stairs, she saw Kitty, fighting back tears of pride and joy, and Marilee, wistful and envious, wishing it were *she* in the spotlight. And Kit could see her brother, a mixture of emotions on his face as he realized perhaps for the first time just how grown up his "little" sister really was.

Then her heart skipped a beat as she saw her father step forward from the crowd. She could see that his gray eyes were shining with—what? He didn't look angry as he walked slowly up the stairs to meet her.

There was the shadow of a smile on his lips, and Kit realized that he was trying to suppress his delight as he reached her side and held out his arm to escort her the rest of the way. "I'm afraid, my darling daughter," he leaned close to whisper, "that your scheme backfired."

She looked at him and blinked, bewildered.

He nodded, ever so slightly, to where Jade stood looking up at them. There was no mistaking her pride. "This is what she's dreamed of—for you to be the center of attention, a star, as she was. I'm afraid you really don't know your mother, Kit. She's not a prude. She's a lady through and through, but never would she turn up her nose at high fashion. So, instead of shocking her, you've made her quite proud . . . and myself as well," he added with an adoring smile.

The orchestra had faltered when everyone stopped dancing, but had quickly recovered with the lilting strains of a waltz.

Colt led his daughter to the middle of the ballroom,

and everyone stepped back to let them pass. They began to dance, and the crowd watched in admiration, for they were an impressive sight—proud, handsome father with his stunningly beautiful daughter.

"You saved me the cost of a formal debut," he teased her, enjoying her astonishment that her plan had failed.

"I . . . I thought you'd be mad," Kit admitted.

Colt laughed. "Why should I be mad? Of course"—he glanced down at her gown, giving his head a slight shake—"I think you chose a dress that is a little bit old for you, but when I heard that your grandmother went shopping with you, quite frankly, I expected as much, and so did your mother. And by the way, you two didn't fool either one of us with that little act about not being ready on time and insisting we go on without you."

Kit sighed, disappointed. "Well, I'd hoped that Mother would be so mad she'd never dare nag at me again."

Colt's expression was sympathetic. "I know. She wants to take you back to New York. Sometimes I agree with her, but I also realize that you're all grown up, Kit, and you've got a mind of your own. I'm caught in the middle, but I want you to know that I'm holding out for your sake. For how long, though, I don't know. I won't make any promises."

Colt nodded toward several young men standing to one side of the room, their eyes devouring Kit as they waited for their chance to dance with her. "You've attracted the attention of every bachelor in Spain. Maybe there's one out there who'll make you a good husband, then your mother couldn't object to leaving you here when we do go home."

Kit groaned, making a face. "The last thing I want

to do is get married. I just want my own little ranch, my own life, to live as I want to.''

Colt stared down at her thoughtfully. ''You mean that, don't you, kitten?''

She nodded solemnly.

''Well, I can't agree with that,'' he told her sternly.

Kit did not respond, because she was not about to abandon her dream. She was grateful that just then the dance ended.

Travis was waiting to take his father's place. ''Thought you were doing something cute, didn't you?'' he teased her as they danced. ''Well, you had just the opposite effect on Mother. She's tickled to death . . . says she's never been prouder.''

Quietly, firmly, Kit told him, ''I'm not going to live in New York, Travis. They may make me move there, but sooner or later I'll find a way to come back here.''

He sighed. ''You are stubborn, little sister, and I think I'd better let you in on a little secret—they *know* how stubborn you are, so unless you find yourself a wealthy husband, you won't have the money to stay here . . . or their blessing,'' he added grimly.

Kit stiffened, momentarily losing the rhythm of the dance. She quickly recovered and demanded, ''What's that supposed to mean? I've got my trust fund, the money Grandpa left me, and—''

''And Dad is the trustee,'' Travis informed her. ''I heard them talking, and there's no way you'll get your hands on that money until he says so. You know he'll never agree to your using it to stay in Spain. The best thing for you to do is get used to the idea of living in America again.''

Kit tossed her head haughtily, not about to let Travis upset her. Besides, he wasn't telling her anything she did not already know. Her eyes found Kitty, beaming happily, as they swirled about the floor. She felt secure in the knowledge that she had options, whether her parents knew it or not, and when the time came, she would be ready.

"I know what you're thinking," Travis interrupted her private thoughts, "and I don't think it's fair for you to ask her."

Kit looked at him sharply. "Just mind your own business. It's my life."

Travis sighed, grateful that the dance was ending, for a lovely blond in a turquoise gown had caught his eye.

In the shadows of a leaf palm, a man stood alone watching. He, too, was glad their dance had ended, for he had personally asked the orchestra leader not to play another waltz. He wanted to dance with the girl with the shimmering golden-red hair and unusual lavender eyes that smoldered with mysterious rebellion and sensuality. He had a feeling that she could dance something other than the impotent waltz.

Travis escorted Kit toward a group of eager young men. The music began slowly, yet the beat of the drums grew steadily faster as the rhythm quickened to a feverish pace.

People exchanged curious glances. They knew the tango when they heard it, but few could perform the intricate steps.

The man with the dark, brooding eyes watched as one of the young embassy aides moved forward, unable to wait any longer for a chance to hold the loveliest girl at the ball in his arms. He eagerly took Kit by the hand and as they began to move, the man smiled to himself. He had been right. She *did* know

how to do the intricate steps—but her partner did not.
He was stiff, awkward, a pathetic dancer.

He stepped forward into the light. He was tall and
well-built, his broad shoulders and sinewy muscles
encased in a tight suit of black velvet. His shaggy
raven-black hair was swept back from his forehead,
unruly locks curling at his collar. His lowered lashes
were surprisingly long, veiling coffee-brown eyes that
missed nothing. The play of a dimple to the left of
his mouth marked a crooked, often taunting smile. A
tiny scar just below his right eye only made him more
attractive.

He crossed the floor to where Kit was trying piti-
fully to match the awkward rhythm of her inept
partner. When he reached them, Kit's partner was
so stunned at the intrusion that he just stopped
dancing and stood there, a questioning look on his
face.

Kit stared up at the stranger. She drew in her breath
softly, assailed by a feeling she had experienced only
in her private, secret dreams of love, when a faceless
stranger held her and took her to ethereal heights of
passion. He was unforgettable—so handsome, yet he
emanated a sense of feral power that she found
strangely desirable.

Kit met his probing gaze. For one flickering instant, it seemed as though he could see right through
her black velvet gown to her bare flesh. A mysterious
little smile touched his lips, as if to say that he was
pleased with what he saw there.

He did not look at her partner as he declared huskily, "It seems the lady has a special need."

With a movement so swift that Kit had no time to
object, he swept her into his arms, whirling her completely around and dipping her backward, so low that

her long hair brushed against the floor. He held her there for an instant, his dark eyes proudly challenging. "Kurt Tanner," he casually introduced himself, swinging her up, forward and back into a dip once more. "Can you dance with me?"

Kit was tingling from head to toe with anticipation. She sensed that this savage of a man could match her every step in a way no other partner ever had before. With a provocative laugh, she gave a high kick as he swung her once more, her gown falling away to reveal a long, shapely leg. There was no mistaking the soft gasps of their audience. "I think," Kit said with a bold wink, "the question is—can *you* dance with *me?*"

"There's one way to find out, mi *princesa.*" He returned the wink, announcing, "Milonga, my princess, the outlaw Spanish tango!"

He drew her up to stand tall and straight before him as the throbbing cadence of the music made the very air about them seem to vibrate with emotion. They were unaware that other dancers had given up their attempts to do the intricate, difficult dance and had backed from the floor. All in attendance ringed the room to watch the stunning couple. The crystal and gold chandeliers bathed their bodies in shimmering light. They were a vision of sensuality in black lace and velvet, whirling together through the charged atmosphere.

Kurt Tanner slid his right hand from Kit's shoulder down her back and along the curve of her hips. Their fingers interlocked as their cheeks turned first left, then right. Kit allowed him to bend her effortlessly backward once more, her bare leg kicking up and out of the velvet slit, sending a ripple through the onlookers once more.

As one they sidestepped to the left, made a swift kick, and turned abruptly. Kurt moved with precision, guiding her through breathless dips and swings. Then he lifted her up in the air with one arm, holding her aloft as he turned round and round. Kit balanced regally, legs outstretched, arms high above her head in an arch. Then suddenly he dropped her, to the awed cries of the crowd, catching her easily to swing her about in a wide sweep. He brought her almost to the floor and leaned over her, his breath warm against her cheek. His eyes met hers in a fiery challenge of dance and lust. And although no one else could see, he slid his thumb up from her waist to touch her nipples through the soft velvet bodice of her gown. Kit instantly felt the sensation, and he saw in her eyes that she enjoyed it. He smiled that arrogant, taunting smile once more.

The music ended with a crashing crescendo, and the room exploded in cheers and applause.

Kurt held her tightly, dipped low in his arms. He saw in her eyes a myriad of emotions—the frightened look of a trapped animal giving way to the fierce determination of a survivor. This woman offered a dangerous challenge of her own.

"As I said"—Kurt gave her a lopsided grin—"the lady has a special need." He dared to brush his lips boldly against her throat, touching his tongue against her warm flesh.

Kit was too proud to struggle in his arms. She would not give him the pleasure of letting him know the desperate fear and hunger that churned within her—a hunger that he had awakened . . . and she knew, without doubt, that he could satisfy. He was arrogant, insolent, and conceited, but he was also devastatingly handsome. Yet she was secure in her dignity. She was not about to be one of his fawning female admirers. "And the question was, *arrogante*, can you dance with me?"

Kurt raised her up, set her on tiptoe, and kissed her soundly. "Time will tell." He winked. Nodding, he turned quickly and disappeared into the crowd.

Chapter Five

IT was the first week of January 1913, and the holiday of Dia de los Reyes, the Procession of the Three Kings, when children received their Christmas gifts. Kit was lonely, because Carasia had been given time off to enjoy the holiday with her family. They were as close as sisters, and Kit especially missed her on her daily ride, because Carasia always hurried to finish her work so she could accompany her.

Alone or not, Kit was not about to stay around the house with her mother, especially since the embassy ball. Her scheme had backfired all right, and her mother was worse than ever, nagging her to have parties and socials. The young men who were constantly calling were also a nuisance. On this particular day, Kit was determined to be away, because Esteban Yubero was in town and her mother had invited him to have tea. So, before the first light of day, she had packed a knapsack with cheese, fruit, and a canteen, and quietly sneaked out of the house to saddle Belle and be on her way before her mother awoke. She planned to ride all the way to the Río Turia—to retreat from the world and dwell in her dreams, if only for a little while. She would face her mother's anger later.

Kit now crossed the back pasture and rode alongside the creek bank, moving to a knoll at the rear of

Doc Frazier's land where she could watch the ever awesome spectacle of the sun's victory over darkness. It was a lovely morning, blue and gold, the sleeping winter fields a blanket of bronze.

She dismounted and leaned against a jutting rock, enjoying the splendor around her. How she wished that she knew for certain she would never have to leave. Her mother hadn't said anything about going back to America since the embassy ball, but that didn't mean she had changed her mind.

Kit's mind drifted back to the ball . . . and she cursed herself for once again feeling a sensuous, warm flash of desire as she thought of Kurt Tanner, despite her dislike of the man. Oh, he was arrogant! The nerve of him kissing her right there on the dance floor, but the worst had been the way he had boldly caressed her nipples, staring down at her with knowing, laughing eyes.

Kit had not seen him since. She did not want to, ever, but she had been curious enough to ask Carasia about him. She learned that his ranch was not far away. It was north of Valencia, between Sagunto and an area called the Castellon de la Plana, sometimes called the Costa del Azahar for the sweet fragrance of the orange blossom that drenched the countryside. Carasia had delightedly told her that Señor Tanner was said to own over two thousand acres of land, extending from the shores of the Mediterranean eastward to the section the Phoenicians had called Spagna, meaning "the hidden land," because of the menacing mountains along that rugged coast. It was the region beyond where Señor Tanner raised his prize cattle.

"He is very, very wealthy," Carasia had said, "one

of the richest men in all of Spain. He has *mucho* gold
. . . and many women.''

Carasia had giggled, but Kit had not been amused.
When Carasia saw her look of disgust, she asked what
was wrong. Kit told her about the dance and the kiss,
but not the way he had touched her so intimately.

"Caramba!" Carasia had squealed. "What *I* would
not give to have such an *amante!"*

She had then lowered her voice to an intimate whisper. "They say he knows how to make a woman
happy beyond her wildest dreams. They say the richest
women in Europe have tried to buy his love, but of
course, he is above that. They say that for a time he
was engaged to a princess from Denmark, a golden-
haired beauty with blue eyes and the face of an an-
gel.''

Kit had cursed herself for her curiosity, but she
could not resist asking, "Why didn't he marry her?"

Carasia felt superior with her knowledge of Kurt
Tanner, and airily disclosed, "Her name was Princess
Nedjelja, but he called her Nebula, because, it was
said, he found her to be as beautiful as a star. Near
Sagunto, there is a place where the ramparts of a
medieval castle extend for over a kilometer across the
hilltop of an ancient acropolis. You can see the be-
ginnings of the new castle he was going to build for
her there when they married.''

Kit wondered what it would be like to be so loved
by a man. She quickly pushed such thoughts aside
and pretended only mild interest. Shrugging as though
it didn't really matter, she asked, "So? What happened to the great romance?"

"No one knows for sure, but it must have been
something terrible, because they say Señor Tanner
forbids anyone to mention her name. It is as though

she never existed." Carasia's eyes glittered as she hurried to share her gossip. "My aunt is his housekeeper, and she said there was a portrait of Princess Nedjelja on the wall above the big stone fireplace. One morning when she went to work, the portrait had been slashed to ribbons."

Curious, Kit had asked, "Why is Señor Tanner living in Spain? He's an American."

"There's a story about that, too."

Kit had sighed, again pretending that she really didn't care. "Well, you might as well tell me the rest, I suppose."

So Carasia had told her the rumor about how Señor Tanner was said to have been a wanderer, and happened to be in Texas at the same time as Francisco Madero, who had just escaped from jail in Mexico. The two became friends, and Tanner had aided Madero in his successful attempt to unseat Porfirio Diaz and become President of Mexico. Afterward Tanner could have stayed on in Mexico, an important friend of the government, but revolution and politics were not to his liking. Madero had understood and rewarded him for his loyalty and help by deeding him over a thousand acres of valuable land in Spain. Tanner had, in a short while, become one of the wealthiest ranchers in the country.

Kit now chided herself for dwelling on Kurt Tanner again. The sun was high, and she'd wasted too much time thinking about the brazen Señor Tanner already!

She mounted Belle and was about to ride on when she saw vaqueros in the meadow below. She paused, curious, when she heard excited shouts. Then she saw two riders galloping side by side across a clearing to where a man waited to mark the finish line. She watched as one pulled ahead of the other to win the race.

Kit trotted Belle down the slope. She had many friends among Doc Frazier's vaqueros and always enjoyed riding with them. She had even raced with them, winning often, because Belle was quite a horse. Suddenly the idea of having fun with them was more inviting than her intended ride to the river.

Kit approached at a fast clip. Catching sight of her, one of the men yelled to the others, *"Hola!* Señorita Coltrane!''

They all turned to greet her, surprising her with their enthusiasm. Doc Frazier's foreman, Riguero, cried excitedly, "Señorita, you must win back our gold for us. He has beaten our best!''

Kit dismounted, pushing her felt hat back on her forehead and loosening the lanyard beneath her chin as she looked around. She saw several men she didn't recognize, wearing smug expressions. Her old friends seemed quite upset. "Maybe,'' she said quietly, "you'd better tell me what this is all about.''

"They come, these strangers,'' Riguero said with an accusing wave toward the strangers who stood watching in amusement, "with their leader. They challenge us to race, and he beats us and takes our money. You can win it back for us.''

Kit frowned. She had dash-raced many times, but never for money. If Doc Frazier knew what his vaqueros were up to, he would not like it one bit. "I don't think so,'' she told him curtly.

"But you must, *señorita,''* another of the vaqueros spoke up. "Belle is the fastest horse on the ranch, and you ride her so well. You are our only chance!''

Kit sighed in disgust. "Why did you race for money

in the first place? You know that Doc would never approve.''

''You do not understand,'' Riguero told her with an angry glance at the strangers as they laughed among themselves. ''The strange hombre, he comes in with his horse and says he is the best. He goads us. Makes us feel like cowards if we do not accept his challenge. And so we do, and we lose.''

''Well, was it a fair race?'' Kit wanted to know.

Doc Frazier's vaqueros nodded reluctantly. Shuffling their feet, they exchanged miserable glances.

''Well, then, let it be a lesson to you not to bet in the future.'' She swept the strangers with an angry look. ''Especially with people you don't know anything about.''

''Maybe when you know them, you will like them.''

Kit whirled about to see a man behind her astride a horse. It was not the rider who caused her to stare in wonder, even though her first glance told her he was not an average vaquero. Doc's men did not wear bandoleers—cartridge belts criss-crossed on their chests. This man looked formidable, was perhaps a true *bandido*—but it was his horse that caught Kit's attention. He was the finest animal she had ever seen.

The man leaned forward in his saddle to stroke the great horse's neck proudly. Flashing gleaming white teeth from beneath a bushy black mustache, he grinned knowingly and said, ''Ah, you like the horse, *sí*? He is one fine animal, *sí*?''

''Beautiful,'' Kit breathed in admiration, ''absolutely beautiful.''

''Allow me to introduce myself.'' The man removed his sombrero and gave her a sweeping bow from the saddle. ''I am Galen Esmond, and I have to tell you never have I met so lovely a *señorita* in all of Spain.''

''*Gracias,*'' Kit responded quietly, unimpressed.

Then she asked brusquely, ''Why did you come here and goad these men into betting their hard-earned pay?''

To the delight of his men, who were chuckling as he spoke, he pretended innocence. ''Ah, *señorita*, do not judge me so harshly. I am but a poor *gitano*—a gypsy, wandering through Spain. I come here, and these men, they goad *me* to race *them.*''

Frazier's vaqueros shouted in protest, and Kit waved them to silence. Galen Esmond spread his hands in mock despair. ''Is it my fault they do not recognize a fine horse, and do not realize they have no chance to beat me?''

Kit said, ''I don't believe they challenged you, any more than I believe you're just a poor, wandering gypsy. I *can* believe, however, that they've never seen a Hispano before. There aren't that many in Spain, because few people can afford them.''

''Ah ha!'' he cried, looking around at his men in pretended delight. ''The *gringa* knows something about horses, and I thought she only knew how to do what *gringas* do best—wag her tongue!''

His men laughed again, and Kit bristled, quickly informing him, ''I know much about Hispanos, *campesino*. They're quite rare, the result of breeding Spanish Arab mares to English Thoroughbreds, producing a horse with more pronounced Arabian characteristics than the average Anglo-Arab. It's intelligent, has great courage, and is known for an agility that makes it a popular competition horse in every branch of equestrian sports. The Hispano can take the challenge that an ordinary horse can't.''

Esmond threw back his head and laughed. *"Mi Dios!* The *señorita* knows her horses!"* Then he abruptly fell silent, turning black, penetrating eyes on her as he challenged, "Why did you not teach your *compadres* about such a fine horse, *señorita?* Then they would not be so *estupido* as to think they can race against my Hispano and win."

Kit met his cold, condemning stare with one of her own. "Do not call them *estupido* because they have confidence in their own horses, hombre. After all, that's what you were counting on to get them to bet so you could take their money."

"Oh?" He raised an eyebrow, exchanging amused glances with his men. "Are you also so *estupido* as to have such confidence in your own horse, *señorita?"*

"Sí, hombre." The sound was like the hiss of the prairie rattler.

He threw back his head and laughed, "Ah, so you are not *estupido!* You know my horse is tired after so much racing. Naturally you wish to race him now. You would easily win."

"Race any horse against me you wish."

His grin faded. He swung his right leg up and over the saddle, landing with both feet on the ground. He commanded to no one in particular, "Bring me the fastest horse. I will show it takes no special horse to beat a mere *gringa!"* To Kit, he snarled, "What shall be your stake? You do have money to wager, do you not? Galen Esmond does not waste his time for nothing."

At that, a ripple of laughter went through Doc Frazier's vaqueros. Riguero called gloatingly, "She is a Coltrane, hombre, and her family has more money than you will ever see."

Galen Esmond's insolent gaze did not waver as he coolly said, "So be it, *rica gringa*. Name your wager."

"All the money you have taken from my *amigos*," Kit replied.

Galen pulled a cheroot from his shirt pocket. He bit off the end, spat, and lit it, his narrowed black eyes fixed on her. He had already given away much of his winnings in payment of old debts, but it made no difference—he was confident a *gringa* could not beat him. Finally he shrugged, his lips curving in a taunting grin beneath his bushy black mustache. "So shall it be, *señorita*. Only make sure," he added with a wink, "that you have the money, for I can think of other ways you can pay me."

His men laughed raucously. Kit seared them with a look of contempt, then mounted her horse. Galen's friends quickly chose the fastest and strongest horse, and led it to him. He swung up into the saddle and followed Kit to the starting line. Riguero stood to one side, holding his gun up in the air. "You both know the rules. To where Carlos stands—" he said.

"No!" Galen interrupted harshly. "We circle him and come back here. The *gringa* thinks she is such a great rider—let her prove it!"

There were a few cries of protests. "That would be nearly two miles," Riguero pointed out.

"Does the *gringa* object?"

Kit said that she did not, adding saucily, "Let him feel he tried very hard to win!"

Everyone laughed at that—except Galen and his men. "Let us begin," Galen snarled. "I wish to join the rest of my *amigos* at the cantina to celebrate such a rich morning."

Riguero asked Kit anxiously, "Are you ready, se-ñorita?"

She laughed. "Oh, yes, Riguero. Quite ready."

"*Uno . . . dos . . .*" and then he fired the gun.

The horses charged forward side by side, and a cheer exploded from Galen's men as his horse bolted ahead. He pulled away by inches, then half his length, then a full length. Kit had raced the course many times. She knew her horse, knew when to let her out. She held back, fighting against Belle's thundering plea to let her go, let out the reins, let her overtake the pompous, arrogant hombre.

Carlos loomed ahead, and even from a quarter mile away Kit could see the disappointment on his pudgy face. Galen was nearly two lengths ahead of her now. Would Belle be able to catch him when Kit finally let her go? Did she dare restrain much longer? Her hat had blown away and her hair flew wildly about her face. It was harder to hold back than to give Belle her head, but she gripped the reins and gritted her teeth. When she reached Carlos and swept around him, Galen had already passed and was now three lengths ahead.

"*Mi Dios! Mi Dios!*" Carlos screamed out at her, waving his sombrero at her as he jumped up and down. "Go! Go! Go!"

It was all Kit could do to hold Belle back. She was like a bridled demon. In every other race she had always been allowed to charge freely. Now she was confused and angry. Her eyes were wild in the wind whipping in her face and her hooves cut into the ground with frustrated frenzy.

Galen stretched his lead to five lengths. He dared in his confidence to turn and look back at Kit, and laughed out loud at the large margin between them.

They were nearing what would be the three-quarter mark. Kit could hear Galen's men shouting triumphantly in the distance. She dug her knees in tight to Belle's side and leaned forward. Her heart pounded furiously as she dropped the reins, dug her fingers into her horse's mane, and cried, "Now, Belle! Now!"

Belle surged ahead, closing the gap by one length, then two, then three. Galen looked around with disbelieving eyes. He saw instantly what was happening, and drew blood as he kicked his spurs brutally into his horse. He whipped the reins across its rump in a frenzy, screaming and cursing in Spanish as he realized that he was losing his grip on victory.

Another length closed, and then they were side by side. Riguero stood just ahead, waving his sombrero, his men jumping up and down, cheering Kit and Belle onward.

Belle made a final charge, as though to twist the knife of defeat deeper into the man who had dared to challenge her . . . and crossed the finish line two full lengths ahead of Galen Esmond.

Kit reined in and trotted back to where the vaqueros were waiting, their happy roar almost deafening. She dismounted to join them in revelry, reminding them to let it be a lesson never, ever, to bet their hard-earned wages again.

Galen Esmond was momentarily forgotten in the excitement. It was only when Carlos rode up to them yelling angrily that they looked around to see Galen and his men riding away, a cloud of dust behind them as they disappeared over a ridge in the distance.

"*Bandidos!*" Carlos was screaming in rage. "*Bandoleros!* They have no honor!"

"What are you talking about?" Riguero cried. His

face grew livid with anger as he realized what was happening. "They have run away without paying their debt?"

Carlos threw a small burlap bag to the ground and said furiously, "They say this is all that is left of their winnings."

A grumble went through the men, and someone cried in frustration, "We cannot take this! Any of it! The *señorita* won it. It is hers."

Kit quickly shook her head. "I'm not keeping any of it. Divide it among those of you who lost your money. Let's just be grateful we were able to get this much back."

Riguero gave her a grateful smile. "You are very kind to us, *señorita*. Then he added regretfully, "But you race so hard for nothing for yourself."

"No!" Carlos told them. "The hombre, he say the *señorita* deserves a prize of her own, so he leave for her . . ." All eyes turned in the direction he pointed.

Tied to a bush stood the regal Hispano.

"He say to tell you," Carlos said with a sneer, "that he is a man of honor . . . and always pays his debts."

Kit's mouth dropped open, and her heart skipped a beat. Galen Esmond had paid his debt all right, and she was now the proud owner of her very own horse!

Chapter Six

KURT Tanner squinted against the sun. It was the middle of January and the weather should have been cold, but wasn't. Winters in Spain could be as unpredictable as a woman. Hours ago, he had taken off his leather coat, rolling and tying it on his horse's rump. Now he yanked off his neckerchief to wipe the perspiration from his forehead. He had been riding hard, having heard that the man he was looking for had been seen in a cantina in Valencia—nearly two weeks ago. He'd left his vaqueros to take care of things on his ranch, riding out alone in the hope that the trail was not too cold for him to follow.

He reached for his canteen and took a long drink of lukewarm water, momentarily closing his eyes against the heat and dust. God knew he thrived on the ruggedness of the country, but there were times when he had to admit that he missed the pleasures he enjoyed when he visited Madrid.

As in November.

Kurt kept his eyes closed, picturing her in his mind—those lovely lavender eyes fringed with thick, almost golden lashes; her wild, fiery hair flying about her face as she danced so passionately. She could dance the tango, all right. A smile touched his lips. He had an idea that that was not all she could do well.

He'd known who she was—Kit Coltrane, the daughter of one of the American emissaries, Colt Coltrane. After the ball, he'd made other inquiries, wanting to know more about the lovely young lady. It had been like opening a wonderful gift wrapped in black velvet, finding within an ivory treasure—a woman with more life and fire in her eyes than any he'd ever known before. Many times, he reflected without conceit, he had stared down at a woman in his arms, her eyes hot with desire. But no woman emanated the smoldering passion he'd felt in Kit Coltrane.

Kurt opened his eyes. The lovely vision was gone, in its place the knowledge of what he had learned from his men about the spirited *señorita*. It was said that her mother, Señora Jade Coltrane, blood relative to the Czar of Russia, thought her daughter wild. She was infuriated because Kit rode with vaqueros like a man. Kurt chuckled to himself. From what his men hold told him, the fiery beauty could not only ride as well as any vaquero around, but could rope and brand. And, it was rumored, she knew how to use a gun . . . and use it well.

A frown creased his forehead as he touched the scar beneath his eye. To him, it was not the mark of a wound, but a brand—a brand to remind him forever that women were never to be trusted, never to be loved. They were good for one thing, and one thing only—the pleasures of the flesh. If a man wanted children, a son to carry on his name, then he should take a wife and breed, but never, goddammit, love the woman.

In the distance, Kurt could see the pens where young men studied and practiced *tauromaquia*—the art of bullfighting, in the hopes of one day becoming a great matador. Usually he enjoyed the action, but today he was not interested. He had allowed his mind to drift back to another time, another place—and his first insight into the treachery of which women were capable.

He had grown up in Springfield, Illinois, a pleasant enough place . . . until violent race riots exploded in the summer of 1908. Kurt had never been a man of prejudice. His closest boyhood friend was a black man named Guthrie Hadden. The two had hunted and fished together, sharing dreams of one day setting out to explore the world. But dreams have a way of fading into the realities of life, and Kurt had gone off to college to study to be a lawyer like his father. Guthrie's family was poor so he had gone to work in a local store, sweeping and cleaning. Toiling nights as well as days, he'd saved enough money to manage the down payment on a tiny farm just outside town. He married and had a baby. By the time Kurt came back to open his own law office, his parents had died. He was alone—except for his old friend Guthrie and Guthrie's wife, Janie . . . and a comely young lady named Edwina Chandler, whom he planned to marry.

Edwina was pretty—and spoiled, the daughter of one of the richest men in Springfield. She was destined to be a society queen like her mother, and her fiancé's choice of a best friend was not to her liking. It was a bone of contention between them.

Then came the hot August night Kurt would remember until his grave—the night he was scarred on his face—and on his soul.

Guthrie had gone into town to get some medicine for his sick baby. A group of drunks started picking on him, breaking the precious bottle of expensive medicine he'd just bought with hard-earned money.

Guthrie lost his temper and fought back. He landed a blow to the chin of a redneck who fell backward and hit his head on a rock. The drunk didn't get up. Though the man eventually woke up with only a terrible headache and a vague memory of what had taken place, his friends decided instantly that he was dead, and that the Negro who had killed him must be lynched.

Guthrie had run away. He tried to find Kurt, the one person he could depend on to help him. He went first to his office, then to the rooming house where he lived, not knowing that Kurt had stopped in a saloon for a drink. Finally, in blind desperation, Guthrie went to Miss Edwina, hoping that there he would find Kurt. He had no idea that to Miss Edwina he was just a Negro, and by her standards, worthless. It made no difference that he was the lifelong friend of the man she was engaged to. She had told him that Kurt wasn't there but that she would try to find him, directing Guthrie to hide in the cellar. Only she never called Kurt; she called the sheriff instead. One of the crazy-drunk rednecks looking for him was there, and overheard the conversation. The sheriff could not hold back the angry, blood-crazed mob that quickly formed. They dragged Guthrie, terrified and pleading for his life, out of Miss Edwina's cellar.

That was when someone finally went into the saloon and told Kurt what was happening. He ran to the hanging tree at the courthouse square . . . and was nearly beaten to death for daring to interfere. He woke up with Edwina leaning over him, sobbing as she stared down at his bloodied, battered face. Nearby, swinging from a rope tied to a tree limb, was the body of his friend.

"Oh, why did you have to interfere?" Edwina had

cried. "Why didn't you just stay out of it? I told them where to find him, and he got what he deserved, and—"

They told him later that he'd tried to strangle Edwina. He might have killed her if they hadn't pulled him off her, but he didn't remember any of it in his mindless fury. The next morning he had awakened with a blinding headache . . . and the realization that he didn't want to spend another day in a town so full of prejudice and hatred that such a nightmare could have happened. He went to the bank and took out what money he had, giving it to Janie Hadden. She was in such shock that it would be days before she realized that a small fortune had been bestowed upon her.

Then Kurt left town, never to return.

He had drifted for over a year, not caring where he went, what he did. He earned enough money to eat by doing odd jobs, construction work, railroad work, finally learning to herd cattle as he worked his way southwest. Then he met Francisco Madero.

He had been living well. He enjoyed his success, and he enjoyed women, keeping his guard up, however, against falling in love.

The he received the invitation from King Alfonso for a gala weekend at the royal palace in Madrid. The festivities were being held in honor of visiting royalty from Denmark. Kurt accepted the invitation. It was a fateful decision, for that was when the seductive Princess Nedjelja came into his life, to mesmerize him with her deep indigo eyes and with her passion to melt away his resolve never to fall in love. She was sunshine and light, happiness and mirth. She brought him more joy than he'd ever believed possible, despite her many, and ever-changing, moods. She could be childlike and playful one moment, petulant and willful the next. She was capricious, headstrong, and spoiled. He had never met anyone like her, and it did not bother him at all that she was so experienced in lovemaking, boldly teaching him how to please her in ways that other women of her class might be too inhibited to enjoy. She hypnotized him completely, rendering him helpless to her charms.

She took him to the top of the mountain of ecstasy . . . then threw him mercilessly down to the pits of heartache and despair.

She had told him that she was going into Valencia to shop. He had planned to spend the time working on his ledgers, but later decided that it was too nice a day to waste indoors. So he rode over to where he was building what his beloved fondly called their Palace of Love. Nothing was happening at the moment, because they were waiting for special pink marble to be shipped from Italy before starting the construction of the outer walls. Kurt was puzzled to see two horses tethered outside a storage shed—one of those horses being the golden palomino he had given his princess.

His raging brain battled with his heart, pleading for reason. He had forced himself to move slowly, to dismount a good distance away and walk. But when he was perhaps still a hundred yards from the shed, he heard the unmistakable moans of pleasure that Nedjelja could never suppress.

Instant fury consumed him. He kicked open the door, reeling at the sight of the two naked bodies, tangled together on the floor. They stared up at him in frozen surprise. Everything that happened after that seemed but the shadows of a nightmare—glimpses of horror. Mercifully he was not quite able to recall every lurid detail. He had grabbed the man, a migrant

worker from nearby vineyards, and beaten him sense-
less. He probably would have killed him had Nedjelja
not grabbed a nearby shovel and hit him soundly over
the head. Later, when he had awakened, the man was
gone. Nedjelja had remained behind, not to beg forgiveness, but to tell him what a fool he was. Did he
really think that he was man enough to satisfy her?
She had laughed in his face. No man lived who could
give her all she wanted. That very morning, before
she had left on her fictional shopping trip, Kurt had
made love to her twice, yet it was not enough.

Even with the throbbing pain and the blood oozing
from her blow, he had managed to counter with a jeer
of his own—did *she* really think that he believed her
to be a true princess? He had known all along that
she was not of royal blood. She was actually a member of the middle class—social climbing by using a
phony royal title to gain acceptance. Kurt had known
this because he made it his business to know everything about everyone he dealt with, but he'd loved her
just the same.

She had paled beneath his verbal assault, toppled
from her pedestal. Kurt silently admitted however,
that she was victor, for she had torn down the wall
he had built around himself . . . and made him fall
in love with her.

Enough reminiscing, Kurt chided himself now,
looking once more toward the pens. Maybe the man
he was looking for was hanging around down there.
He cantered over in that direction.

Kurt saw her even before he reached the wooden
corral. She was sitting on a top rung, and her golden
hair streamed down her back, gleaming in the mid-
morning sun. She was wearing tight denim pants, a
fringed suede jacket, boots, and leather gloves.

Completely absorbed watching the young man swinging his cape before a hot-eyed bull, Kit Coltrane did not notice Kurt Tanner, even when he hoisted himself up to sit beside her on the railing.

The young matador performed well, earning the applause and cheers of the spectators as the picadors drove the bull from the ring.

"So, the lady goes from dancing to bullfighting."

Startled, Kit jerked about. She felt a sudden flush of surprised pleasure, but managed to calmly say, "If you knew anything about bullfighting, Señor Tanner, you would know that it's a form of dance in itself." The shadow of a smile touched her lips. "At the end of a series of veronicas, when the matador holds the cloth of his cape to his waist and twirls as the bull passes, the cape stands up like the skirt of a pirouetting dancer. It's called a *robolera,* and if he's good at it, the matador has the grace of a prima ballerina."

Kurt's eyes moved over her hungrily. It had been a long time, and she was ravishing. "Watching ballet doesn't arouse quite the same emotions as a bullfight, *cara,*" he murmured.

"Oh, I think it depends on what you're searching for. Beauty, as well as savagery, can be found anywhere. It's all in how you view it."

Their eyes met and held. Kurt wondered whether she would let him kiss her if they were alone . . . while Kit felt a tremor deep within her as she remembered how it had felt when he did.

Around them, the crowd shouted over the matador in the ring, but they were oblivious to it all. Finally Kit gave herself a mental shake. She swung about easily, effortlessly, to drop the few feet to the ground below. She did not want him to see the effect he was having on her, and was afraid that if she tarried, he might.

Kurt followed her, as she had feared . . . and hoped he would.

"I'm wondering what brings you here," he said.

"I like to watch the matadors practice."

"Strange interest for a young lady."

"Why? Women attend bullfights."

"But they don't hang around the pens with the men, wearing men's clothing."

Kit laughed. "Who says that men are the only ones who have the right to wear denim?"

"You seem more at home in black velvet."

She stopped walking and turned to look up at him, frostily declaring, "You were out of place that night."

Kurt pretended to contemplate her accusation. "You're right. *It was* out of place. I can think of other places for that kind of . . . *dancing.*" His tone, the heat in his eyes were filled with sensuous innuendo.

"I don't call that dancing," Kit snapped.

"No," he agreed somberly. "I think it's called . . . *desire.*"

"Then that explains why you don't understand the similarity between dancing and bullfighting!"

Kurt did not respond, and she thought perhaps she'd bested him in their war of wits. She reached out to untie the reins of her powerful chestnut Hispano, and swung up into the saddle. She turned to stare down at him in triumph, but her grin quickly faded.

He was furious! His face was red; his nostrils flared ever so slightly. His eyes glittered with rage as they swept over her stallion. "Where'd you get that horse?" he demanded hotly.

Kit trembled beneath his wrath although she did

not know why. She suddenly felt strangely defensive and shot back, "He's mine!"

"I asked you where you got him."

"That's none of your business."

Kurt reached up and grasped her around her waist, and pulling her roughly from the saddle. As he set her on her feet he growled, "Dammit, woman, I asked you where you got that horse!"

"And I told you," Kit hissed at him indignantly, jerking out of his grasp, "it's none of your business." She tried to mount once more, but he grabbed her arm. She whirled about, intending to slap him, but he caught her arm and held it.

"I'm going to ask you one more time, goddammit," he said between clenched teeth. "Where'd you get that horse?"

Kit kicked him in the shin, and he held her so that her back was against him as she struggled in his arms.

A few men passing saw their struggle and stared but continued on their way. They knew that she was the señorita Coltrane, and he was Kurt Tanner; they weren't about to stick their noses in *his* business.

Kurt gave her a rough shake. "Okay, little tiger, we'll just go talk to the local law and see what they do to *señoritas* who steal horses."

Kit stopped struggling and cried, "What did you say?"

"That's my horse."

Kurt released her, and she turned to face him, saying incredulously, "What do you mean—this is your horse?"

"That's a Hispano, little girl," he informed her furiously, "and I paid a lot of money for him. I had him all of two days before he was stolen, right from the barn outside my house."

Stunned, Kit bounced back to challenge, "Where's your proof? He's not branded."

"As I said, I only had him two days. I hadn't got around to putting my brand on him. Where's *your* proof? Where's your bill of sale?"

Kit started to tell him how she'd come to own the magnificent horse. Then she reconsidered and asked instead, "Where is *your* proof, Señor Tanner?"

"I have a bill of sale from a breeder in Morocco. I bought him at a ranch just outside Tangiers. Now . . ." Kurt drew in his breath and let it out slowly. He did not want to lose his temper, but she had his horse, which meant that his quest was only half over, goddammit. He intended to find the bastard who'd stolen him. One of his hands had told him that a known *bandido* by the name of Galen Esmond had been hanging around that day, asking for work. He had disappeared about the same time as the horse. "So, are you going to tell me where you got him, or do I have you arrested for horse stealing?"

Kit gave her long hair a haughty toss. Lifting her chin defiantly, she said, "He's not your horse. He's mine. I won him in a race, fair and square. If you don't believe me, ask Dr. Frazier's vaqueros. They are my witnesses that I'm the legal owner. And if he was stolen from you, which I don't believe for one minute, I suggest you take that up with the man I beat in the race, because it's no concern of mine."

Kit swung up into the saddle again. "Pegasus is mine now." For emphasis, she tugged the reins sharply and dug the heels of her boots into the great stallion's side. He reared up on his hind legs, forelegs slashing the air menacingly, Kurt leaped back out of the way.

He watched her ride away. For the moment he decided to do nothing except talk to Dr. Frazier's men and learn what he could about how Kit Coltrane had won his horse—and about the man she'd won him from. But eventually, he silently vowed, feeling the muscles in his jaw tighten, he'd have his horse . . . and Kit Coltrane.

Chapter Seven

KIT could hear the music from downstairs. Her mother was having a small dinner party for some friends visiting from Barcelona. She'd been polite and genial throughout the evening, but had feigned a headache so she could slip away before coffee and cognac. Escaping to her room, she locked the door and worked feverishly on the letter she was writing to Kitty. She had found paradise . . . but she needed her grandmother's help to make it exclusively *hers*.

That morning, after the unpleasant encounter with Kurt Tanner, Kit had just wanted to be alone. The last place she could expect solitude was at home where her mother was always entertaining guests, so she had ridden to one of her favorite sanctuaries—a spot just across the Rió Turia north of town. There on a knoll with a breathtaking view of the river, she spent the golden afternoon contemplating the idiotic charges of the brash and presumptuous Kurt Tanner. His claim was absurd. Where was his proof that the magnificent horse was his? But what was his motive for lying?

Kit had shaded her eyes against the sun as she looked toward the horizon where a little farmhouse stood. Kit had known the old man who had lived there, Gaspar Gaspencia. She had enjoyed visiting him, and sometimes he'd invited her to share a simple meal of tortillas, fish, and his own special blend of gazpacho. Kit smiled wryly to think how she loathed her mother's sumptuous dinner parties, yet was delighted to eat country fare with Gaspar.

They had been friends, and she had loved to hear him talk of his past as a wanderer, a special glow in his eyes as he related faraway adventures. He had finally settled here, buying the little farm with his life's savings, eking an existence from the field of golden carnations he grew so lovingly to peddle at the flower market in Valencia. He talked of one day planting a vineyard on the slope to the river, for he said the soil was fertile and rich, and he could produce grapes to make the best wine in the region. Only that dream did not come true, and Kit had been saddened to hear of his death recently when she had gone to visit.

As she stood there that morning, fate had stepped in. She had turned at the sound of a carriage approaching. A man dressed in a plain brown suit, with friendly eyes, had waved at her amiably. He had asked if he had reached the Gaspencia farm, and Kit had replied that he had. Then he had taken a wooden post and hammer from the carriage and pounded the post into the ground. On top of that he nailed a sign. Her interest piqued, Kit walked over to read the notice. It proclaimed that the property was to be sold for back taxes.

Suddenly an idea hit her. Kit had quickly asked the man how much taxes were owed. He told her, explaining that he was only posting the sign because the law required it, but he was probably wasting his time since the man who owned the adjoining land had already made a bid for the property.

When he left, Kit's heart had pounded with excitement. This was the answer to her prayers. Twenty acres! She didn't need a larger place. With a little fixing up, the house would be fine. She'd have room for a few horses, and what was to stop her from making Gaspar's dream come true? She could plant a vineyard, and she would certainly keep the field of carnations. And she would not be isolated, because it was not far to Valencia.

She mentally calculated the amount she needed to offer just a bit more than the bid the adjoining landowner had made. The tax office man was not supposed to have told her the amount, but he was a talkative sort, and it hadn't taken much prodding. If only she could use a little of the trust fund her Grandpa Travis had left her, she could buy the property. She had forced her racing brain to calm down, reminding herself that the money was not to be hers until she reached her twenty-first birthday. And even if she could persuade her father, who was the trustee, to release some of it, her mother would be violently opposed.

That was why she was now writing her Grandma Kitty. All Kit needed was a loan until she was old enough to claim her inheritance. Kitty would understand, she always did. Of course, there would be quite a ruckus when her parents found out, but decided that she would worry about that later, after the papers were signed. It might take some time, but sooner or later they had to realize that she intended to live her life the way she wanted.

She finished the letter, sealed it, and laid it aside to mail first thing in the morning.

She opened the glass doors to the terrace and stepped outside. It was a chilly night, but lovely, with a honey-colored moon creating thousands of dancing lights upon the sea beyond. It was, in fact, such a glorious night that she felt a sudden urge to go once more to the ranch that she hoped soon would be hers. It was perhaps a half hour's ride, and the road was good. As a precaution against danger she would wear the gun and holster she kept hidden in the barn. Her mother would have a fit if she knew that her daughter carried a gun, much less knew how to use it, Kit mused with a grin.

She put on denim trousers, a flannel shirt, and her worn leather jacket and boots. Then she tiptoed down the back hallway and stairs. As she was making her way through the kitchen, Carasia came in from the dining room with a huge tray of dirty dishes. "Where are you going?"

Kit held a finger to her lips. "Riding. Leave the back door unlocked so I can get back in."

Carasia shook her head. Giving her a look that said she thought Kit was crazy, she went on her way to finish cleaning up from the dinner party. Kit could hear the sounds of the party—music, laughter, the clink of glasses. Her mother loved to entertain, and people enjoyed her parties. Kit would not be missed.

Hurrying to the barn, she wondered what her father would say when he came home that weekend. If her mother had even noticed Pegasus, she no doubt thought he was just another horse from Doc Frazier's ranch. Her father, however, would know that Pegasus was rare and expensive. He'd ask questions—questions that she would have to answer truthfully. He was not going to like it when he heard that she'd been racing and betting with vaqueros. Well, Kit was not one to worry about the future—she faced problems as they came along. She had stories of her Grandpa Travis to thank for that philosophy. "Play the hand you're dealt, Kit," he'd say, "and don't worry about the next deal of the cards till they're shuffled."

She saddled Pegasus, who pawed the ground in anticipation. They left the barn and skirted across the back pasture lest one of the guests be outside for a breath of fresh air and see her in the moonlight. Then, when she was a good distance away, Kit turned back to the main road, which would lead her toward the river.

She passed dense groves of orange trees and breathed in the sweet fragrance. Kit loved the peace and quiet of the night, the gentle breeze that kissed her face as she rode slowly, lost in thought, lost in the sheer joy of being alive in a world she adored.

She soon reached the little ranch, delighted by the sight of the dilapidated house perched on the hill. Why, she mused curiously, did houses fall apart so quickly once no one lived in them any longer? It was as though the very spirits of the inhabitants kept the walls alive, and once they left, there was nothing to hold the structure together. Well, she'd take care of that soon enough. Necessary repairs would be made, and by spring she'd have flowers blooming in window boxes. The grass would be green and soft, and she'd walk barefoot, delighting as clover tickled her toes. The barn, now a dull gray color, would have to be painted bright red. Pegasus would have a special stall, and . . .

Kit stopped, nerves suddenly taut.

Excited over being at the ranch once more, she had dismounted and tied Pegasus to a tree. She had begun to walk up the hill toward the house when she heard a sound—like someone stepping on a twig in the dense forest to her left. Drawing her gun, she moved quickly into the shadows and waited..

She heard only silence, broken occasionally by a nightbird mournfully calling his mate. Chiding herself for being so jumpy, Kit reminded herself that once she moved in, she'd be all alone here. She would have to get used to noises or she'd be a bundle of nerves.

She stepped from the shadows and began to walk toward the house again. She wanted to see the view of the river in the moonlight. Reaching the porch she thrilled to the breathtaking sight. It was as lovely as she'd imagined. No wonder the old man had loved it here.

Kit stepped from the porch and began to turn around and around dreamily, arms wrapped about herself. Humming quietly, she began to dance in the dappled nighttime wonderland.

"You're even more beautiful by moonlight."

Kit instantly drew her gun, whirling about to aim it at the ominous shadows of the house. "Come out . . . or I start shooting," she tersely commanded. Kurt Tanner stepped out into the moon's luminous glow. An amused smile was on his lips as he came toward her. "I've got an idea you wouldn't miss, either."

"I never miss," she assured him, "and I've a mind to prove it. What the hell are you doing spying on me?"

When he stood a few feet away from her, his smile faded. "I like to keep an eye on my property, *señorita,* and that Hispano belongs to me, regardless of how you came by him."

Kit holstered her gun and laughed. "Are you so greedy that you have to make up lies to try and get what you can't have? I hear you're rich. Why didn't you offer to buy him?"

"I already bought him once," Kurt grimly reminded her. "I hear that your family also has money, so I didn't figure that a rich spoiled brat like you would be interested in any amount I offered."

She was stung by his insult. "That's right. I don't want anything you've got."

He raised an eyebrow and grinned lazily. "How do you know?"

Fury snapped within her like a whip. "Because I find you an insufferable, egotistical bastard, Kurt Tanner! You may be used to getting your own way, but not from me! The Hispano is mine, I won him fair and square, and if he *was* stolen from you—which I doubt—then I suggest you question a man named Galen Esmond. How *he* came into possession of the horse is no concern of mine."

"I have a bill of sale."

Kit narrowed her eyes. "I don't believe you."

Kurt reached into the pocket of his leather vest and took out a folded slip of paper. "See for yourself," he said, handing it to her.

Even in the dim light Kit could see that it was indeed a bill of sale for a horse whose description matched Pegasus.

"How do I know it's the same horse?" she asked, not yet ready to concede ownership.

"You have to take my word for it."

"Why should I? I won the horse from Esmond, and nothing else concerns me."

"It should, seeing as how he stole Pegasus from me. You've no legal right to him."

Kit turned thoughtful. If he was telling the truth, then she would have to give up the horse. Even though she didn't trust Kurt Tanner, she felt instinctively that he was being honest.

"Very well," she relented. "I suppose I've no choice but to give you the benefit of the doubt. But that doesn't mean I intend to turn my horse over to you just like that!" She snapped her fingers, her lavender eyes sparkling defiantly in the silvery light. "I'm willing to make a deal." Her voice was a taunt. "Are *you?*"

"You're in no position to make a deal, *señorita,*" Kurt responded. "I might find you irresistibly beautiful"—his gaze passed over her appreciatively— "but that doesn't mean I'm going to let you keep my horse. All I have to do is show this document to the local law, and you'll have to turn him over. I don't even have to go to that much trouble—I have a feeling Colt Coltrane wouldn't approve if you refused."

"You'd go to my father . . . or the law," Kit said scornfully, "because you're afraid to accept a challenge from a woman. You'll dance with a woman, and dare to kiss her, but when it comes to real courage, you don't know what it means."

Her taunts smarted, but he could not help being impressed by her boldness. "What kind of wager did you have in mind?"

"One that proves I deserve to own such a fine horse," Kit replied confidently.

Suspicious, Kurt prodded, "Go on."

"Hispanos are known for their courage and agility, that's why they're used in the *acoso y derribo.* It's dangerous, but the Hispano can stand the challenge of an angry bull better than the average horse. It takes an experienced rider to handle such a spirited animal.''

Kurt chuckled. ''And you think that just because you're a good rider you deserve to keep my horse?''

''No. I want to prove that I deserve to own him.''

''That's going to be rather difficult, since I can't think of anything you could do to change my mind.''

''What if I fought a bull?''

Kurt shook his head, certain he'd heard her wrong. ''What did you say?''

''I said, what if I fought a bull? Surely you will agree that if a woman has the skills of a matador, she deserves to own a horse also known for prowess in the ring. Oh, I'd never use Pegasus for that,'' she hastened to add. ''I'll fight the bull like any matador, on my feet.''

He stared at her, incredulous. ''You're crazy! You don't know anything about bullfighting.''

''Then you don't have anything to worry about, do you? I'll go in the ring, make a complete fool of myself—''

''And get yourself killed!'' he exploded. ''No. I won't accept this deal.''

''I'm merely asking for a chance to prove my courage by making a few passes—not an official bullfight.''

Kurt shook his head, repeating, ''You are crazy!''

''Maybe.'' She grinned up at him. ''But if you don't agree to my challenge, I can assure you I'll spread the word that you were afraid to wager with a woman . . . because you were afraid you'd lose.''

''I don't care about that,'' Kurt declared. ''There's no way you can win, *señorita*. It's a waste of time.'' He reached out to cup her chin with his hand. ''Maybe a waste of *you*, and that would be a shame.''

She knocked his arm away angrily. "Don't touch me! You seem to think you can do anything you want to a woman, Kurt Tanner."

He grinned. "I've never done anything to a woman she didn't want me to . . . or that she didn't enjoy."

"Then I'm the first, you bastard," Kit exploded, "because I didn't enjoy what you did to me at the ball."

"Yes, you did. You just won't admit it—to me . . . or to yourself."

Kit was struggling to control her temper. "Stop changing the subject, damn you. I made a challenge. Are you going to accept it?"

Kurt was sure she was bluffing. She would ultimately back out, and so he decided there was no harm in going along for the moment. "All right. When?"

"You agree that if I can defeat the bull, you'll make no further claims on Pegasus?"

Kurt nodded.

"There's an old bullpen behind Doc Frazier's ranch that's hardly ever used. His vaqueros will set it up for me and won't say anything—I don't want my parents to hear about this."

"I don't blame you," he agreed sarcastically. "What you're doing is not exactly a compliment to your femininity."

"You'd best be worried about your masculinity," she retorted.

He stiffened. The little vixen had a tongue as sharp as cactus juice. "I asked *when,*" he growled. "I'm tired of wasting time. I want my horse."

"I'll have someone send word to you when it's all set." Kit turned to go, then paused to add curtly, "By the way, it won't be necessary for you to follow me anymore. I'm certainly not going to run away with the horse. Why should I? After all, he's going to be mine.''

''I can think of a lot of reasons to follow you,'' Kurt murmured, wrapping an arm around her waist and pulling her close against his chest, ''but believe me, I wasn't. This is my land . . . or soon will be.''

He kissed her, but she jerked from his grasp, looking at him with wide eyes. ''What . . . what did you say?'' she managed to ask.

Puzzled by her reaction, Kurt repeated, ''I said this will soon be my land. I might build a new house in this spot, and I rode over to see the view in the moonlight.''

''You . . . you live near here?'' she asked.

''My land joins at the ridge, up there,'' he said, pointing, then asked curiously, ''Why?''

Kit shook her head, trying to compose herself. ''Señor Gaspencia . . . I knew him. He was a dear friend. I . . . it hurts to think the land isn't his anymore.''

''It's being sold for taxes. As soon as they post it.''

Kit thought of the sign she'd pulled from the ground that morning and hidden in a clump of weeds by the river. Now she was doubly glad she'd been so sneaky, because Kurt Tanner had no idea that probate time was up and the land was ready to be sold.

Once again she turned to go, for there was no need for further conversation. It bothered her to think that her property would adjoin his, but it really made no difference. Kurt Tanner had two thousand acres or more. He'd hardly be close.

''I'll be waiting . . .'' he called after her softly, ''to see what you can do.''

Kit whirled about, ready to hurl an angry response, but he was gone. There was no sound but the wind in the branches and the tumultuous beating of her heart.

Chapter Eight

THE next morning Kit woke early and immediately sent Muego to post the letter to Kitty. Then she dressed and was going out the back door when her mother called from the breakfast porch. With a silent groan, Kit turned around and went to her.

The room was filled with dozens of miniature orange and lemon trees, planted in bright pottery. The furniture was white wicker, and a peach-and-blue hand-loomed rug covered the mosaic tile floor. It was Kit's favorite room, offering a splendid view of the rolling sea from its point on the bluff.

Jade looked fresh and cheerful in a pink silk dressing robe, but when Kit walked in, her smile changed to a gasp of dismay. "Oh, good heavens, Kit, look at you! You look like . . . like one of those gypsies, all rags and tags! Whatever can you be thinking, going out in public like that?"

Kit sighed, struggling for patience. "Mother, I'm going riding. I have on *riding* clothes."

"Those aren't riding clothes!" Jade's gaze swept her with contempt. "Ladies were riding *habits*—not shabby men's clothes. You just go back to your room and change. No, on second thought, I don't want you riding at all today. You need to start getting ready for the party tonight."

Now Kit groaned out loud. "Are you having another party, Mother? Really, it seems that every night—"

"*I'm* not having the party," Jade was quick to inform her. "If you paid any attention to your social obligations, you'd know that tonight's Anaya Esteban's birthday party. Not just anybody has been invited, but *you* have, and you're going. Do you understand me?"

Kit could not stand Anaya Esteban. She was a horrid girl, snobbish and conceited. But she was pretty and rich, and young men vied to court her. Society-minded girls strove to be invited to her many parties and socials.

Stubbornly Kit declared, "I don't want to go. Every time I'm around her I have to bite my tongue to keep from telling her just how hateful and mean she is."

Jade sighed. "I don't know what I'm going to do with you. It just isn't normal for you not to enjoy dressing up and going to balls and parties."

Kit knew it was a waste of time to tell her mother she was wrong. She actually did enjoy fine gowns and lavish parties, but *not* when they were forced upon her, and *not* in the company of people she didn't enjoy. "I don't see why I have to go places where I know I won't have a good time."

"If you had your way, you'd do nothing but ride with vaqueros and tag along after Doc Frazier. It's just a shame I didn't give birth to identical twins, so you could've been a boy like your brother."

"Maybe then I'd have some freedom," Kit tossed back saucily.

"And what would you do if you had it?"

"Be a veterinarian like Doc Frazier."

"That's ridiculous! Who ever heard of a woman being an . . . an animal doctor!"

"Then I'd like to be a rancher."

Jade exclaimed, *"Marry* a rancher, my dear! Marry someone of your background and blood . . . *royal* blood," she reminded Kit soberly.

"You know," Jade went on, "I made some inquiries about the handsome man you danced with at the embassy ball. His background is a bit shadowy, but apparently he's received by the best families in Europe, even royalty. He's quite wealthy, one of the biggest landowners in Spain, and—"

"And he's insufferable!" Kit interjected.

Jade ignored her. "I thought he might be perfect for you, so I invited him to several parties here—"

"You didn't!" Kit gasped.

"I did," Jade told her coolly, "but he refused. Obviously he wasn't as smitten with you as I thought, or," she added tartly, "perhaps when he realized that you're the little gypsy who rides like a man, he was disgusted—as any gentleman would be."

"He's no gentleman," Kit advised hotly, "no matter how much money he's got. Believe me, if he ever does show up here, I will not receive him! I won't suffer the company of that . . . that reprobate!"

Kit's expression turned conciliatory. "I really have something I need to do this morning, Mother. I won't be gone long, and when I get back, I'll spend the rest of the day getting ready for Anaya's party, if it'll make you happy. I promise."

Jade was adamant. "No. I won't allow you to leave this house dressed like that. If you want to go riding, then you'll have to change, and—"

"I have a headache," Kit suddenly announced, sinking into a nearby chair. "I think I'm going to be sick, so I'll just go to bed. I don't think I'll be able to go to the party tonight after all.''

Jade's eyes narrowed. Kit's dramatic act was a ploy Jade herself would have used in her younger days, so she recognized it for what it was, and, weary of confrontation, conceded. ''Oh, really? Well, I'll just bet a nice ride in the fresh air and sunshine would make you feel a lot better, wouldn't it?''

Kit couldn't suppress an impish grin. ''It probably would.''

''Then go,'' Jade said frostily, ''but I'm warning you, young lady, I'm doing all I can to persuade your father that we need to leave this place, and get you in a more civilized atmosphere, and I *will* succeed.''

But it won't matter, Kit thought as she hurried from the room, because I'll be the owner of my own ranch, and no one will ever tell me what to do again!

The ride to Doc Frazier's was a blur as Kit wrestled with her anger. Doc was preparing to leave, but he waited as she approached. ''So that's the Hispano I've heard so much about!'' he cried as she reined up beside him. ''My men told me about him. You done yourself proud, girl. I've heard of Hispanos . . . never seen one till now. A fine, fine animal, indeed.''

''What, exactly, did they tell you?'' Kit asked.

''Everything.'' Doc snorted. ''Believe you me, girl, I put the fear of God in 'em, and there won't be any more race betting on my land. They wish now they'd kept their mouths shut, but they were so proud of you they just had to share it with me. What have you told your folks about how you came by that horse?''

''I suppose Mother thinks he's just another horse of yours I borrowed, because she hasn't asked. Daddy hasn't seen him yet. I've never lied to him, so I hope he'll assume the same thing as Mother.''

"He won't. He knows I don't own a horse that fine, and if I did, I wouldn't loan him out."

Kit shrugged, pretending she wasn't worried, even though she knew there would be hell to pay when her father heard the story.

Doc had to laugh, because he knew her so well. "He's more understanding than you think. You just tell him the truth, and he'll understand. It's your ma I'd worry about, nagging that you're wild and need to be locked in your room till you come to your senses."

"Not locked in my room," Kit wryly corrected, "just moved to New York where I'll be exposed to all the culture and refinement a young lady of my class needs." She made no effort to hide her derision.

Doc nodded toward Pegasus, envy in his voice as he said, "Well, you got yourself one fine horse there."

Kit's eyes were shining with pride. "I still can't believe he's mine." And he's going to stay mine, she vowed silently. She dared not tell Doc of her plan. He would be against such a contest, especially on his land.

"So . . ." Doc changed the subject, "what brings you here today? You going to make a few calls with me?"

"Can't," she answered regretfully. "I came to see Riguero."

"You'll find him in the bullpen out back, I suppose. We're trying to breed old Sancho with Diablo Padreio's cow and having a tough time, because old Sancho is just that—*old!*" He winked. "Gotta go now. You take care . . . and take care of that horse. He's a prize!"

Kit headed for the pen, disappointed that it was being used. She spotted Riguero perched on a railing.

He grinned as she approached, tipping his sombrero. *"Buenos dias,* Señorita Kit. It is a fine sight to see such a beautiful lady on such a beautiful horse."

Kit was riding bareback. She slid easily to the ground, looping the reins over the railing and climbing up beside him. *"Gracias,* Riguero, but he might not be mine much longer. It seems that Galen Esmond was more of a *bandido* than we thought—he was a horse thief. Pegasus was stolen."

He stared at her in disbelief, then threw his sombrero to the ground and cried furiously, *"Condenar! Bastardo!* I should have known! How did you find out?"

"His owner recognized him."

"But he has no brand!" Riguero argued.

"The owner had a bill of sale."

He fell silent for a moment, looking from her to the horse. Then he grinned. "But you straightened everything out, no? You still have the horse. So why did you say—"

"That I might not have him much longer? Because, *amigo,* his legal owner wouldn't give him up, even though I won him fairly. I had to make a wager for him."

"A race? There is nothing to worry about—"

"Not a race," Kit corrected him. "A bullfight. If I can best a bull, Pegasus is mine. If I lose, then I must give him up."

Riguero was fuming. "What kind of man would make such a challenge to a woman? Why did he not just let you buy the horse?"

"He didn't challenge me, Riguero. *I* made the wa-

ger.'' She dropped to the ground, Riguero following.
"I'm not worried about it. You've seen me defeat bulls
many times. I learned the skill well, but only you and
a few of your men know that. Pegasus's owner
doesn't, and I plan to keep it that way. But I need
your help.''

"Just tell me what you want me to do," Riguero
said.

"I want a good, spirited bull," she told him. "And
I want to get it over with quickly so there's no more
disagreement about Pegasus being mine. How soon
can we do it?"

"I would say we can be ready day after tomorrow."

"Good." Kit was relieved. "But don't pit me
against old Sancho. I want a *good* bull. Spirited and
mean. Can you find one?"

He beamed. "We have one. The men call him
Malo, because he is that—evil. His owner brought
him here last week to be bred to one of the doctor's
cows, and he has not yet sent for him. We can use
him, and no one will know . . . unless you are in
danger, and then Malo must be . . . stopped," he
grimly finished.

"That won't happen," Kit assured him. She had
heard of the fierce bull. He was a formidable foe and
would provide a good show for her to demonstrate
her skill. She would certainly not be accused of tricking anyone by fighting an old or cowardly bull!

She turned to leave, but Riguero suddenly asked,
"*Señorita*, the man the horse was stolen from, what
is his name? Do I know him?"

Kit drew in her breath, and let it out in a sigh of
disgust. "Probably. It's Kurt Tanner."

"*Mi Dios!*" He crossed himself.

* * *

Kit thought that walking into the Salon de Cortes of the Palacio de la Generalidad was like entering a Faberge box. The gleaming enameled walls and glittering silver and crystal chandeliers created a dazzling effect. In the center of the room was the largest birthday cake she'd ever seen—at least ten layers tall, with eighteen candles in delicate gold filigree holders.

Anaya and her parents received their guests as they passed through the entryway. Kit had to admit that, despite her unpleasant personality, Anaya looked lovely. She was wearing a blue satin gown that matched her eyes and complemented her honey-colored hair. She also wore sapphire and diamond jewelry, but, Kit reflected, her fine attire could not mask her cold, vain attitude.

"Kit, how nice . . ." Anaya drawled, a sarcastic twist to her smile. She took the gift Kit handed her with casual disinterest and passed it to a waiting servant. "It's so good of you to come. I would've thought you'd be out riding with your cowboy friends."

Kit lifted her chin and met Anaya's impudent gaze. "Well, Anaya, I feel it's important to mingle with *patricians* now and then. It gives me a lesson in humility."

Kit moved on quickly, afraid she would start laughing. It served the snob right!

Anaya paled at her response.

Kit saw Rosamonda Huenciad, one of her favorite friends in Valencia, at the lavish buffet table and joined her. They found a little table in a corner, and sat. "Everyone is waiting for the Princess Anaya to fall," Rosamonda confided. "They say this time, she has met her match. Her new love is the real reason for this party. Her parents had planned to send her to the Greek islands for a holiday, but she said no, because she wanted to show off her new beau to everyone.''

"I'll just be glad when the formalities are over, because I don't intend to stay long. It's a boring party," Kit commented.

"They can't have the toast till he gets here."

Kit frowned. "Who is this wonderful man who, I hope, will break our cobra's heart?"

Rosamonda nodded toward the door. "There . . . he just arrived."

Kit turned . . . and froze at the sight of Kurt Tanner.

Chapter Nine

KIT watched as Anaya hurried to greet Kurt, glancing about to assure herself that everyone saw him kiss her outstretched hand. Kit had to admit that he was strikingly good-looking in his suit of bold black leather, red silk shirt, and black string tie.

Rosamonda moaned enviously, "Oh, he's so handsome! He takes my breath away! Why does *she* have to have him? She's so mean and hateful—she doesn't deserve such a man."

"Who says she has him?" Kit softly remarked.

Rosamonda looked at her quizzically.

Kit lifted her chin ever so slightly. "Some men collect art. From what I hear, Kurt Tanner collects women."

"I had forgotten!" Rosamonda cried, snapping her fingers. "He danced with you at the embassy ball in Madrid. All the girls talked about the passion in your dance. Someone said they thought he even kissed you. So, are you saying that since then—"

"No!" Kit's quick denial was too loud, and a few people looked her way curiously. She lowered her voice. "No, I did not see him after that. I don't know anything about him except what Carasia told me—that he's a womanizer. I don't want anything to do with him."

Rosamonda giggled, watching Kurt adoringly as he stood talking with Anaya and her parents. "From what I hear, it's the other way around. It's the *women* who chase *him* . . . and I can see why!"

"Well, here's one who won't be added to his list." Kit suddenly decided to leave, even though the formal birthday toast had not been made. If she had known that *he* would be there, she would never have come, despite her mother's wrath. "I'm going to slip out a side door. I really can't stand being here."

Kit stood, then sank miserably back into her chair when she realized it was too late to escape. Delhy Esteban was clapping his hands for attention, and everyone in the parlor turned in his direction. Waiters began to move quickly about the room with glasses of champagne for the celebratory toast. For the moment, Kit was trapped.

With a great flourish, Señor Esteban announced, "Thank you, one and all, for being here tonight to celebrate the birthday of my beloved and beautiful daughter, Anaya . . ."

On and on he went, singing Anaya's praises, as Kit impatiently tapped a satin-slippered toe, looking everywhere but at the Estebans. She did not want Kurt Tanner to think that she was looking at him.

All of a sudden, Rosamonda gasped. She leaned closer and whispered furtively, "He's looking at you. He glanced around the room, but then he saw you, and this strange expression came on his face, almost as if he were angry. He hasn't taken his eyes off you since."

Kit's heart began to pound. She would not look in his direction, and wished desperately that she could leave.

People were standing and raising their glasses, and

Kit had no choice but to do the same. There were cheers and more toasts. Then, mercifully, it was over, and the guests began to talk softly among themselves. The band resumed playing and Kit murmured a quick good-night to her friend and headed for a side door.

She was halfway across the room when she heard her name being called. She pretended not to hear, but suddenly a hand reached out for her arm. She vaguely recognized someone she knew telling her, "Señorita Coltrane, our hostess is calling you . . ."

Once more she was trapped. She could do nothing but turn and face Anaya—who was holding on to Kurt's arm and pulling him along with her. Kit could see that he appeared as reluctant as she for an encounter.

Anaya's eyes glittered like those of a snake about to strike. "You've met my friend Kurt Tanner, I believe," she cooed sweetly. "I seem to recall that you danced with him at the embassy ball in Madrid."

"Your memory is partially correct, Anaya," Kit countered frostily. "Actually, *he* danced with *me.*"

At that Kurt smiled. His gaze upon her was downright lecherous, Kit thought heatedly. It was as if he were looking right through her clothing, could see her nakedness, *feel* it. She hated him for it . . . and for the way he was making her feel inside.

"Yes, and it was a spectacle, as I recall," Anaya went on, "but some people enjoy being the center of attention, I suppose."

"Did you want something?" Kit snapped impatiently. "I was just leaving. Thank you for inviting me to your party, by the way . . . and happy birthday," she added dryly.

"Yes, as a matter of fact I did." Anaya moved

closer to Kurt, who continued to watch Kit with a penetrating gaze. "A horse was stolen from Kurt."

Kit stiffened, and Kurt looked puzzled.

"I thought we should tell you about it, since you ride with those trashy vagabonds who would do something like that. Should you happen to see the horse that resembles the one stolen from Kurt, well, you could inform the authorities. Describe your horse, Kurt," Anaya commanded.

Kurt quietly said, "I see no need for this, my dear."

"Oh, but you're wrong, Kurt darling. You see, Kit has you fooled. She really does know the kind who would steal a horse. Why, no doubt her mother forced her to come to my party. She much prefers riding with vaqueros—like a man. So she might be able to help you find your horse, because she keeps company with such common riffraff."

Swallowing her anger, Kit crisply retorted, "Rest assured, Anaya, I don't know a soul who possesses anything that isn't rightfully theirs. Now, finally, I bid you good-night." She turned to go, then paused to add, "But you are right about why I came. I'm afraid that my mother doesn't know you as well as I do."

Anaya's eyes flashed fire, and Kit continued briskly on her way. She was furious, but proud that she'd held her tongue and not told Anaya that she had absolutely nothing to fear—the last thing in the world she wanted was Kurt Tanner!

She had just reached the door when she heard her name spoken in a low, masculine voice. She froze.

A hand touched her arm, and she knew instinctively that it was he.

"I'm sorry. I didn't know Anaya was going to do

that. She's unpredictable, and very jealous. . . ." he
added with a hint of amusement in his tone.

Kit brushed his hand away. "She has no reason to
be jealous of me."

He raised an eyebrow. "I'm not so sure of that."

"*I* am." She tried to leave, but he caught her arm
again. She looked from his hand to his face, then
scathingly said, "If you don't leave me alone right
now, I'm going to scream. Unless you want a scene,
I suggest you go back to the party . . . and Anaya."

Kurt released her. "You really are determined to
hate me, aren't you? Okay. Have it your way. I never
was good with children."

"How dare you—"

"You're a spoiled brat, Kit Coltrane," Kurt said,
his face hard. "What I'd like to do is turn you over
my knee and spank your beautiful bottom, but instead, I will have a word with you about tomorrow."

"Have you decided to withdraw your ridiculous
claim? If so, I'd be willing to reimburse you for—"

"Hell, no!" he exploded angrily. "That damn
horse is not for sale. Now how about calling off this
mad dare of yours? It's gone far enough!"

Kit looked at him long and hard, then said, "Tomorrow you'll find out how far is far enough!" And
before Kurt could mutter more than a nasty oath, she
was gone.

Once home, she changed into her riding clothes,
going straight to the stables—and her beloved horse.

She rode to the beach below her house. The pebble
beach glistened like silver satin in the crystal moonlight. The water was a dark and mysterious ribbon,
dancing and shimmering out to the distant horizon.
Dismounting, Kit leaned against a large rock, drink-

ing in the peace and tranquillity. She tried not to think of Kurt Tanner, but she knew that was why she had come here—to be alone and try to sort out her feelings. He affected her like the dreams she sometimes had—dreams so alive with passion that they frightened her.

The tide was coming in, and her boots were getting wet. After making sure Pegasus was securely grazing on some nearby weeds, she scrambled up onto a huge rock and stretched out.

The dream came over her, inspired, as always, by the beauty and freedom of her moments alone in her beloved countryside. Kit gave into it with a sigh, flinging her arms above her head in complete submission to the fantasy. Her mystery lover came to her on a silver horse. The man was naked, his body as powerful and magnificent as the mythical Adonis. He lifted her up easily and folded her against a rock-hard chest. Once on the ground, he stretched out beside her, his fingertips tracing a ribbon of tantalizing fire over her yearning body. She surrendered to the overpowering desire, revelling in the feel of him against her skin as they became one.

The dream usually ended abruptly, but sometimes it went on and on until a strange feeling came over her—a white-hot wave of delicious ecstasy. She would awaken damp, warm . . . and almost, but not quite, fulfilled.

Now Kit felt his lips on hers—warm, searching, possessive. She yielded willingly, eagerly . . . Suddenly she opened her eyes. Pushing him hard, she stared in disbelief. Her dream had vanished. She was sitting on a rock, in the mystical moonlight, by the sea . . . with Kurt Tanner gazing down at her.

"Why are you so surprised? I know of no man who

could have resisted such a beautiful sight as you lying here, waiting to be kissed.''

"But not by *you!*" she told him vehemently. "Why did you follow me here?"

Kurt hoisted himself up beside her on the rock. "We didn't finish our conversation."

"Oh, yes, we did. And tomorrow, we finish any business between us, and then I never want to see you again."

She started to slide off the rock, but he held her back. She looked at him warily.

"I don't want you to be angry, Kit. I find you very, very desirable. I'd like for us to forget all this business about the Hispano and start over again, be friends."

"Why?"

"Because"—he smiled roguishly—"I can think of so many other things we could do . . . together." He kissed her hard, hungrily, his tongue touching hers.

Kit was furious with him for his brashness, and with herself for responding, for there was no denying the liquid fire moving through her veins. She wanted desperately to let herself melt against him, to allow her dream to come alive.

He pressed her gently back upon the rock, his hand moving over her breasts, stroking her lightly. "So lovely," he murmured. "I want to touch you, kiss you . . . all over. . . ."

Kit was waging an internal battle. Her brain commanded her to resist, to deny the longing in her heart, but her body refused to obey, wanting more. . . . Never had she felt so drawn to a man.

He devoured her with his eyes and lips and fingers, and despite her turmoil, Kit's hands began to caress him, exploring the wonders of his magnificent body.

His tongue moved down her throat as he nimbly unbuttoned her shirt, and her breasts became vulnerable to the hungry warmth of his mouth. She moaned deep in her throat and clutched him tightly against her. He used his knee to gently spread her thighs, and she could feel his hardness against her.

He raised his head to gaze down at her, hunger evident in his eyes. "I want you, Kit, more than I've ever wanted a woman before. . . ."

He paused, then continued in a low voice, "But I want more than your body, Kit. I want you . . . your friendship, for a start. I want us to stop fighting. Forget the silly wager. I'm going to settle things by giving you the Hispano's firstborn."

Kit came back to earth with a crash. "What . . . what did you say?" she gasped, pushing him away and sitting up.

Kurt repeated his offer quietly.

"Don't *patronize* me!" Kit hissed. "We made a pact—how dare you try to seduce me into backing out? Who do you think you are, that you can trifle with me this way?"

Kurt cursed himself for ruining the tender moment, his own anger rising. "I made you a generous offer, Kit. I don't *have* to offer you anything. That horse is mine, and you know it. It's you who've been trifling with me, and I damn well don't appreciate it. As for my supposed attempt to seduce you, I was pretty sure that we wanted each other. If calling it seduction lets you save your honor, suit yourself. I've been accused of much worse," he added with a brittle laugh.

"I can believe that!" Kit scrambled to her feet and straightened her shirt, informing him hotly, "I'll see you tomorrow in the bullpen. After I've won the wager, don't ever come near me again!"

Without another word, Kurt mounted his horse and rode into the night, breathing hard with anger. He'd known plenty of women, in many ways, but never one like Kit Coltrane. She was fire and ice, and passion and beauty. He knew that if he ever decided to give another woman a chance, she'd be the one for him.

Kurt smiled to himself. She wanted that horse because she was used to getting anything she wanted.

Well, so was he.

So when she got in over her head and made a fool of herself, he'd be ready to console her.

She wanted the horse.

He wanted her.

Maybe they could do some trading in private.

Chapter Ten

*S*EÑORITA . . . Kit . . . wake up . . ."

Kit opened heavy eyelids and blinked against the sudden burst of sunlight as Carasia opened the drapes.

"You must wake up. There is big trouble!" Carasia's black eyes were round with fear. "Your mother sent me to tell you to dress and go downstairs at once. Señora Esteban arrived perhaps a half hour ago and—"

"Oh, no . . ." Kit groaned, covering her face with her hands and falling back on the pillows. She was beginning to understand. "Go on."

"Señora Esteban demanded to see your mother. I took her in, but then I listened at the door, because I knew Señorita Anaya's mother coming so early the day after her birthday party was not good."

"How right you are," Kit had to agree.

"Well," Carasia rushed to continue, "Señora Esteban was crying. She said you ruined Anaya's party, that you caused some trouble between her daughter and her escort. Anaya locked herself in the bathroom and would not come out. She said she was too humiliated to face her guests, because *you* had said terrible things to her that everyone heard, and you had tried to take her man away."

Kit was incredulous. "That's a lie!"

Carasia shrugged. "The guests finally left, and only then could her parents persuade her to come out. So now, Carasia finished with a sigh, "the *Señora* has come to demand an apology from you and your family. I do not think I have ever seen Señora Jade so furious."

It was already so late! She had no time to waste on this nonsense with Señora Esteban. If she wasn't at the ring, Kurt would be only too happy to declare her a coward and demand possession of Pegasus. She'd be damned if anything was going to stop her from proving him wrong. Flinging back the satin coverlet, she jumped out of bed and began to dress.

Soon, she stepped out of her dressing alcove wearing trousers, an old jacket, and boots, fitting a gun into her holster as she walked to the door.

Carasia threw up her hands in horror. "If you go downstairs dressed like that, your mother will drop dead!"

"I'm not going downstairs. Give me a few minutes, then say you've looked all over the house, but you can't find me." She swung open the doors to the terrace, about to climb over the balcony railing and down a nearby tree.

"You are going to be in big, big trouble, Señorita Kit," Carasia admonished. "Who is this man that Anaya says you tried to take from her?"

"Someone I wouldn't have if he were the last man alive—Kurt Tanner." Kit dropped the last few feet to the ground, dusted herself off, then ran toward the stable as fast as her legs would carry her. Damn Anaya and her lies, she cursed silently, and damn Kurt Tanner for all the misery he's caused. Oh, she couldn't *wait* to show him up.

Once on Pegasus and out of sight of her house, she began to relax. It was a beautiful day, all blue and gold, and it was only going to get better—she could just feel it. She leaned forward to give Pegasus a pat, assuring him that in a few hours he'd be legally hers.

Riguero was at the pen when she arrived. He greeted her enthusiastically. "I have just enough men to act as picadors and banderillas—but without the lances and darts, of course," he assured her with a broad grin.

Kit nodded her approval, then asked, "Did you take my note to Joselito?"

His happy expression became one of deep concern. "*Sí*, I found the old *torero* at his casa by the sea. He read the note you sent him, and he was very happy. He packed a box for me to bring to you, and he also sent his muleta. I must ask you, *señorita*"—his eyes narrowed suspiciously—"how far do you plan to take your little joke?"

"Far enough that Señor Tanner will feel like a complete fool," Kit curtly declared. "Don't worry, Riguero. I know what I'm doing, and no one will get hurt—not me, not Malo. Just have the men ready to help me if I need it, and everything will be fine." She turned toward the barn. "I'm going to do the *faena*—the footwork, the passes."

Riguero protested frantically, "No, no, not the *faena, señorita*. It is too dangerous. You could be killed, or we may have to kill the bull. He does not belong to this ranch, and the doctor-vet, he will be furious. He will have our heads for allowing such a thing to happen, and—"

"You musn't worry. You've seen me in the ring before, Riguero, and you know I'm good. Everyone knows I'm good—except the pompous Señor Tanner, and he'll find that out soon enough.'' She grinned, imagining his reaction, then suddenly frowned. ''I think you'd better have a couple of vaqueros close by, just in case he gets any ideas about stopping me. I want to make sure he learns something from being so stubborn.'' She winked and hurried on her way.

Kurt Tanner was on time. He wanted to get this contest over with, and claim his horse.

Riguero greeted him, inviting him to take a seat where some benches had been set up in the shade. ''I'll stand,'' he said curtly. ''I've a feeling this won't take long. Has the *señorita* even shown up?''

Riguero nodded happily. Señorita Kit was right. This man needed to be taught a lesson.

Kurt pulled a watch from his vest pocket. ''It's time,'' he announced as a cry erupted from the group of vaqueros around the pen.

Kit appeared, and Kurt shook his head in disbelief. She was wearing the clothes of a matador—a shirt-waist of hand-drawn linen lace, a short jacket, and knee-length skintight trousers of blue silk, richly embroidered in gold and silver. His stunned gaze took in the coral-pink silk stockings and flat black slippers. Perched atop her hair was a *montera*—a *torero* hat made of tiny black silk chenille balls.

''A perfect fit, no?'' Riguero beamed. ''She borrowed the costume from her friend, the retired *torero*, Joselito Gomez.''

''Fine,'' Kurt said brusquely as Kit walked toward him. Raising his voice loud enough for her to hear, he said, ''But I didn't come here to look at costumes. She said she was going to fight a bull, so let's get on with it.''

Kit reached him, saucily grinning. She rested her

elbows on the railing in front of him and said co-
quettishly, "Welcome, *señor.* I'm glad you could
make it. It's frustrating to put on a show without an
audience."

His jaw tensed. How far was she going to go, dammit? "Then let the show begin, *señorita.*"

Kit suddenly pretended surprise. Wide-eyed, she
asked, "Did you know that five years ago the Spanish
government declared it illegal for women to perform
in bullrings?"

So this was the trick! She was going to tell him that
he'd goaded her to do something against the law. Before he could say anything, she rushed on, "Yes. They
did. Why, when the law was passed at the turn of the
century, La Reverte, the famous *señorita matadora,*
was forced to take off his wig and reveal himself as
a man! Can you imagine that?"

"Is that what you're going to do?" he snickered.
"Or just back out of our deal by saying it's illegal?"

"Neither." Kit smiled innocently. "I just thought
you'd want to hear a little history before the performance.

"Did you also know," she continued, enjoying
herself immensely, "that one of Goya's etchings de-
picted a female *torera* performing in the Saragossa
arena?"

Kurt said nothing, merely regarded her with cold
eyes.

"So," she finished triumphantly, "it would seem
that you have much to learn about women, *señor.*"

"And you have much to learn about me," he
snapped impatiently, "such as how I don't like game-
playing. You made a wager. Keep it, or give me my
horse."

Kit's violet eyes flashed with rage. She raised her

hand to signal the waiting vaqueros. Taking the red satin cape and ornate silver sword from Riguero, she turned on her heel and began to walk toward the center of the pen. She waved the cape at Kurt and cried, "Did you know that bulls are color-blind? They charge the matador if he uses a red or a white cape. You're like a bull in so many ways, Tanner! In your own stubborn way, you're just as blind!"

Kurt suddenly swore at Riguero, "Goddammit, what kind of trick is this? She's going to get herself killed, unless you run a blind, crippled bull in there—"

"No, no, *señor.*" Riguero laughed heartily. "You will see. Just watch."

Kurt had had enough. There was no way he would stand there and watch that foolish girl get herself hurt . . . or worse. "Enough!" he roared as the bull was about to be released. He raised himself up to swing over the railing. "That's Malo. I know that bull, and he's mean."

He suddenly felt a gun pressed against his side. Riguero was smiling apologetically. "Sorry, *señor,* but the *señorita,* she say you are to watch, so please get off the railing and do as she asks."

Kurt had no choice but to obey.

The bull roared into the ring and went straight for Kit. She spread the cloth in front of his snout and swung it smoothly by her side as he charged. Malo followed the cape past Kit. Then he turned and charged anew. Again she swung the cape, and the bull came frighteningly close to her slender body. As the bull made another charge, Kurt observed how deftly she worked, with complete control over the bull. Finally she gathered the cape against her body. Confused, the bull stopped short. Kit boldly turned her back in the traditional pose of mastery. The vaqueros rewarded her with a roar of *"Olé!"*

Kurt rubbed his eyes as if to dispel the amazing spectacle before him. There was no way he could deny that Kit knew exactly what she was doing. She displayed her mastery by letting the beast's horn actually graze her chest!

Furiously Kurt's hands clenched at his sides. So he'd been tricked by a woman once again! The little vixen had known exactly what she was doing when she had goaded him into accepting her challenge. He felt like a fool. He was a fool. The vaqueros standing there gloating would make sure that everyone heard about his humiliation. That, however, did not cause him concern. He'd never cared what others thought; he didn't like the way he felt about himself. "All right," he quietly told Riguero. "She wins."

He turned to go, but the gun pressed against him once more.

"She wants you to see it all," Riguero told him.

"Twist the sword in me instead of the bull, right?"

Riguero shrugged and turned his eyes back to the pen. "She's going to go to the *faena*," he said, sounding worried.

At that moment, Kurt didn't care if the bull gored her right in her smart little ass.

She executed a *rebolera*—holding her cape to her waist, she twirled as the bull passed, so that the cape stood up like the skirt of a pirouetting dancer. Kurt marveled at her skill, and, he had to admit, her courage. She swung her cape over her head, a movement that was especially dangerous because it made her lose sight of the bull at a critical moment. She then swept it behind her body, and knelt before him—the ultimate display of skill—and the ultimate laugh at death.

Finally Kit signaled to the vaqueros that she was victorious. She had successfully exhausted the bull. They came into the pen and drove Malo easily into the stable.

Breathless and excited, Kit accepted congratulations from her audience. She searched for Kurt Tanner, eager to enjoy her moment of triumph and glory.

Kit headed toward Riguero, hoping to find Kurt there. He was nowhere to be seen, however. She was disappointed but not surprised. She hadn't really expected him to linger. Reaching Riguero, Kit said tonelessly, "He left."

"*Sí.* He said to give you this."

She took the slip of paper and saw that it was the bill of sale Kurt had shown her earlier. He had signed possession of the Hispano over to her.

"He said nothing." Riguero met her disappointed gaze. "But you were right. He wanted to stop the contest, then he wanted to leave before it was over. My men, they made him stay. Then he wrote on the paper and gave it to me. But he said nothing," he repeated for emphasis. Then, watching her face, he added, "I could tell he was very, very angry."

Kit shrugged. So what? She had won fair and square. It was his own fault if he felt foolish. He'd never even asked if she'd had any experience as a *torera.* Well, that's what he got for being so stubborn and arrogant. "Thank you," she said to Riguero. "You all did a good job for me, and I'll see that you're rewarded."

"There is something else, *señorita.*" Kit looked at him expectantly.

"Your mother, she came looking for you."

Kit reeled, gasping, "Oh, no! When?"

"During the *faena* . . . when you were doing the *rebolera.*"

"Where is she? Has she already gone?"

Riguero shook his head and pointed speechlessly.

Kit followed his gaze to a shady spot beneath a tree. Her mother lay on the ground, surrounded by vaqueros anxiously fanning her with their sombreros.

She had fainted.

Chapter Eleven

KIT felt like a prisoner. She *was* a prisoner, she fumed, in her own home! Pacing up and down her room, she paused occasionally to peer out the window at the guard posted below her balcony. Kit hoped that Carasia didn't lose her job for lying. She'd only been obeying orders. Her mother had been so angry when none of the servants would tell her anything that she'd gone to search for Kit herself. When she'd awakened after fainting, the nightmare had really begun. Kit had been waiting almost two days now for the family conference with a growing sense of dread.

Her father had arrived from Madrid a few hours ago, leaving the embassy right after receiving her mother's frantic cable. Oh, damn, damn, damn, Kit cursed as she continued to pace. Why did her mother have to arrive at that moment? She had already been furious beyond the point of reason, and the sight of her daughter in the pen with a charging bull was more than she could take. Kit regretted the incident more than anything in the world, but what could she do now except apologize?

She heard a knock on her door as a carriage rattled into the circular driveway. She dared to peek out the window and felt a rush of hope at the sight of the

family arriving—Kitty, Travis, and Marilee. It didn't
bother Kit that her mother had summoned them. Kitty
would be on her side, as always. She would also have
received Kit's letter by now.

The knock on her door was louder and more insis-
tent. "Whoever it is, I'm sorry, but I can't let you in.
I'm a prisoner, in case you didn't know," Kit called
out dryly.

"I have the key, Kit. Is it all right for me to come
in?"

It was her father. Kit's anger fled, and she said
quickly, "Yes, please do. I didn't know it was you."

Colt walked in, his expression serious. Kit faced
him nervously, not knowing what to do or say. Then
he held his arms open to her. She went to him immediately, gratefully accepting his hug as he told her
what she already knew. "You've really done it this
time, little girl. I don't think I've ever seen your
mother so mad."

"I know," Kit murmured against his broad shoulder. "I'm terribly sorry, but what can I do?"

He father motioned for her to sit down on the divan
by the fireplace. "It's a bad situation, Kit. You know
that your mother has been after me for a long time to
move back to New York."

"And now you agree with her."

"It's not a matter of agreeing or not. She won't
be put off this time. Besides," he added grimly,
"there are serious rumors of war breaking out in
Europe. I think it would be safer for all of us to
leave Spain."

"But that's not fair to me, Daddy!" Kit cried. "I'm
nearly eighteen. Many women my age are already
married, with babies. I'm old enough to take care of
myself and live my life the way I want—and I *don't*

want to go back to New York." Kit searched his face,
desperately seeking some sign that he understood, that
he would yield and take her side.

"And I know all about the rumors of war," she
rushed on. "I know that the government of Spain says
that if war does come, they'll declare neutrality, so
I'd be safe here."

Colt frowned. "Safe doing what? Where would
you live, Kit? What would you do?" He shook his
head. "No, I feel that the family would be safer in
America, and this time I've got to agree with your
mother that it's time to get you away from unhealthy
influences.

"Quite frankly," he went on, anger suddenly flashing in his steel-gray eyes, "I'm pretty upset with you
myself. The idea of my daughter playing bullfighter
does not make me happy. I let you ride with Doc's
vaqueros because I didn't see any real harm in it. But
bullfighting?" He raised an eyebrow. "I'm afraid that
you've gone too far this time.

"And," he added coolly, "I don't even want to
discuss the accusations the Estabans made about how
you ruined their daughter's birthday party."

"Well, that's all a lie, anyway. Let's talk about me
and my life." She then said slowly, "Just what *do*
you and Mother have planned for my life, since you
think it's perfectly all right to tell me how to live
it."

Ignoring her sarcasm, Colt said, pursing his lips,
"I haven't had time to really plan anything yet, Kit.
This came about a bit suddenly, you know. Frankly,
if your mother had her way, she'd have you on the
next ship for New York, but there are details to be
taken care of. I've got to resign my position with the

embassy and tie things up there before I can leave, and there's the ranch to sell.''

''And then?'' she snapped.

''We move back to New York.''

''And where do we live?''

''Until we find a suitable house, your mother wants to take an apartment in the Osborne Building. It's in a good location—on Fifty-seventh Street. The new apartments have fourteen rooms and six bathrooms—quite luxurious.''

Kit leaned back on the divan and folded her arms across her chest. Staring into the fireplace, she said with cold resolution, ''I won't go.''

Colt was unmoved. ''Yes, Kit, you will. You don't have any choice.''

Kit stood up suddenly, her eyes blazing with rebellious determination. ''Oh, yes, I do! I have my trust fund, and I can use that to buy my own ranch. I've got it all figured out. Marilee is going away to finishing school, and Travis will go to West Point. Grandma can live with me. How could you object to that?''

''In the first place, I want you to be with me and your mother. In the second place, you don't have the trust fund, not yet . . . not till *I* say so.''

''You mean not till *Mother* says so!'' Kit said hotly. ''Seems to me that *she's* making all the decisions.''

''Don't be impudent, Katherine,'' Colt warned her.

Kit cringed inwardly. When he called her Katherine, it meant he was dangerously close to losing his temper, and she knew that nothing would be accomplished then. ''I'm sorry. It's just that if the decision were up to you, you'd be more understanding.''

''Your mother and I don't have that kind of marriage, thank goodness. We have equal say in decisions concerning you children.''

Kit's lavender eyes flashed. ''I'm not a child! That seems to be the whole point here, doesn't it?''

Colt sighed, thinking how badly he needed a brandy. Jade had been absolutely incoherent, trying to describe the terrifying sight of the bull charging Kit. He couldn't blame her for being upset, and the only way he'd managed to calm her down was to agree to return to America. But he hated seeing Kit so unhappy. It was a miserable situation all the way around. ''We'll talk more about this later, Kit. We're both tired and upset right now.''

He headed to the door, but turned when he heard his daughter's voice. Tears were running down her cheeks, and her lips were trembling.

''I love you, Daddy,'' Kit whispered tremulously, ''but I swear to you, I'll run away before I'll go back. My life is here now.''

Colt sighed, his heart going out to her. ''Later, Kit.''

She ran to him, and he wrapped her in his arms once more. ''Just promise me that you'll at least consider letting me stay here.''

''I'll consider it,'' he promised, ''but let's have a family conference first, all right? We are a family, you know,'' he reminded her with a warm smile. ''And, speaking of family, they're all here. I know they'd like to see you, so dry those eyes.''

Despite her misery, Kit managed to joke, ''Well, I guess you'll have to give them the key, won't you?''

He reached in his vest pocket and took out the key. Laying it on the table by the door, he winked. ''Somehow I've got a feeling that with your old man around you won't be climbing out any windows to go fight bulls.''

He turned to leave, then remembered to ask, "By the way, that magnificent horse in the barn—where'd you get him?''

"He's mine," she informed him proudly. "I won him in a race.''

Colt smiled, unable to hide his pleasure that his daughter was such an accomplished horsewoman. "Congratulations. Does your mother know you've been racing for wagers?''

Kit shook her head.

"Well, we won't tell her. I'm afraid she can't take any more at the moment." With another wink, he left.

Kit started pacing her room again. She desperately wanted to see Kitty, but she knew that her mother would be hysterically relating her side of the story. She'd have to wait.

After an hour passed, Carasia came to tell her that tea was being served on the summer porch, and she was expected.

Kit hurried downstairs. She blinked back tears of joy when Kitty stepped into the foyer, holding her arms open in loving greeting. She ran to her grandmother and hugged her tightly. "Oh, I'm so glad to see you! I've never needed you more!''

"Shush now. Don't you dare cry. Everything's going to be all right, I promise, and—''

"Kit! Kitty!''

They both turned at the sound of Jade's sharp voice. "In here, please.''

As they went in, holding hands, Jade glared at Kitty. "I thought you agreed that we'd have this family conference before you went behind my back and took sides against me.''

''When have I ever gone behind your back to take sides, Jade? You know I've always been very open with my opinion that you smother Kit.''

Jade stiffened and looked to Colt for support. As always, he glanced away, not willing to get involved in a confrontation between his wife and his mother.

Travis was sitting by the window, looking bored. He gave Kit a polite nod, but she saw at once that his eyes held condemnation.

Marilee sat on the wicker lounge, eyes wide with excitement.

No one said anything as Carasia nervously served the tea and sandwiches. When she left, closing the door behind her, Jade said, ''Let's get this over with. Everyone knows what Kit has done, and I think everyone agrees that it's best we move back to New York, and take her away from such harmful influences.''

Kit objected angrily. ''Well, *I* don't agree, and it's my life we're talking about. I love Spain, and I don't want to live anywhere else.''

Travis got to his feet and faced her, his expression stern. ''What you did was foolish and dangerous, Kit. You weren't thinking of anybody but yourself, and you were wrong to cause Mother so much distress. I agree that it's time to get you away from here, because you're turning into a spoiled brat, if you want to know my opinion.''

''I don't care what you think!'' Kit cried furiously. ''What I do is none of your business, Travis, and I'll thank you to stay out of it.''

''Now wait just a minute, young lady,'' Jade said.

"This is a family conference, and everyone has the right to speak his mind."

"You all know how I feel," Kitty put in. "I think it's time Kit was allowed to make her own decisions. You can't force her to live a life she doesn't want to live."

"She's my daughter, and she'll do as I say." Jade walked across the porch to stand before Kitty. Her green eyes glinted with anger. "Kitty, you know I've always had the utmost respect for you, and I've loved you like the mother I can hardly remember, but quite frankly, there have been times when I've resented your interference with how I raise my daughter. I'm going to have to ask you to stay out of this."

Kitty was undaunted. "She's my granddaughter, and my namesake, and I'm not going to stand for her being made unhappy."

Jade was appalled. "Do you mean to tell me that you approve of your granddaughter fighting a bull? Risking her life?"

Kitty shrugged. "From what I hear, she did a good job. I'd say you should be very proud of her."

Jade threw up her hands, turning to Colt in disgust. "Oh, why do I even bother arguing with her?"

Kitty ignored Jade's outburst. Addressing Colt, she said, "What if Kit compromises?"

Kit stared at her in astonishment, but Kitty went on. "Suppose . . . just suppose that Kit agreed to go back to New York—"

"Wait a minute!" Jade interrupted. "I don't have to make any bargains. She's my daughter, and she'll do as I say, and—"

"Please, Jade. Hear her out."

Her eyes widened as she looked at her husband.

Kitty smiled at her son, then gave Jade a patronizing nod. "Now then, you know that if Kit makes up her mind not to go to New York she'll find a way to stay here, even if it means running away. You also know that if it came to that, I'd help her."

"You . . . you wouldn't dare . . ." Jade sputtered indignantly.

"Yes," Kitty said quickly. "I would, and you know it, so stop pretending you're shocked. You'd best listen to the compromise I propose."

Jade gripped the arms of her chair. "I'm listening," she said tightly.

"The compromise is that Kit will go to New York on the condition that if she is absolutely miserable, you will let her return to Spain."

"Never!" Jade objected loudly.

"Return . . ." Kitty announced slowly, "to the ranch I'll buy for her. And I'll live there with her since Marilee and Travis will be away at school."

Jade shook her head adamantly. "That's absurd!"

"Is it?" Kit exploded, leaping to her feet. "I think it's a fair compromise. I'll agree to it. Why won't you?"

"Because . . ." Jade's fiery green eyes met her daughter's defiant gaze, ". . . because I don't have to compromise."

Colt slowly got to his feet, wearing a determined expression. "Yes"—he looked at Jade—"we do, because otherwise, like it or not, Kit will do something drastic. I suggest we accept this plan and just hope that Kit comes to her senses and decides to remain in New York with us. I don't see any other alternative."

Jade turned on Kitty. "If this doesn't work out, I don't think I'll ever be able to forgive you."

"It's settled," Colt stated. "We're going back to

the States in time for the inauguration. Meanwhile, arrangements will be made for Kit's debut. Now . . .'' He sighed, heading for the door. ''I'll see everyone at dinner. As far as I'm concerned, this discussion is closed.'' Everyone filed slowly after him, leaving Kit and Kitty alone. They threw their arms around each other and danced a little jig around the porch, laughing with joy.

Kit cried, ''I love you! You're my best friend in the whole world.''

''And I love you, too, my precious,'' Kitty said, her lavender eyes sparkling. ''Oh, how I wish I was young now, to have all the wonderful opportunities you have—''

''The ranch! What do you think?'' Kit asked excitedly. ''Please, don't say we've got to wait to buy it. I don't care what we told Mother. If we wait, we'll lose it, because there's someone else after it.''

''Of course we aren't going to wait,'' Kitty assured her. ''Do you think *I* want to stay in New York with your mother?'' She made a face, then grinned. ''I've wanted to live on a ranch again for some time now, and this is my chance. Tomorrow morning we'll go into town and make all the arrangements. As for your mother . . . '' She paused to wink, lowering her voice conspiratorially. ''We didn't tell her *when* we'd buy the ranch.''

Kit was trying very hard not to cry. She had never loved anyone more than she loved her grandmother at that moment.

''Don't you get emotional on me!'' Kitty commanded. ''Now that that's all settled, I want to talk to you about something else.''

''Anything.'' Kit grinned happily.

''That handsome devil you danced with at the embassy ball. There was just something about him that reminded me of your grandfather . . .''

Kitty went on talking about what a striking couple they'd made, not noticing how Kit had stiffened. She didn't know she'd struck a nerve . . . and that Kit had no intention of discussing Kurt Tanner.

Chapter Twelve

As they had previously agreed, Kitty remarked at breakfast that she'd love to go horseback riding. She said wistfully that the ranch was the only place where she could do real range riding. According to plan, Kit offered to go with her.

Jade immediately voiced her objections. "We have far too much to do if we're going to leave in just two weeks—packing, putting the ranch up for sale—"

"Two weeks!" Kit cried, stunned.

Colt continued to read his newspaper, Travis groaned, and Marilee watched them all with bright eyes.

"Two weeks," Jade repeated. "Your father and I talked it over last night. He made some calls, and we've already booked passage to sail two weeks from today. It's going to take some doing for him to finish up his work at the embassy, but we think it's best we leave as soon as possible. If we're going to be able to arrange your debut to coincide with all the inauguration parties, we've got a lot of work ahead."

"If you're going with us," Jade said to Kitty, "you don't have much time to get your own affairs in order."

"Be that as it may, I don't see anything wrong with

Kit and me riding for a few hours this morning,"
Kitty said.

Jade's face turned stony. "She doesn't have time.
There's something else she has to do."

Kit warily asked her mother what she was talking
about.

"I would like for you to visit the Estebans and
apologize for whatever you did at the party that has
everyone so upset."

Kit instantly exploded, "Apologize? Oh, you can't
ask me to do that, Mother! Anaya is the one who
owes me an apology!"

"Well, it would smooth things over . . . and end
it. Muego will drive you over when you've finished
eating."

Kit stubbornly shook her head.

Jade sighed, exasperated. "Really, Kit, it's just a
matter of propriety. After all, you were an invited
guest, and it was Anaya's birthday, and you could
have been a little more tactful."

"Tactful!" Kit snorted with unladylike disdain.
"You weren't there, and you didn't hear the nasty
things she said to me. Why, she's lucky I didn't push
her into the champagne fountain."

Colt could not resist murmuring under his breath,
"Your mother would have!"

Jade suppressed a smile and tried to give him a
furious look. He grinned, not at all contrite. Forcing
a straight face, Jade said to Kit, "I really wish you
would, dear. I don't like them talking about you, and
if you'll just apologize, this whole misunderstanding
will be over with."

"Please don't ask me to do this, Mother."

They all looked then to Colt. He knew he had to
take a stand whether he wanted to or not. "I have to

agree with Kit, Jade,'' he said without remorse. ''We weren't there, so we don't know what happened. I do know that the Esteban girl has a reputation for being rude and spiteful. If Kit says that she doesn't owe her an apology, then I think we should stand by her. She's more important to me than what the Estebans think.''

Jade drew in her breath and let it out slowly. Finally she shrugged her acquiescence.

Not twenty minutes later, Kit and Kitty were riding toward the Gaspencia ranch. It was a cold day, with gray skies that threatened rain, but they ignored the weather as Kit led the way, her heart beating excitedly in unison with Pegasus's thundering hooves.

When they reached their destination, Kit gave her grandmother a hurried tour of the house and barn and pointed out the property boundaries as best she could. Kitty remained silent until they were standing on the front porch, gazing out at the breathtaking view. ''It's for us, Kit!'' she exclaimed. ''I can feel it. It's as wonderful as you said it was, and you know something else? It reminds me of my land back in North Carolina. Oh, the terrain is different—this is rolling and hilly, and my land is flat, sandy. But there's just something about it. Maybe,'' she mused, a faraway look in her eyes, ''it's the atmosphere, the peace that you can just feel in your heart.''

Kit was trembling with happiness. ''I knew you'd love it. There's lots of work to do—the house isn't much, and the barn needs repairing and painting— but fixing it up will be fun. We won't have to buy much furniture, and we can make curtains to give it a homey look. It's not fancy, certainly not what you're used to, and—''

''What I'm used to?'' Kitty echoed with an indignant laugh. ''Why, I thought you knew I grew up in a cabin a lot shabbier than this one. That's where your grandfather and I began our married life together, after the war.

"Frankly," she went on, her voice soft and warm with nostalgia, "I don't think we were ever happier than we were back then, when we didn't have anything but each other. I think you're going to find as you grow older, Kit, that memories of a simpler life are somehow always the nicest."

Kit was curious. "You've never told me about your land. Why haven't you sold it by now?"

Kitty looked aghast that she could even suggest such a thing. "That land has been in the Wright family for three generations now, Kit. When I die, it'll go to your father, then to you and your brother. I promised my daddy I'd never sell it. 'Don't ever sell this land, Kitty girl,' were his very words. 'I'd rather see you starve to death than sell the Wright land.'

"He said," Kitty continued, the memories carrying her away so that it seemed she was talking more to herself than to Kit, "that he'd rather have his land than all the gold on earth, because the land will be here forever. With money, you can't be sure."

Kit said, "I'd never sell it, Kitty, and neither would Travis. You don't have to worry about that, but what are you doing with it now? What's happened to it?"

"I rent it to the Duke family," Kitty explained. "They, in turn, let tenants grow tobacco on the land. Daddy always said the future of North Carolina lay in tobacco, and as usual, he was right."

She proceeded to explain how the Duke family had built a multimillion-dollar tobacco industry near Durham. "Cigarettes are big business in America now. And don't you ever tell a soul," Kitty confided with wicked delight, "but I smoke now and then."

How like her, Kit thought, impressed and amused.

Kit told her that Señor Gaspencia had harbored dreams of growing grapes in the sandy soil near the river. Kitty thought it was a wonderful idea. ''When we get to New York, I'll have some scuppernong vines sent up from my farm, and we'll bring them back here with us. Wouldn't that be wonderful? To plant North Carolina scuppernong grapes in Spain and make our own Rosé? Oh, Kit, we're going to be so happy here, I know it!'' She hugged her granddaughter tightly.

Kit shared her joy, but wished she could renege on her promise. ''I don't want to go to New York. Not even for a little while.''

''It won't be so bad. And remember,'' Kitty gently chided her, ''your parents are only doing what they think is best for you. Give them a chance, you owe them that much. We'll stay long enough to be fair, and then there won't be any hard feelings when we leave. All right?'' She pushed a strand of golden hair back from Kit's forehead, thinking that looking at her was like gazing into a mirror of the past.

Kit sighed, capitulating. She then said, ''When I get my trust fund, I'll pay you back. I promise.''

''We'll worry about that later; right now I think we'd better get into town and take care of the legalities. You say that someone else wants to buy it?''

Kit nodded. She did not want to explain that!

Kitty persisted. ''I hope there won't be any resentment, but I suppose it can't be helped. We're buying fair and square. They had their chance.''

Kit quickly changed the subject. She did not want to think about how she'd hidden the sign. Nor did she want to think about how angry Kurt Tanner was going to be when he discovered she'd tricked him—again.

Maybe, she decided, leaving Spain for a while wasn't such a bad thing.

By midafternoon the papers were signed, and they went to a respectable cantina to celebrate. The conversation went from the ranch, to the life Kit dreaded in New York, to her mother's plans for her to marry soon, someone *respectable*.

"I don't know about that respectable business," Kitty remarked, to her granddaughter's surprise. "You're too much like me, dear—wild, rebellious, free-spirited. You need a man like your grandfather."

"Ah ha!" Kit couldn't help teasing. "Then you're saying I'm as wild as you were . . . and I need a man to tame me!"

"No," Kitty replied, her voice serious. "Travis wasn't like that at all. He let me be myself. I think that's why I loved him so. He let me glory in being a woman, without feeling that it made him less of a man."

To Kit's dismay, the image of Kurt Tanner suddenly appeared in her mind.

Why had *he* invaded her thoughts at that moment?

She despised him!

Did she?

Didn't she?

Lately, he was constantly stealing into her thoughts. She vividly remembered his warm kisses and soft caresses. Whenever she heard music, she thought of dancing in his arms, the way their bodies had molded together so naturally.

What would it be like, she wondered, to surrender, to let him lead her to those mysterious pleasures she knew only in her passionate dreams? His touch drove her wild. She could still feel the shivers of delight that had rippled over her when he'd touched her where no man had before. He was irresistible, and he was also dangerous.

"Kit!"

The sharpness in Kitty's voice roused Kit from her reverie.

"Darling, what . . . *who* were you thinking about just now? Your cheeks are flushed." Kitty's eyes narrowed suspiciously. "You know you can tell me anything. Who is he?"

"Nobody . . . nothing," Kit stammered. "I was thinking of the ranch . . . Pegasus, a million things. Not a man, though."

Kitty continued to look at her thoughtfully. Quietly she confided, "I've seen myself look like that in the mirror, when I was thinking about your grandfather."

"Well, I wasn't thinking about a man," Kit repeated.

Kitty pushed back her chair. "I'll be leaving early tomorrow morning. It's a long trip, and I dread to think of all I've got to do if we're to be ready in two weeks."

Stepping out into the late afternoon sun, Kit shut her eyes against the sudden assault of light. "I didn't realize we were in there so long," she said, adding with a giggle, "and I'm afraid I had one sangria too many, because I'm almost tipsy. Mother is going to want to know what we were celebrating, and—"

Suddenly Kit collided with someone and stumbled slightly. Her heart turned over as she looked up into the warm, mocking eyes of Kurt Tanner.

"Well, *princesa,* it seems fate decrees we meet again."

Kitty looked from Kurt to her granddaughter. In that instant, she knew that this was the man who was preoccupying Kit, and she instinctively approved of him. "Señor Kurt Tanner," she said pleasantly, when Kit merely glared at him in icy silence. "I believe we met at the embassy ball in Madrid last November."

He took her hand. "Madame Coltrane, isn't it? It's very nice to see you again." He then asked Kit if she was all right.

"I'm just fine, thank you!" She responded curtly. She began to walk past him, but he moved to block her.

"How's my horse?"

"He's not your horse!" she fired back indignantly. "You signed him over to me. I won the wager, remember?"

"It depends," he drawled, "on whether you consider treachery an honest victory."

Kit was aware that her grandmother was listening to every word. She would no doubt have some explaining to do later, but at that moment, she was too angry to care. "I didn't trick you. You never asked me if I had any experience. You were too busy behaving like the pompous egotist you are. Now, good day!"

Again Kit tried to pass him, but he stepped in front of her. "You did trick me, Kit."

"If you don't get out of my way—"

"Kit, really!" Kitty admonished. She then said to Kurt, "It's obvious you two have a difference of opinion over something, but this certainly isn't the time to discuss it. Maybe you can call on Kit before she leaves for New York and straighten things out."

"New York?" Kurt raised an eyebrow. "You're going to New York?"

"Yes, my family is moving there," she replied airily. "Now, since you and I have nothing further to discuss, perhaps you'll stand aside, and let my grandmother and me continue on our way." She cursed herself for looking at his lips, remembering how wonderful they felt pressed against her own. She hoped he could not hear the excited pounding of her heart.

"What about the horse?"

"What about him?" she snapped.

"Are you going to sell him?"

"No. I'm taking him with me."

Kitty gasped. "You're taking that horse all the way to America? Why, when you—" She caught herself. Kit looked at her in horror—Kitty had almost given away their plans to return to Spain!

"If you don't get the hell out of my way, I'm going to scream!" Kit warned Kurt through clenched teeth.

He stepped aside, his face a mask of barely contained rage.

Kit swept by him without another glance. Once they rounded the corner Kitty demanded, "Will you please tell me what that was all about?"

Kit was walking fast, trying to escape not only him, but her own turbulent emotions. "The bullfight. I did it to win Pegasus from him. He's so conceited and arrogant he just can't accept the fact that a woman bested him."

Kitty laughed. "Oh, child, he doesn't care about that horse."

Kit slowed, not sure she'd heard correctly. "What did you say?"

"I said he doesn't care about that horse. It's *you* he wants."

"That's absurd," Kit scoffed. "Kurt Tanner doesn't care about anybody but himself."

Kitty could well remember the time when she felt only contempt for Travis. If anyone back then had told her she was falling in love with him, she'd have said he was crazy. So she kept silent and did not say what was on her mind, or in her heart.

She did not tell Kit just how much Kurt Tanner reminded her of Travis Coltrane.

Neither Kit nor Kitty was aware that when they turned the corner and disappeared from his sight, Kurt had crossed the street and gone into the tax collector's office.

By the time they reached the spot where Muego waited with the family car, he had come out of the office.

And everyone who saw him stepped out of his way, for the furious look on his face said he was a man not to be crossed.

Chapter Thirteen

THE next two weeks passed in a flurry of activity as the Coltranes prepared for their return to America. While Kit pretended to help with the move, she slipped away every chance she could, making her own arrangements for her return.

Since she didn't know just when she'd be coming back, she'd asked Riguero to secretly look after her ranch. It made her feel easier to know that he would be protecting her interests for the next few months, and surely it would be no longer than that before she could get on with her life—the way *she* wanted to live it.

Kit did not like being so deceitful, but she knew it was necessary. She'd felt real guilt at her father's delight when she asked to take Pegasus with her to New York. He'd viewed it as a sign she'd given up her idea of returning to Spain. But she certainly could not confide that she was afraid Kurt Tanner would steal the prize Hispano when he found out she had bought the land he wanted.

A lavish dinner party was being held their last night in Spain, at the home of Señor Ortega Monolete, a very rich and important diplomat. Kit looked forward to the evening, for she had many friends in Valencia. In a festive mood, she selected a stunning gown of emerald velvet. Carasia piled her shimmering golden hair atop her head and fastened a necklace of pearls and sapphires around her neck.

As she descended the staircase, Jade exclaimed proudly, "Oh, Kit darling, you're so pretty. You should be the titled princess in this family!"

Colt stepped from his study to greet her, having just arrived from Madrid. "She *is* a princess"—he grinned at Jade—"whether the Czar officially titled her or not. She's the image of you—"

"No!" Jade said sharply. Her husband and daughter looked questioningly. She continued quickly, trying to cover her unusual response. "She . . . she's never looked like me, darling. We've always said she looks like Kitty, *your* side of the family . . . not mine at all."

"Your mother!" Colt said to Kit in mock exasperation. "Always afraid that someone will think you take after her and not me. Why, I don't know—she's beautiful, and so are you."

Jade turned away, lest her anxiety show on her face. As much as she wanted to return to New York, ever since the decision had been made the old fears had been creeping back to haunt her . . . fears she'd vowed, on the day her children were born, never to think about again. That was why it was so important that Kit and Travis resemble the Coltrane family, and never doubt who their father was.

Before leaving for the Monolete castle, Colt opened a bottle of champagne to celebrate their last night in Spain. By the time they arrived at the party, Kit was as bubbly as the wine.

"I didn't know there would be so many people here," Jade remarked as they stepped into the massive marble entrance hall. They could see into the large ballroom beyond, packed with gaily dressed guests. A small orchestra provided soft music that rose above the laughter and conversation.

Colt was beaming. "Señor and Señora Monolete have really outdone themselves. I'm very touched by all this."

Kit saw the way her parents looked at each other. This was their night, an evening they would always remember.

Señor Monolete and his wife greeted them warmly. For the next hour, Kit stood with her parents, exchanging pleasantries with old acquaintances. Then she closed her eyes and groaned softly as she recognized Esteban Yubero. For one hysterical instant, she thought of trying to escape—but it was too late. His hand, warm and clammy, was holding hers, and decorum decreed that she look up into his shining black eyes and force herself to smile. "Ah, *señorita*, I am a man of mixed emotions this night."

Kit braced herself, wondering irritably why such an attractive man would make himself so obnoxious.

"I have not been able to get you out of my mind, and I have counted the minutes until we could be together again, but—" He closed his eyes dramatically, cocking his head to one side and gazing at her with longing. He whispered, "You are leaving Spain . . . and leaving Esteban, and my heart now bleeds."

"How sweet of you, Esteban," Jade said approvingly.

She did not see Kit's annoyed expression as they all proceeded into the dining room. Kit and her parents sat at the table of honor. She tried to escape Esteban, but he made a special plea to Señora Monolete, and Kit was horrified to find him seated next to her. Oh, how could he be so bold, she fumed inwardly. What had started out to be a wonderful evening had suddenly turned into an ordeal, and she just wished it was over.

Waiters began serving the food—*faisán, perdiz* and *cordonices*—pheasant, partridge, and quail; *champiñones al ajillo* and *alcachofas con jamon*—mushrooms sauteed in garlic and artichokes cooked with ham. For dessert there were sweet baked orange slices, drizzled with flan—a creme caramel sauce.

Normally Kit would have enjoyed every bite, but tonight she might as well have been eating sawdust. All she was aware of was the way Esteban kept rubbing his leg against her knee. She desperately wanted dinner to end, because she wasn't sure what she would do if he dared put his hand on her leg as he had at his parents' home in Madrid. She refused to look at him, at his hungry, lust-filled eyes. The only thing that helped ease her wretchedness was the delicious wine.

When dinner finally ended, Señor Monolete announced there would be dancing in the main ballroom, and then flamenco dancers would perform.

As everyone began to make his way from the dining room, Esteban caught her arm, his breath hot against her ear. "I want so much to dance with you, to feel you in my arms . . ."

His words were slurred. Kit decided that what they both needed was some fresh air. She nodded toward the door and suggested they take a little walk before the evening's entertainment began. Esteban grinned, trembling with excitement that she wanted to be alone with him. He'd find out otherwise soon enough, Kit thought dryly.

As they walked he bragged, "I know this castle well. Once upon a time I courted Señor Monolete's daughter, Lanida, but she was not so pretty. I adore pretty women—like you, Kit. . . ."

He tried to put his arm around her and pull her close, but she jerked away. "I didn't ask you to go for a walk to have you pawing me, Esteban. We've both had too much to drink, and we need some air."

He laughed as if she were joking, but made no move to touch her again. They had reached a side door when he suddenly caught her and shoved her roughly to the other side of the hall, where a heavy wooden door was bolted. Kit had played in the castle with Lanida when they were children, and remembered that there were stairs to ancient dungeons—no place for them to be.

"What are you doing?" she cried, struggling. He held her with one hand, fumbled with the bolt with the other. "Esteban, let me go!"

The bolt slid back, and he opened the door and shoved her inside. Kit tried to scream for help, but he covered her mouth with his hand, pushing her into the dark shadows. "You don't have to be afraid. I'd never hurt you, Kit, but I can't have you screaming, giving people the wrong impression. We're on a landing, above the steps going down to the dungeon. We're quite safe, and we're alone, so I can tell you how much I adore you . . . and want you . . . and how much I want to love you . . . really love you."

Kit realized that struggling was useless. He was easily pressing her against the cold stone wall, pinning her arms behind her back and silencing her cry of protest with a nauseating kiss.

Kit brought her leg up to knee him, but he leaped back, avoiding the full brunt of the blow. Still, she hurt him, and he stumbled backward, releasing her as he grabbed the splintery wooden railing. Holding on to support himself, he gasped, "Why . . . why did you do that? I only want to love you—"

"You only want to maul me, you slimy little toad!" Kit cried, pushing by him furiously. She shoved open the heavy door and stumbled out.

The hall was empty, and Kit imagined she could hear the echo of her own heavy breathing. Behind her, from the other side of the door, she could hear Esteban trying to get out. Without a moment's hesitation she slid the bolt into place. He yelled in frightened protest, but she ignored him. He deserved to be shut away with the other rodents, she thought as she walked quickly away.

As she approached the main part of the castle she could hear the clicking of castanets as the dancers performed a furious fandango. Kit suddenly decided that she no longer wanted to be there. Sooner or later a servant would hear Esteban yelling, and she just didn't want to be around when he got out. Instead of joining the merriment, she went out a side door and skirted around to the front of the castle, where Muego waited with the family car.

He was surprised to see her so early, but she offered no explanation. "Take me home, please, and then come back for my parents." She instructed him to tell no one about her early departure until her parents asked, then to say she'd had a sudden headache.

Carasia had left a few lamps on, and the soft light created an eerie effect. Walking around the white-draped furniture was like passing tombstones in a cemetery. The only sound was the rain that had begun softly falling. By the time Kit went to her room and changed from her ball gown to her nightgown, the wind had picked up, angrily rattling the windows and patio doors.

It was a nostalgic time, Kit reflected, not at all sleepy. This was her last night in the only home she had ever known. The future was exciting, but why did she feel a strange, churning hunger within, like the nagging need for answers to unknown questions? Why was she so restless? It was not because Esteban had made her angry, and she certainly wasn't worried about repercussions for locking him in the wine cellar. She doubted he'd even admit she was responsible. Nor was she upset about leaving Spain since she'd soon be coming back. No, there was something else bothering her, and Kit knew she'd find no peace until she determined what it was.

Kit jumped as lightning split the sky with forked fingers. Thunder exploded, shaking the floor beneath her. The wind screamed ominously and rain splashed against the windowpanes. A violent storm was bearing down, and Kit thought of Pegasus, alone in the barn and probably terrified.

She knew she would get no rest until she made sure that Pegasus wasn't tearing down his stall in panic. What if he crashed into something and broke a leg? Snatching a poncho that had not yet been packed, she ran outside, momentarily blown backward by the gale-force wind. Lightning streaked across the sky, illuminating the way. Ducking her head against the storm, she charged into the night. It seemed that for every step forward she took, she was blown back two. The poncho whipped open, and she was immediately drenched, her robe and gown plastered to her skin. Shivering, she plunged onward, determined that no harm should come to her horse. The barn appeared as a vision in the distance, seen in flashes, only to be swallowed into darkness as the storm crashed around her. Kit finally reached the doors and struggled mightily to push them open. Then, stumbling in, she heard Pegasus snorting and stamping above the din. She fumbled for a lantern and matches, but they were missing. Moving by instinct she felt her way through the stable. She finally reached the stall. In a flash of lightning, she saw the rearing horse, his hooves wildly slashing the air. Unafraid, she called to him gently. He began to calm down, finally standing still and allowing her to rub his nose. She continued soothing him. "You'll be all right, boy. Just calm down. Nothing to be afraid of. The storm is almost over—"

"Is it?"

Her fright changed to anger as another flash of lightning lit up the stable, revealing Kurt Tanner standing on the other side of Pegasus's stall.

"You!" she gasped. "What are you doing here?"

"I asked *you* a question," he said, his voice as ominous as the thunder. "Is the storm almost over? I don't think so. Actually, I think it's just beginning."

He stepped inside the stall. Instinctively Kit retreated, maneuvering so that Pegasus was between them. "I'd advise you to get out of here, Tanner. You're trespassing. How dare you sneak up on me like this? Are you drunk? Get out!"

He snorted. "Not till we talk, *princesa*. You *are* a little princess, aren't you? Romanov blood!" he said mockingly. "I made some inquiries. You see, I like to know what kind of neighbors I'm going to have," he added sharply.

So he knew! Well, he was bound to find out sooner or later. Kit knew she had to get him to leave before her parents came home. "We have nothing to talk about. I had as much right to buy that ranch as you did!"

Kurt emitted a bitter laugh. She could see the na-

ked fury on his face and the narrow look in his dark
eyes.

"You took away my right when you hid that goddamn sign, you sneaky little vixen. I went by the
office to find out when the land would be posted.
That's when I learned it already *had* been posted—
and bought—by your grandmother, for you, of course.
I rode out there and discovered the sign hidden in the
bushes—where you put it the day the tax man was out
there. He told me how he'd met you that day . . . said
who could forget so beautiful a woman," Kurt added
with a sneer.

Drawing in a ragged breath, he said, "It didn't take
much to figure out your scheme—pacifying your parents by making them think you're seriously consid-
ering moving to America permanently. But don't
worry, I won't give you away. I only came to let you
know that you're not as smart as you think you are,
and I'm sick of your deceit. I'm going to enjoy watching you fall on your smug little face, because you'll
never make it as a rancher, baby. Sooner or later
you'll get what's coming to you."

"Oh, really?" Kit stepped around Pegasus. She
stared up at him undaunted, her hands on her hips.
She was so angry she gave no thought to how she
must look, her sheer nightgown wet and clinging to
her body.

"Get one thing straight, Señor Tanner—Pegasus is
mine, and I'm taking him with me so you can't steal
him. And another thing, you pompous ass. Why is
it that when a man does something sharp and cunning
it's shrewd, but when a woman does, it's *treachery?*"

The storm had picked up in intensity, and was now
directly overhead. Kurt stared down at Kit, her face
shimmering in the glow of the lightning that streaked

the sky outside. His eyes raked over her, following
the curve of her breasts beneath her damp gossamer
gown. Without a word he stepped up to her and
cupped her breasts. He pulled her close against him,
and she could feel the sudden swell of his desire
against her. It was as if he had hypnotized her with
his steady, burning gaze. She could only stand there
helpless, allowing delicious waves of passion to course
through her body, shaking her as profoundly as the
thunder that crashed around them.

"It's *my* turn to make a challenge, *princesa*," he
whispered huskily. "I defy you *not* to want me. . . ."

His lips covered hers possessively, urgently. She
could taste the whiskey on his mouth, and her blood
began to race with liquid desire. She was aware of a
trembling deep within her and cursed herself for the
wild longing that had taken over her senses. No longer
did she have a will of her own. She was helpless before the intense yearning he had ignited.

The kiss seemed to last forever, and she prayed it
would never end as she reached up and put her hands
around his neck.

Then suddenly he released her. Taken by surprise,
Kit stumbled backward. She was furious—with him,
and with herself. She had realized in that moment
why she had been so restless lately. Kurt Tanner was
on her mind, in her blood, even though she despised
him as she looked up into his triumphant face. Despite herself, she was drawn to him in a way she could
neither explain nor deny.

"This time, *princesa*," he said smugly, "*I* win,
and one day, I'll claim the full prize. Have a nice
trip." He saluted her impudently, then turned on his
heel, leaving her staring silently, furiously, after him.

The cool rain beat down on his smiling face as Kurt

headed into the storm. For once, he was glad his temper had gotten the best of him and kept him from telling her that President-elect Wilson had sent him a personal invitation to the inauguration. He'd be going to America too, as a successful and wealthy man. He'd thought maybe the vixen and he could have declared a truce, but he decided that it had all turned out for the best. He'd just show her a few tricks of his own—she certainly had it coming.

Kurt let her image take over his senses, and he marvelled, remembering the sensuality that slumbered in those smoky lavender eyes. He had known that she wanted him as much as he wanted her. Whether she liked it or not, he was a part of her private dreams.

As she had become a part of his.

Chapter Fourteen

THE voyage from France to England had been pleasant. They arrived late in the day, and Kit was disappointed when her father immediately whisked them away to a hotel in the city. She had wanted to check on Pegasus's transfer to the ship they were taking to America, but Colt would not hear of it. When they arrived the next morning to board, he kept a firm hand on her arm as they went up the gangplank, to keep her from heading to the ship's hold.

They were sailing on the White Star Line's magnificent ocean liner *Olympic*. With a slim hull of forty-five thousand tons, the ship was known for its smooth ride across the rough Atlantic.

Upon entering the grand reception room, the Coltranes were greeted by a smiling, friendly young lady who introduced herself as their hostess, Miss Jane Aberdeen. An attendant stepped forward to present each of the women with a small bouquet of roses, and a white-coated waiter offered champagne and caviar. Miss Aberdeen then escorted them to their quarters, leading them down a wide, plushly carpeted hallway.

Miss Aberdeen paused before a set of double rosewood doors and said with a broad smile, "You have the Imperial Suite—one of our finest." Then she guided them into a foyer, which held a huge vase bursting with red and white roses.

Their suite included a drawing room, a dining room, a parlor, three bedrooms, and a bath, as well as a dressing room.

After showing them around, Miss Aberdeen said, "On behalf of the White Star Line, we are proud to have such prominent and important passengers. You'll be receiving a formal invitation to dine with the captain at his table."

She then reminded them of the bon voyage party on the promenade deck a half hour before sailing and moved toward the door. Kit followed her outside and whispered, "Can you tell me how I can get to the cargo hold?"

"Why would you want to go there? It's dirty, and there are rats, and the men aren't exactly used to having a young lady around."

Kit looked over her shoulder anxiously, fearful that one of her parents might overhear, and she led the curious hostess a few more steps down the hallway. "I'm taking my horse with me to New York—"

"Oh, of course," Miss Aberdeen exclaimed. "Why didn't you say so, dear? Lots of passengers ship their animals and pets. They're put in a special part of the hold. It's nicer there, so the owners can visit." She gave Kit directions before going on her way.

Kit watched her turn the corner, then broke into an unladylike run. She knew that the family was about to go on deck to meet Uncle Drakar, who had come from Paris to see Marilee off. Kit wanted to see him too, but first she had to make sure that Pegasus was all right.

It took a while to maneuver her way through the

huge ship, but she finally reached the cargo hold. She was delighted to see comfortable stalls with fresh straw and hay. A young attendant who introduced himself as Norman Thatcher led the way to where Pegasus was stabled. He was eating happily, and Norman assured her that she had no reason to worry, and was welcome to visit any time.

Kit gave Pegasus a few hugs and let him know he had not been abandoned. When a horn blasted, Norman told her that the bon voyage festivities were underway.

Kit found the promenade deck crowded with passengers drinking champagne and waving to people down on the dock. Confetti and streamers were being thrown wildly, and a brass band was playing a rousing march. Kit pushed her way along, spotting her parents standing against a railing. Uncle Drakar was talking to her mother, and Kit saw that Jade had tears in her eyes. She knew how close they were, how they'd been best friends when her mother was growing up in Russia. Marilee clung to her father, torn between her excitement at seeing America, and her pain at leaving him behind.

After a few moments, Kit saw her uncle and cousin move away, to have some time alone. She stepped forward and met her mother's scolding eyes. "Where have you been?"

"I had to see to Pegasus. He's fine. Sorry," Kit said contritely. Kit wondered what was wrong that her mother seemed so worried, so preoccupied. She seemed almost sad to be leaving Spain, yet that was all she had talked about for years.

Colt met Kit's bewildered eyes and attempted to explain. "This is a time of mixed emotions for all of us, sweetie. Try and understand. I'm a bit torn myself. Europe has been our home for so long, yet my heart's always been in America.''

In a sudden wave of nostalgia, he recounted his first trip to Europe, to regain the family fortune after being swindled. Kit knew the story well, just as she knew that her father had loved other women before her mother. That was all right though. She was not naive. Then he told how he'd met Jade on his second visit to Europe, and they'd married. Kit knew the rest of that story, too, about their tragic sea voyage, and the dark time they spent apart. Colt made his third trip to Europe with Jade by his side, to forge a new start and try to forget the past.

''I never dreamed I'd end up staying in Spain and loving it, but new challenges and new dreams keep a man young. I guess it's time for another adventure before I wake up one morning and find myself an old man.''

Jade suddenly lifted her face to receive his kiss, and managed a smile. ''You'll never grow old, Colt Coltrane. You're forty-eight now, but you might as well be sixteen.''

Colt seemed to glow with renewed enthusiasm at going home. He then asked, ''Do you think we'll be able to find Andy? We haven't heard from him since he wrote last year that his mother had died, and he hasn't answered any of my letters. I'd like to see him. It's been a long time . . .''

Kit melted away into the crowd, sensing that her parents needed to be alone. Besides, she didn't particularly like being reminded that long ago her father, suffering from amnesia, was tricked into believing that he had not only married another woman, but had fathered her baby—Andy, who was now twenty years old. Even after Colt had learned the truth—that the boy was not his—he'd kept in touch with Andy, whom he had grown to love like a son. Kit had nothing against Andy, had actually liked him when he'd visited. But she still found the situation awkward, and that dark past of her parents' lives painful to contemplate.

Kit found Kitty standing above by a railing and was not surprised that she, too, seemed melancholy. Kit slipped her arm around her waist and said gently, "You're thinking about Grandpa, aren't you? That you're going home and leaving him behind."

Kitty gave her an incredulous look. "I'm never without Travis, child. He lives in my heart. Forever."

"But you seem so sad—"

"I guess it's because part of my life is ending, but"—Kitty gave her granddaughter a quick hug—"another part is beginning, and that, I'm looking forward to. And do you know something else? We're going to have fun in New York. With our sense of adventure, we'll either search it out, or make our own!"

Just then, Kitty spotted her friend Amelia, an ardent crusader for women's suffrage. Kitty called to her and started to make her way through the crowd. Kit saw Travis and began to walk over to him. Then she saw that he was engrossed in conversation with a lovely blond with round blue eyes. The girl was staring up at him as if completely entranced. Kit decided not to intrude.

Soon the ship's horn blew long and loud, and everyone cheered as the mighty liner began to move slowly from the dock.

Although she was surrounded by hundreds of people, Kit realized that she had never felt more alone in her life. It was as though something was missing, but what? She'd always been independent, never really needing anyone. Yet there was an odd feeling of emptiness in her.

A wave of awareness then swept over her. Dammit, it was Kurt Tanner again! She could close her eyes and see him—his dark, beautiful eyes, mocking and devouring . . . and his lips, so sensuous, almost chiseled in perfection. She could feel his strong arms around her, warm and protective, and remember how well their bodies curved together when he held her.

But why?

Why did she have to be haunted by a man who obviously had only one use for women?

Because, a voice within her taunted, *he's the only man who's ever made you feel like a woman, and you're afraid you'll never feel that way again with anyone else.*

She jumped, startled, as the horn sounded again. She turned from the railing, determined to enjoy the crossing and not allow her mind to dwell on thoughts of Kurt Tanner. And the little voice within her challenged, *but can you?*

Miss Aberdeen came to the Coltranes' suite promptly at seven to escort them to the captain's quarters. They met two other couples also invited for the evening, Mr. and Mrs. Vincent Grenoble and Mr. and Mrs. Peter Horing, all of London. Miss Aberdeen had confided on the way that both gentlemen were members of Parliament.

They were served champagne and iced Russian caviar, and they chatted amiably among themselves. Captain Braden Pawley soon came in, resplendent in white dress uniform, four black bars on each broad shoulder denoting his rank as master of the *Olympic.*

He was friendly and charming, yet reserved, as befitting his high position of authority.

Kit was wearing a clinging gown of shining green satin, edged at the bodice and hem with tiny seed pearls interspersed with ruby chips. Her mother's diamond tiara perched regally atop her carefully coiffed hair.

Kit saw Miss Aberdeen occasionally glance nervously at the door, as if she were expecting more guests. Finally she came over and said it was time to go into the dining room; protocol dictated that she lead the way and make sure that everyone was properly seated. The captain would make his entrance a few moments later.

The captain's table, with seating for twelve, was positioned on a slightly raised platform in the middle of the spectacular seven-hundred-seat dining room that glittered like a Christmas tree, with gold and silver and crystal appointments, satin-papered walls, and gold and white furniture. The other passengers had already taken their seats, but looked up curiously as the captain's guests filed in, as it was understood that only the most important were invited to dine at his table.

Marilee nudged Kit, pointing to the empty seat on her other side. For the first time Kit realized that there might be a stranger seated beside her.

"Whoever it is"—Marilee sniffed airily, very impressed with herself for being at the table of honor—"I hope he or she gets here before the captain makes his grand entrance. It'd be so rude to come in after him. I mean, if he can't get here on time, one should just not show up at all."

Miss Aberdeen, standing behind her, suddenly sighed with relief. "Our last guest just walked in."

Unconcerned, Kit looked over the menu, trying to decide between chocolate-covered strawberries or a lemon souffle for dessert. Only when she heard Marilee's gasp did she look up. . . .

. . . into the dark impenetrable eyes of Kurt Tanner.

Chapter Fifteen

SUDDENLY Kit knew what it must feel like to be struck by lightning, for in that infinite moment, when the world around her ceased to exist, with Kurt Tanner's seductive eyes on her, she was electrified. Only when Miss Aberdeen began the introductions was Kit able to gather her wits. Taking a deep breath, she managed to smile politely as Kurt explained that they had already met.

"I know all the Coltranes," he said, acknowledging them with a gracious nod. "We're neighbors in Valencia," he added, looking at Kit.

Kit avoided his eyes and reached for her wineglass. She took a large sip as he sat down beside her. Dear Lord, surely he wasn't going to try to get his revenge now!

On her other side, Marilee whispered eagerly, "He's so handsome, Kit. You have all the luck!"

Kit silenced her with an icy glare. Her mother was graciously correcting Kurt. "We *were* neighbors of Mr. Tanner's in Valencia, but unfortunately we didn't have the pleasure of making his acquaintance until recently."

"At the embassy ball in Madrid," Kurt said. "It's a shame I missed out on getting to know such charming people, and now I understand that you're all moving to New York.''

"I invited you to several socials, Mr. Tanner, but you declined," Jade reminded him.

Kurt grinned sheepishly. "That's true. I'm afraid each time I had another obligation.''

"A shame." Jade looked from him to Kit, aware of the tension between them. "Perhaps you'll find time to call on us in New York.''

"Tell me, Mr. Tanner," Colt said pleasantly, "what takes you to America? Is this your first trip back since leaving Springfield?''

Kurt was not surprised that Colt Coltrane had delved into his past. After all, he had a beautiful daughter and was no doubt wary of any man who showed an interest in her, especially one who'd dared dance with her the way he had at the embassy ball. He evaded Colt's mention of Springfield, instead replying, "I was invited to attend the inauguration. I also thought it would be a good opportunity to keep tabs on my interests.'' Crossing his legs, he deliberately brushed against Kit. She raised her napkin and whispered sharply, "Just make sure it's *your* interests you keep tabs on, Mr. Tanner.''

He gave her an insolent smile that made her burn with anger, and other emotions she could not define, fired by his nearness. She could not help noticing his broad shoulders and the way his muscles strained against his white dinner jacket. Her fingers ached to touch him, for she *had* touched him, and she knew how wonderful it felt. She yearned to brush back the unruly curls that tumbled rebelliously over his forehead. Despite his uncanny ability to irritate her, she was inexplicably drawn to him. He excited her in a way she'd never before experienced . . . and she cursed herself for her susceptibility.

Kurt launched into a spirited conversation with Colt about Mr. Wilson's policies. Jade listened with polite interest, and Travis glanced across the room at Valerie, the little blond he had met earlier. She stared at him dreamily from where she sat with five other young girls going home from fancy European schools, prune-faced chaperones keeping eagle-eyes over them all. Marilee looked expectantly from Kit to Kurt. Kit continued to sip her wine, wishing fervently that the evening would quickly end.

Finally Captain Pawley appeared, and everyone stood respectfully as he made his way to his table. He greeted each of his guests, then took his seat between Jade and Kitty.

The dinner conversation was lively, and even Marilee turned her attention to the others. Suddenly Kit was all too aware of Kurt's presence. It was as if they were alone, hidden from the others by a curtain of intimacy.

Softly, his voice like a cool caress upon her warm cheeks, he murmured, "Would it upset you if I accepted you mother's invitation to call in New York?"

Kit shrugged. "My mother is very convivial. She invites everyone she meets to visit."

His laugh was gentle. "I wouldn't be calling on *her,* and we both know it."

Kit turned to look at him sharply, praying that she could hide the heat churning within her at his nearness. "Why would you wish to call on me, Mr. Tanner? I think that by now it's obvious we just don't bring out the best in each other."

"I haven't had a chance to show you my best side, and although I haven't seen yours, I'm sure I won't be disappointed . . . ." He allowed his gaze to rake over her insolently. Then he continued boldly, "We've spent all our time in a war of wits. Don't you think it's time we call a truce and see if there's anything we *like* about each other? After all," he reminded her pointedly, "we *are* going to be neighbors, remember?"

Startled, Kit quickly glanced about to see whether anyone had overheard them. She was relieved to find everyone still engrossed in Captain's Pawley's stories. "Please . . ." She hated to plead but she knew she had no choice. "Don't say anything to my parents about my plans. I can't let them know. Not yet."

He raised an eyebrow. "Oh, Miss Coltrane . . . or Kit, if I may? We might as well be on a first-name basis since . . ."

Kit clutched his arm. "Please . . ." She beseeched him with her eyes. "Don't torment me this way."

Kurt laughed softly. He covered her hand with his and caressed her with dark, hungry eyes, "I've no intention of betraying you, *princesa*. That's not my way. Your secret is safe with me."

But am *I* safe with you? Kit wanted to ask. She feared that she already knew the answer. She would have to make sure that he never realized the power he had over her. Even as their eyes met and held, she remembered the way it had felt when he kissed her, held her. Angry with herself, she picked up her glass of cognac, trying to keep her hand from trembling.

Suddenly she burst out, "Since you consider yourself so noble and trustworthy, why didn't you tell me you had booked passage on the same ship with me?"

"Why would I? I seem to recall we were discussing another matter that last night—*your* treachery."

"Call it what you wish," Kit fired back. "What I did was a shrewd business maneuver."

"Remember that."

Kit turned to look at his quizzically. There was something unnerving about his tone. "What is that supposed to mean?"

He regarded her with cool confidence. "There are all kinds of maneuvers in life, Kit honey, for all kinds of situations. According to you, the end justifies the means. I just want you to remember your own doctrine."

Kit shrugged indifferently.

"You didn't answer my question."

She sighed, annoyed. "What question, Mr. Tanner?"

"Kurt. We might as well pretend to be friends."

Kit glared at him again. "I asked you what question you want answered . . . Kurt."

"Would you mind if I accept your mother's invitation to call on you in New York?"

She was about to admit that she might like that very much, when he added with a tigerish grin, "Maybe you'd be kind enough to allow me to ride my horse in Central Park."

Kit bristled. "When are you going to get it through your thick head that Pegasus is *my* horse? Don't you ever admit when you've been bested, Mr. Tanner?"

He shook his head. "Not when I haven't been, Kit."

"Oh, you!" she hissed, thoroughly exasperated. Then she turned her head resolutely and attempted to ignore him for the rest of the dinner.

Finally Captain Pawley stood and thanked them all for being his guests.

Pushing back her chair, Kit said to Marilee, "I'm

so glad we can finally leave.'' Marilee looked at her in surprise. ''I'm not leaving—I want to go dancing with everyone else.''

Taken aback at her cousin's sudden assertiveness, Kit told her, ''I have a headache, and I want to go to bed. Now come along.''

Marilee lifted her chin defiantly. ''Then you go on without me, because I want to have a good time.''

Kurt was enjoying Kit's displeasure. He gallantly extended his hand to Marilee. ''Of course you do. Are you sure you don't wish to join us, Miss Coltrane?''

''I suppose I have no choice,'' Kit muttered, falling into step behind them.

They entered the grand salon, a large room with marble floors and mirrored walls that reflected the dazzling light of crystal chandeliers. Couples were dancing to a slow waltz. Kurt led the ladies to a small table.

He ordered champagne, then led Florence Grenoble onto the dance floor.

''Why don't you like him?'' Marilee suddenly hissed.

Kit blinked, at a loss for words. Finally she retorted, ''Just because I don't fall at his feet like every other woman, doesn't mean I dislike him. He doesn't suit my taste in men, that's all.''

Marilee smiled coyly. ''I don't believe you.''

''Well, I don't care what you believe,'' Kit said airily. Then she added sharply, ''And the next time you pull a stunt like this—dragging me along because you know I'm not supposed to leave you—I swear I'll refuse to go anywhere with you ever again. I didn't want to come here, and you know it.''

''Yes, you did.''

"What?" Kit gasped, unable to believe her ears.

Just then Kurt returned to the table, spinning a breathless Florence Grenoble into her chair in one smooth gesture. He held out a hand to Marilee, which she eagerly accepted.

Kit was surprised to see how well Marilee danced, but Kurt was a strong dancer himself and could probably lead almost anyone.

"Oh, he's wonderful!" Marilee said upon returning to her seat. "Being in his arms is a dream come true."

"Marilee, you're behaving like a silly child," Kit exploded. Watching Kurt dance with Madeline Horing, she whispered furiously, "Kurt Tanner has a terrible reputation where women are concerned. He's too old for you, too experienced for you, and you're playing with fire to chase after him. If you don't stop, I'll have no choice but to talk to Kitty about it . . ." Kit's words trailed off when she saw the amused way Marilee was looking at her.

"What's so funny?" Kit demanded. "I'm not joking about this, Marilee."

"You're funny." Marilee giggled. "Because even in this room of mirrors, you can't see yourself."

Kit reached over and took away Marilee's glass of champagne. "I think you've had enough."

"I haven't. I just see through you, Kit, that's all. You don't want to admit it, but you're attracted to Kurt Tanner. You're fighting it because you're scared."

Kit stared at Marilee incredulously and sputtered, "Why . . . why that's the silliest thing I've ever heard! Why would I be afraid of a . . . a conceited womanizer?"

Marilee was no longer smiling. She seemed older,

as she said solemnly, "It isn't Kurt Tanner you're afraid of, Kit. It's yourself. You're afraid of being rejected."

Kit laughed. "That's absurd."

"Is it?" Marilee drew circles on the tablecloth with one finger. "You're afraid of men like Kurt Tanner, because you know they're the most dangerous kind . . . the kind that can break a heart like that." She snapped her fingers, meeting Kit's eyes.

Trembling with indignant fury, Kit exploded, "You don't know anything, Marilee, and I'll thank you to stay out of my business and keep your opinions to yourself."

Marilee looked beyond Kit to the dance floor. "He's coming this way. If you aren't afraid of him, dance with him," she challenged.

"Afraid?" Kit echoed, laughing scornfully. "I'm not afraid of any man, Marilee, but if it will make you happy I'll dance with him, for heaven's sake."

She rose from her chair as Kurt whirled Madeline Horing into hers, but he did not reach out to take her in turn. Instead he bowed ever so slightly. Smiling apologetically he declared, "Ladies, if you'll excuse me, I'd like to have a brandy and cigar before retiring. Good evening to you." With that he left.

Chapter Sixteen

THEY were blessed with unusually good weather their last day at sea. The winds were not as strong, so most passengers put on warm clothing and went out on the decks to get a breath of fresh air.

Kit did not want to go out on deck. Since her encounter with Kurt, she had made every excuse imaginable to remain in their suite. Marilee said nothing, but her accusing looks told Kit that she knew Kit was avoiding Kurt.

No one else seemed to notice her unusually quiet demeanor. Her mother was still behaving strangely, as if lost in a world of her own. Travis appeared only at mealtimes, so Kit was surprised that last day when he invited her to join him for a walk on deck.

"Why?" she asked blankly. "Did you and Valerie have a fight?"

He shook his head, but his gray eyes were worried. "I just want to talk to you about something, okay?"

Sensing he was troubled, Kit hurried to get her wool cape. Reaching the railing, they stared toward the misty horizon.

Finally Travis spoke. "It's about Valerie."

"Then you did have an argument—"

"I wish it were that simple, but it isn't. The truth is, I'm in love with her."

Kit stared at him incredulously. "You're not serious! Why, you've only known her for three days!"

"Four," he corrected. "And it wouldn't matter if I'd only known her four hours. In fact, I think I did love her four hours after I met her . . . maybe even the *second* I met her."

Travis gripped the railing so tightly his knuckles turned white. Kit moved closer to him and squeezed his arm. "I've never known a girl like her before," he continued. "She's beautiful, but lots of girls are beautiful. There's something else about her, something I can't really explain, but she's everything I've ever dreamed about. Does that make sense?" He looked at her hopefully.

Kit nodded silently. She knew exactly what he meant. Kurt Tanner was everything *she* had ever dreamed about.

"I guess it couldn't have happened at a worse time."

"You aren't thinking about not going to West Point, are you, Travis?"

He didn't answer.

"You aren't going to ask her to marry you, are you? Mother and Dad would be devastated. They'd never forgive you, and they'd blame Valerie. That's no way to begin a marriage."

"Mother doesn't like her anyway, and she doesn't even know how serious we are." Travis looked miserable. "When I introduced Valerie, Mother was so cold! It was as if she just turned to ice the second she looked at her. Valerie noticed, of course, anybody would have. Later I tried to smooth things over and told her that mother's been acting funny since we left Europe. She said she understood, but I know her feelings were hurt."

"Did you talk to mother later and ask her why she acted like that?"

"Of course I did, but she wouldn't give me a straight answer. She just asked a lot of questions about Valerie's background, her family and so forth."

"Maybe Mother knows more than you think she does," Kit offered. "Maybe she realizes you two have gotten serious, and she's worried about how fast things are moving."

Defiance rang in his voice. "Well, it doesn't matter, because I'm not going to give her up."

Kit frowned. "I don't think anyone would ask you to give her up, Travis. Frankly, I don't think you're being very mature about this. Why do you have to get married now? Why can't you go on to West Point and plan to marry when you graduate? Lots of couples are engaged for that long, and—"

Travis shook his head. "I don't want to wait."

"What about Valerie? Is she pressuring you to turn down the appointment?" Kit was suddenly suspicious. She'd met Valerie, and her first impression was that the girl was as nice as Travis said, but maybe it was all an act. Maybe a ruse to snare someone rich, like her brother.

Travis did not like the implication of Kit's question. He informed her angrily that he hadn't even talked to Valerie about it. "I've told her I love her, and she says she loves me, but other than that, we haven't talked about the future."

Kit spread her hands in a helpless gesture. "What do you want of me, Travis? Why are you telling me all this? Apparently you aren't interested in my opinion."

"I guess I wanted to make sure you're on my side

. . . and it seems I was wrong to think you would be.''

Kit adored her brother, but she had to be honest about the way she felt. "I'm always on your side, Travis, because I love you and want the best for you. If you think I'm going to say you're right to throw away a West Point appointment to marry a girl you just met, I'm sorry, I can't. I hope you'll give this a lot of thought before you tell Mother and Dad, because they're not going to be as understanding as I've tried to be.''

"I don't care!" he growled. Then he walked away.

Kit turned back to stare out at the water.

In the tea salon, Kit's mother also was staring into space, a frown marring her lovely face.

There was something terribly wrong, but it was nothing she could share with her children . . . or Colt. She simply could not tell them that she'd always been haunted by the horrible suspicion that Colt might not be the father of Kit and Travis. And from the first moment she had seen Valerie's face, nineteen years had slipped away and she was looking at the face of a long-ago adversary—Lita Tulane. When Travis had introduced Valerie, and Jade had heard her surname, she felt as if she had descended straight to the pits of hell.

Her name was Valerie Stevens.

And even though Stevens was a common name, Jade *knew* that her father was Bryan Stevens.

"No . . ." she whispered aloud, shaking her head from side to side. Valerie Stevens could not be Travis's half sister. So even if Bryan Stevens had impregnated Jade that terrible night when he'd raped her, even if he was the true father of her son and daughter, he'd been lost at sea nearly nineteen years ago. Valerie couldn't be his daughter; she was too young. Then why, she asked herself, did she harbor such hostility towards Valerie Stevens? Was it merely because she resembled Lita Tulane and her last name was Stevens?

Jade knew that it was because Valerie made her remember things she'd rather forget—like the fact that there had never been any confirmation that Bryan Stevens was dead. His body had never been found, and it was just assumed that he'd drowned at sea. That meant there was a possibility, however remote, that he might have somehow survived.

Kit could hear lively music as she made her way toward the ship's hold. Everyone was making merry the last night aboard, but she had no desire to celebrate. When she made an excuse to leave Marilee, Travis, and Valerie, Marilee had teased that she had no reason to run away—Kurt Tanner was nowhere in sight. Kit had ignored the barb, intent on escaping to the solitude she knew she would find only in the kennel.

Norman Thatcher was not there, and the cargo hold was dark, quiet . . . almost spooky. But Kit wanted to be alone, and this was the only place she could be assured of privacy.

She passed large wooden crates and barrels, and cages containing family pets—dogs and cats staring at her with wide, frightened eyes. She reached the door leading to the horse stalls and was about to enter when she heard what sounded like muffled laughter. A rough pair of hands shot out of the blackness and grabbed her. Terrified, Kit fought back, but her screams were suddenly stifled as a smelly rag was stuffed into her mouth and she was thrown to the floor. Peering up in the faint light, she saw a man standing over her, straddling her while someone else pinned her to the floor. Her assailant was shirtless and dirty . . . and very drunk.

"Looks like we got ourselves a hoity-toity." His voice was thick as he swayed above her. "Now aren't we lucky? Ain't often we get to sample first-class fare!"

The man holding her down laughed. "Makes them long hours in the stokehold seem worth it when we can find ourselves a little fire of our own."

They laughed loudly. Kit realized that they were stokers—the tough men who worked in the hellishly hot furnace room, shoveling tons of coal each day to keep the ship alive. She'd heard that the stokers were a group of savage, ruthless men, and she knew that she was in danger. They were wretched and resentful of wealthy passengers, and their drunkenness made them fearless.

The man standing over her began to fumble with his trousers. "Never had me no hoity-toity pussy. Gonna find out if it's better than waterfront tarts."

Kit tried to scream again, choking against the oily rag. She kicked out at her attacker, but he laughed, reaching down and roughly spreading her legs. Pinning them down with his own, he yanked up her dress with one vicious movement.

The other man begged hoarsely, "Hurry up, will ya? I got a yen that's killin' me—"

Kit saw a flash of steel. A gun struck the head of the man who was just then lowering himself over her. She saw another lightning-quick flash as the gun cracked the face of the man holding her arms. The next moment she felt herself being gently raised by a pair of strong hands.

Kit yanked the rag from her mouth and gasped for

air. "Oh, thank you," she finally managed, then she nearly fainted. It was Kurt Tanner who had come to her rescue! "You . . ." she stammered in amazement.

His dark eyes flashed with anger. "Didn't anyone tell you that ladies don't go tramping around shipholds?"

"I . . . I've been here every day to see Pegasus." Kit struggled to appear composed, despite the excited beating of her heart. "All the passengers visit their animals, and—"

"Not at night, they don't! Especially the last night at sea, when the crew gets drunk and rowdy! You were asking for trouble. It's a good thing I came down when I did, or that second bastard would be having his 'yen' satisfied right about now!" he added mockingly.

Kit's gratitude was overcome by resentment. "Well, I thank you, Mr. Tanner, but I've told you before to stop following me."

He stared down at her fiercely. When she saw the warm look in his eyes, Kit felt no fear, only a reflection of her own desire. She trembled with anticipation.

Pulling her to him with rough possessiveness, Kurt held her tight against his chest. "You want me . . . as much as I want you, but you're too damn stubborn and proud to admit it. One day, though, you will come to me."

Shaken by the whirl of emotions within her, Kit managed to give her golden-red head an arrogant toss. "Will I?" she taunted him defiantly. "Are you so sure that you can charm every woman you encounter, Kurt Tanner?"

His smile was slow and confident. They stood in

the muted light, unseen creatures rustling in the shadows, the boat creaking and moaning in the churning sea. His eyes twinkled mischievously as he confidently assured her, ''I've forgotten all others before you, Kit Coltrane. And yes, with you I'm sure . . . because I feel your desire in every breath you take. I see the heat of passion in your eyes, and I feel it in the warmth of your skin when I touch you. . . .'' He kissed her slowly, deliciously, his tongue gently exploring the delights of her soft mouth.

Kit melted against him, succumbing to what she had dreamed about for so many heated nights.

Kit wondered later what more might have happened, but just then one of her attackers moaned. Kurt immediately released her. ''Go now,'' he instructed.

Kit hesitated, torn by feelings she did not understand.

''Come to me when you're ready, Kit,'' he said quietly, retreating into the shadows. ''I'll be waiting.''

She hurried toward the stairs, blinking back tears of confusion. She could not, would not, admit it, but she knew that she *was* ready . . . and she sensed that Kurt knew it, too.

Chapter Seventeen

K IT shivered in the early morning chill, and her father offered to get her a heavier wrap. She declined, wanting him beside her when the New York skyline came into view. She'd heard it was an unforgettable sight, but the sky was gray and overcast, and she was afraid they wouldn't be able to see anything from a distance. She had wanted her mother to share the momentous occasion, but Jade had declined without giving a reason. Colt said that it was probably too much for her, reminding Kit that the harbor held unpleasant memories for her mother.

It was crowded on the deck, everyone excitedly awaiting their first glimpse of America. Through the mist, they heard the sound of small craft approaching, and watched with interest as a boat sliced its way out of the fog and moved alongside the mighty vessel. A rope ladder was dropped, and two men gingerly made their way up.

"Docking and harbor pilot," Colt explained to Kit. "We must be getting close." He glanced about. "Where's your grandmother and Marilee? They said they'd join us, but if they don't hurry they're going to miss an amazing sight." Someone cheered, and they leaned forward eagerly. The fog obligingly began to lift and the New York skyline came into view, the buildings like an army of great, gray sentinels standing regal and proud.

"That's got to be the new Woolworth Building," Colt said, pointing to the tallest structure in sight. "And that's the Metropolitan Tower, fifty stories, also new. That other big one you see is the Singer, forty-seven stories. They get taller with each one that goes up—makes you wonder just how high they'll eventually be able to build them."

Kit gazed across the water in awe. She'd never seen real skyscrapers, and she could feel the excitement all around her as the crowd took in the splendid sight.

As the pilots navigated the great vessel into the Hudson River basin, the band began to assemble on deck. A flotilla of smaller craft started gathering around their ship. "It's like a parade!" Kit cried excitedly. "Look!" She pointed to the fireboats shooting up great fountains of water, their whistles blowing loudly. Tugboats moved closer to take the lines dangling from the *Olympic,* and Colt explained that they were needed for the intricate maneuver into the slip where they would dock.

The band played a rousing rendition of "Alexander's Ragtime Band," and even though the February day was cold and windy, the crowd on deck began to dance and sing, caught up in the whirling excitement of arriving in America. They cheered and waved at the Statue of Liberty as the boat moved past America's most famous landmark.

Kit and Colt smiled, but they did not join in the revelry, for each was lost in his own thoughts. It was a momentous occasion, and it marked the beginning of a new, very different life.

Marilee appeared suddenly, breathless with excitement. "Isn't this wonderful?" she cried, hugging them both. The she said to Kit, "You're so lucky, you get to stay here! I'd give anything if I could, but I'm coming back as soon as I finish school, right, Uncle Colt?"

"Of course," Colt said, kissing her cheek. "You're part of our family, and don't you ever forget it."

"Oh, this is wonderful!" Kitty joined in, her eyes shining as she looked about in wonder.

Travis walked up, looking worried. "I can't find Valerie anywhere," he said. "I went to her cabin, but no one's there. I think her chaperone deliberately arranged it so that I couldn't see her this morning."

"Why would she do that?" Kit asked.

So Colt wouldn't overhear, Travis whispered in her ear, "Valerie says she's afraid that her parents wouldn't have approved of us seeing each other during the voyage, so I guess she wanted to make sure they didn't see us together when we dock."

"You have her address in New York, don't you?"

"Yes, but not for their estate up in the Hudson Valley. If they go directly there, I won't be able to get in touch with her."

"She can write you," Kit suggested.

"We're leaving for Washington in three days." Travis reminded his sister.

"But isn't Valerie going to the inauguration, too?"

"Well, her parents were invited, but her debut is in two weeks, and she won't know what her parents' plans are till she sees them."

Kit tried to reassure him once more. "Well, I'm sure they won't leave her in New York. She'll go to Washington, and you'll see her there."

"Maybe," Travis said, unconvinced, then he left to look for Valerie again. Kit knew that he was really in love with Valerie, but she hoped he wasn't making a mistake by getting so involved so quickly. She sensed, oddly, that the romance had something to do with their mother's depression.

As the ship made its way to its slip, everyone pressed to the railings, searching for family and friends, and throwing streamers and confetti. Kit was so entranced by the sight of New York that she didn't realize she'd been separated from her family. She stood on tiptoe, but she couldn't see them.

Suddenly a familiar voice, warm and husky, spoke directly behind her. "Has the lady found herself all alone?"

Kit gazed up at Kurt Tanner, and a charge of electric heat surged through her. Oh God, why does he affect me this way? she wondered desperately. Why did she feel that sudden rush of desire, the need to have those soft, sensuous lips upon hers, to feel his possessive embrace? Kit gave herself a mental shake and commanded her body not to betray her as she spoke. "Perhaps by design, Mr. Tanner. I rather prefer solitude to the company of bores."

He laughed. "I know just what you mean. That's how I felt about every woman I knew before you. After all, you have to admit that our times together have been anything *but* boring.

"I've been looking for you," he said, gazing deep into her eyes.

"To say good-bye, I hope."

"To the contrary." His tone was pleasant as he blithely ignored her sarcasm. "I just wanted to say that I unfortunately have to go on to Illinois to visit some friends, but maybe we'll see each other in Washington."

"I doubt it," Kit said, proud of her composure, when inside she was trembling at his nearness. He reached to cover her hand with his, but she snatched it away. "There are dozens of parties being given for the inauguration, and I doubt our names will be on the same guest list."

Marilee appeared, pushing her way through the crowd. Reaching Kit she exclaimed, "Have you ever seen anything so marvelous? The tall buildings, and the people, and the music—I just love New York!" She hugged herself with delight. Realizing that Kurt Tanner was standing next to her cousin, Marilee said, "Are you going to Washington, Mr. Tanner? If you are, you must promise to dance with me!"

"Marilee!" Kit exploded. "That's no way for a young lady to talk to a man!"

Kit's face reddened as Kurt threw his head back and laughed. Bowing gallantly, he promised Marilee that he was looking forward to dancing with her again. Then, with a smile meant only for Kit, he left them and melted into the crowd.

Kitty joined them at that moment, looking thoroughly chilled.

"Maybe you'd better get inside out of this wind," Kit suggested.

"Yes. I think the excitement is over. All we have to do now is wait to disembark."

Marilee refused to go back to the cabin. "I want to walk around and see as much as possible. You two go on."

As they made their way below, Kitty continued to shiver. "Marilee is such a complex child. She has the sweet, demure charm of her mother, yet the wild, reckless spirit of the Coltranes."

"Marilee can take care of herself," Kit declared. "It's *you* I'm worried about."

"I've just caught a little cold—nothing to fret about."

They soon reached the door of their suite and froze at the sound of angry voices from within.

"You aren't being fair, Mother!"

Kit and Kitty exchanged startled looks.

"You don't even know Valerie. She's a wonderful girl, and—"

"And you're so immature you'd throw away an appointment to West Point because of her," Jade cried. "Well, I won't let it happen, and neither will your father."

"I haven't said I wasn't going to West Point!"

"That will come next, after the way you seem to have lost your mind since you met that girl. Just forget about her and concentrate on your future at the Academy!"

"Mother, I'm only asking you to try and like Valerie, and—"

"It doesn't matter whether I like her, because by the time you graduate, she'll be married to another rich young man she'll manage to snare when she realizes she can't trap you. She'll have had three or four babies by then to *keep* him trapped. I know her kind."

"That's not fair!" Travis exploded. "You can't say that about Valerie!"

Kitty opened the door, Kit following cautiously.

Travis fell silent. He was standing in the middle of the parlor, his face flushed and his chest heaving with fury. Jade was standing next to the porthole, tears streaming down her face as she angrily twisted her lace handkerchief with trembling hands.

"Heavens, you two can be heard all the way out in the hall," Kitty said, exasperated. "Can't this wait for a more private setting?"

"It's over," Jade said tonelessly. She turned to stare out at New York, wondering for the hundredth time if she would regret her decision to return. To no one in particular she said, "Get ready to leave as soon as Colt comes back."

They left her silently, and Jade blinked back her tears. She told herself that as soon as they were settled in their new home, and Travis was packed off to the Academy, life would be as wonderful as she'd imagined it would be. She felt no guilt about her feelings toward Valerie. It wasn't merely that the girl innocently triggered painful memories. Travis had no business getting serious about any girl right now.

"Señora . . ." Jade turned at the sound of Carasia's voice. "Since we haven't hired new servants yet, I was wondering if you would mind meeting a girl I met below. She's from Spain also, a very nice girl. She was to have gone to work for a family who have a big estate in a place called the Hudson River Valley."

Jade was stunned. The Hudson River Valley . . . where she had seen Colt for the first time after believing him dead, where they'd succumbed to their overwhelming desire and made love on the moon-shadowed banks of the sultry river, when he'd not known who she was, and she'd dared not tell him. Carasia waited silently, a questioning expression on her face. Jade waved her away, lost in memories.

Bryan Stevens had owned a mansion there. She wondered who lived there now. She'd signed away all claims to his estate, not caring what happened to the money she had no right to inherit, since their marriage had never been valid.

Travis had said that Valerie's parents had a home there. Jade scolded herself for her outrageous fears.

It simply could not be the same family! Many wealthy families lived in the Hudson River Valley. It was a mere coincidence, nothing more. The past was dead and buried, and she refused to let the ghosts come back to haunt her.

That's what she told herself even as an icy chill of foreboding continued to squeeze her heart.

Chapter Eighteen

As first-class passengers, the Coltranes were quickly ushered through customs and immigration. They were soon seated in the two chauffeured Model T Fords that Colt had arranged to have waiting for them.

Although Kit was enjoying the sights, she kept an anxious eye on her grandmother. Kitty was still flushed and her eyes looked feverish. Fortunately, she retired as soon as they had settled into the Waldorf-Astoria, and was still sleeping when everyone came back from a full day of sight-seeing. Kit took a dinner tray in to her, and was alarmed to hear her breathing come as a strange rattling sound. Colt immediately wanted to call a doctor, but Kitty protested.

"There is nothing wrong with me except a little cold. Now if everybody will just leave me alone and let me rest for a few days, I'll be fine!"

Colt sighed, all too aware of how stubborn his mother could be.

The next few days went by in a whirl. Jade took Kit and Marilee on a shopping spree, wanting them all to be outfitted in current New York fashions. Travis spent his time trying to locate Valerie. He went to the address she had given him, but the Stevenses weren't there and the servants refused to tell him anything.

Kit felt sorry for him, but Jade actually glowed with relief, certain that once Travis entered West Point he would forget about his shipboard romance.

The air was crisp and cold the morning the Coltranes boarded the train for Washington. Kitty wrapped herself snugly in a mink cape, a thick woolen scarf about her head. She assured everyone she felt fine. Although her cold did seem better, Kit didn't like the way she continued to cough.

Snow began falling as the train chugged out of New York, and soon the world beyond the windows was a frosty sea. "I hope this doesn't keep up," Jade stewed. "It will be so messy getting out and about. Our hair will be limp, and our slippers will get wet."

"Wear galoshes," Kitty said pragmatically. "In weather like this, you shouldn't care about wearing fancy shoes."

"Maybe you don't care about appearances, Kitty, but I happen to feel that making an impressive entrance is an important social skill," Jade replied.

Kit did not join in the debate. She couldn't care less about social skills or appearances. All she could think about was getting back to Spain and making a new life for herself there. She leaned back and dreamily envisioned the little ranch with its gentle rolling slope to the river. How lovely it would be when there were flowers blooming in the spring.

Travis stepped inside their compartment, throwing himself onto the sofa next to Kitty, leaning back and closing his eyes. Marilee and Kitty exchanged knowing glances. He was brooding over Valerie. Jade watched him for a moment, then, unable to tolerate his mood any longer, said, "Really, Travis, you're letting that girl ruin your trip. In fact, your behavior is ruining everyone's trip."

Travis showed no reaction, and Jade continued. "What is it about this girl that has you so bewitched? It's as if you're obsessed with her. I don't like it one bit. Even if you do find her, your father and I have decided it's best you just forget her."

"You can't do that!" Travis sat up angrily, his eyes blazing. "You can't just tell me who can come and go in my life, Mother. It's *my* life!"

The door opened, and Colt walked in. Glancing about at everyone, his eyes finally rested on Travis. "Would someone mind telling me what's going on here?"

Jade told him while Travis shook his head wearily. There was no point in arguing. He stood to leave, but Colt motioned for him to sit still. "Listen to me, son. I think I know how you feel." He grinned at Jade. "If your mother doesn't want to hear it, well, there are a lot of ladies in the club car having tea. . . ." He gave his wife a meaningful glance.

Jade stood up without hesitation. "You're right, I don't want to hear it. Come along, girls." When they made no move to follow, a look from Colt sent them scurrying. Kitty had fallen asleep.

Travis listened intently as Colt began to tell him of his past love affairs, that there had been many times he'd thought he was in love, only to feel quite foolish later. "But there was one . . ." Colt settled back beside his son, a misty, faraway look coming over his face. He spoke of lovely Briana de Paul and how he had been mesmerized by her rare and special beauty. "The passion was powerful, but it ran its course," Colt confided, looking deep into his son's eyes. Travis was touched by his father's candor.

"The point I'm trying to make, son, is that no matter how much you think you care for this young lady now, there will be many others after her. Just get on with your life and enjoy yourself, because the next four years at the Academy are going to be very, very challenging. But you'll succeed. You can do anything you set your mind to—you're a Coltrane," he finished proudly.

Kitty sat up and grinned. "Your father is right, Travis," she told him fondly. "The Coltrane men all seem to have a heartbreaking romance before they find their true love."

Travis looked from his grandmother to his father, moved by their concern. "I'll be okay," he whispered huskily, "but I want you both to know that I do care about Valerie . . . deeply."

"If it's meant to be, it will be," Kitty said sagely. "I think fate takes care of things like that."

Chapter Nineteen

THE train pulled into Washington's Union Station, and the Coltranes disembarked with the many others who had come to see Woodrow Wilson become America's twenty-eighth President.

Two cars took them to the prestigious section known as the Gold Coast, where they had been invited to stay at the home of a prominent attorney, Wylie Bucher, the nephew of Sam Bucher, who'd been a dear friend of Colt's father. The cars finally stopped in front of a massive white house and Kitty showed renewed spirit when she recognized the man hurrying from the house to greet them. Stepping out of the car, she cried jubilantly, "Wylie, bless your heart, it's been years, but I'd know you anywhere. You're the image of your Uncle Sam." Her eyes glistened with tears of nostalgia.

Wylie embraced Kitty, then he stood back and held her at arm's length, frowning. "My God, Kitty, you've got a fever!" he exclaimed.

"Nonsense. I'm just warm from the car ride."

Colt shrugged helplessly. "Kitty is pretty stubborn, Wylie, but we're going to see that she takes care of herself, whether she likes it or not." He looked pointedly at his mother.

Wylie laughed. "Well, I'll do all I can to help you.

Now I'd like to show you around my home." With that he led them on a tour of the grand house, then made sure that they were settled comfortably in their rooms.

On inauguration day, the skies were again cloudy and overcast. Donning her floor-length mink cape and matching wide-brimmed bonnet, Kit peeked in at Kitty before leaving for the festivities. She was shocked at the way her grandmother looked. Kitty was pale and still, and her breathing was labored. Kit pressed her lips to Kitty's brow and found it hot. She rose to get her father when Kitty's eyes suddenly flew open. Seeing Kit's alarm, she whispered hoarsely, "I'm just tired, darling. You run along and have a good time."

Kit protested. "But I think you need a doctor. You look worse today than you did yesterday, and—"

"And you'll look worse tomorrow than you do today, because you'll be a day older." Kitty's grin was forced. "Now, off with you. I don't need a doctor, just rest."

Kit left her reluctantly, but she went straight to her father. Colt declared that he'd had it with his mother's stubbornness and called their family physician. Dr. Talton came at once and examined Kitty despite her vehement protests. He then called Colt in and announced that he thought Kitty was coming down with pneumonia. Rummaging through his worn leather bag, he took out a small vial of pills. "She should be in a hospital, but she refuses to go, so give her these according to the directions on the label, and I'll come by tonight to see if she's any better."

Making sure that Kitty was comfortable, and safely under Epiphany's supervision, the Coltranes reluctantly left her to attend the inauguration.

On the Capitol plaza, Woodrow Wilson recited the vow that made him President of the United States. He then gave his inaugural address, and his words aroused a sense of admiration in Kit for her parents' native country.

When the ceremony was over, the Coltranes were among the privileged guests invited for a reception and tour of the Capitol. Afterward, they headed home to prepare for the gala evening events.

Marilee was delighted to be wearing her first really sophisticated dress, a rose satin creation that was slightly off the shoulders, with a sweetheart neckline. But when she saw Kit, she wailed, "Oh, why can't I ever wear anything really sophisticated? Now I feel like a bridesmaid!"

Kit couldn't help laughing. "Oh, Marilee, you look wonderful! That is the perfect color for you."

Kit whirled about before the full-length mirror. She loved her gown—it was made of lime-green velvet, the dipping bodice beaded with gold jewels to match her slippers. The skirt was dramatically slit to mid-thigh, a style that, surprisingly enough, Jade had not discouraged. Kit wondered if Jade was hoping that she'd find a competent partner with whom to dance the tango. She knew how proud her mother had been when she'd danced with Kurt at the embassy ball in Madrid.

She wound her fiery hair into a regal chignon. The only jewelry she wore was emerald and diamond ear-bobs. A gift from her grandfather to Kitty, they'd been passed lovingly along to her on her sixteenth birthday.

Finally she and Marilee were ready to descend the spiral staircase to join everyone in a champagne toast. Kit paused, urging her cousin to go on without her.

"I'll be right along. I just want to say good-night to Grandma."

"I'll go with you," Marilee said, and they quietly opened the door to Kitty's room. The canopied bed was silhouetted against the softly crackling flames in the fireplace. Carasia held a finger to her lips and whispered, "She's sleeping very deeply—"

"No, she's not!"

They jumped at the sound of Kitty's voice, then stared silently as she managed to lift herself up against the pillows. Carasia hurried to assist her, but was irritably waved away. "I wish everyone would just stop fussing over me—" Her words were interrupted by a deep, hacking cough.

Kit and Marilee went to stand on either side of the bed. Kitty looked at them critically, then managed a broad, approving smile and declared, "Well, once again the Coltrane women will be the center of attention. Beautiful! My girls are just beautiful!" She held a hand out to each of them.

"Oh, Grandma, please hurry up and get well," Marilee said, her voice trembling. "I can't stand seeing you like this."

"Well, child, I'm not exactly enjoying myself," Kitty informed her crisply, "but every once in a while the Lord puts us flat on our backs so we can appreciate it when He lets us stand on our feet. Now you two have a wonderful time and remember that not every young girl has the privilege of attending the presidential inaugural ball."

They kissed her and turned to leave, but just as they reached the door, Kitty called softly, "Wait, Kit. I have something to say to you."

Marilee left, and Kit went quickly to her grandmother's bedside.

"This young man," Kitty began, "that you're trying to talk yourself out of falling in love with—I think you should give your heart a chance, child. Stop being so stubborn, you waste so much time that way. If it's meant to be, it will be. So unlock the door and let him in."

Kit forced a laugh, determined not to reveal the turmoil churning within her. "Will you please stop worrying about my private life and concentrate on getting well so we can get on with our plans? You know I can't make it without you!"

Kitty's smile faded, and she raised her head from the pillows. Reaching out, she clutched Kit's arm and drew her close. "Listen to me," she whispered hoarsely, looking deep into Kit's eyes. "Don't you ever say that. I've got to believe that you're enough like me that you don't need anybody . . . that you can make it on your own. I'd never have bought that ranch for you if I didn't believe that. You've got a heritage to be proud of, Kit Coltrane, and don't ever forget it. You can do anything you want in this life if you make up your mind to do it. You don't need anybody. Do you hear me, child?"

Kit was shaken; she'd never heard Kitty talk this way. "I'm strong, and I can make it," she assured her grandmother, "but I still need you with me. I want you with me. So please get well."

Against the stark white pillow, Kitty looked like a doll fashioned of delicate bone china. She whispered dreamily, "Dance one for me, my child . . . go and dance one for me . . ." She coughed raggedly, then struggled to go on. "And when he holds you in his arms . . . and your blood turns to fire in your veins . . . think of me. You were born to love . . . and be loved . . ."

Kitty's words trailed off. Kit gasped and felt her wrist for a pulse. She breathed a sigh of relief when she realized that Kitty was only sleeping. Kissing her once more, she cautioned Carasia to take good care of her. Then she left . . . hopefully to fulfill her grandmother's wish.

Chapter Twenty

THE White House was a wonderland of glittering lights and flowers everywhere—roses, orchids, daisies, carnations—their sweet fragrance pleasantly pervasive. Hundreds of guests milled about, the ladies' jewels sparkling amid the dazzling array of gowns. An orchestra played from the second-floor landing, the music drifting above the many voices.

Kit drifted away from her family and wandered about aimlessly for a while. She wanted to memorize everything so she could relive her enchanted evening for Kitty. She took a glass of champagne from a passing waiter and went to stand near the French doors leading out to the east terrace. From there she had a good view of everything that was going on. She could even watch President and Mrs. Wilson as they stood tirelessly in the receiving line greeting guests.

Within moments, Travis was by her side. "I found her!" he cried, his gray eyes dancing happily. "She's here with her parents. They've been up in the Catskills, just as I thought. Where's Mom and Dad? I want to introduce them to Valerie's family."

"Wait a minute, Travis," Kit said quickly. "Aren't you forgetting something? Mother has made it pretty clear that she doesn't approve, and I really don't think now's the time to introduce the families."

"I don't care!" Travis declared vehemently. "I've thought it over, and I know it'd be crazy to give up an appointment to the Academy, but I'm not going to give up Valerie, either. She feels the same way about me. She wants me to go to school, and she says she's willing to wait for me. So I don't see how Mother can have any objections."

Kit suspected that this would not appease their mother. "I don't know, Travis. Maybe this isn't a good time. I mean, we're all worried about Grandma, and—"

"There's Valerie!" Travis waved her over.

Valerie's face was glowing with happiness, and her cornflower-blue eyes shone with adoration for Travis as she took his hand. She tore her gaze from him to look at Kit and shyly say, "It's nice to see you again. I guess Travis told you about our plans. I do hope you approve, Kit, because I really like you, and I look forward to having you for my sister."

Kit hugged her impulsively and assured her that they had her best wishes.

Travis was ebullient. "You two wait here. I'm going to find them," he said eagerly as he headed back into the crowd to search for their parents.

Valerie turned to Kit with a worried look on her face. "Oh, I do pray that your mother will accept me once she realizes that Travis will still be going to West Point. I love him, and I'm willing to wait forever if I have to."

Kit tried to reassure her. "I don't think she has anything against you personally, Valerie. It's just that she hasn't been herself lately. Give her time."

"I will." Valerie nodded with determination. "I'm going to make her like me. After all, if it weren't for her, I wouldn't have Travis to love. I'm not going to be satisfied until she lets me love her, too.''

Kit was warmed by her words. ''I'll help any way I can.'' Suddenly her heart skipped a beat. Kurt was standing in the receiving line, shaking President Wilson's hand. A smile touched her lips, and her pulse quickened. He was devastating in his white tuxedo as he bowed gallantly over the First Lady's hand.

Valerie followed her gaze. ''Oh, isn't that Kurt Tanner? I remember him from the ship. He's quite handsome, isn't he? Travis told me that you danced with him at a ball in Madrid and raised a few eyebrows.''

Kit had to admit to herself that she'd been looking for him. Kitty was right—she was hiding from her own heart, and that was wrong. Yet she was not about to admit her feelings to anyone else. ''He's one of the few men I've come across who know how to dance the Spanish tango,'' she told Valerie. ''It's very intricate, and I guess if you've never seen it, it might seem risque.''

''I'd love to see you dance with him. Would it be proper here? Tonight?''

Kit laughed. ''No, I don't think so. Maybe at one of the other parties in town, but not at the White House.''

''Well, let's ask him to join us,'' Valerie suggested.

Kit was about to say she didn't think that was a good idea, when Valerie whispered, ''Uh-oh! I'm afraid he didn't come alone!''

Kit stiffened as she saw Kurt reach out to introduce an attractive, dark-haired young woman to Mrs. Wilson. He was looking down at her almost adoringly. Swallowing hard, Kit tried to sound flip as she laughed. ''Oh, well, it doesn't matter. I'll admit he's handsome, but I've also heard he's a womanizer. I certainly don't want to get involved with his kind.''

"Yes, you do."

Kit stared at her. "I beg your pardon?"

"Yes, you do," she gave her a quick hug. "Please don't be offended, Kit. It's just that I can tell you really like him. Even though he's with someone, we could still ask him to join us. Then you can decide whether his date is any real competition," she added with a mischievous wink.

"No, I couldn't . . ." Kit said, sounding uncertain.

Valerie was looking past her. Suddenly she grinned. "Well, you're going to get your chance anyway, because he spotted you, and they're coming over here."

"No . . ." Kit moaned. She looked about frantically and saw the doors leading out to the terrace. "I'm going outside. Tell him I've gone to the powder room if he asks for me." She hurried away before Valerie could stop her.

Even outside in the cold, crisp air, Kit felt flushed and overheated. Walking to the edge of the terrace, she looked out at the lights of Washington and wished she were anywhere but there.

Suddenly she felt a hand on her bare shoulder, and she shivered. He had moved through the night like a stalking panther. "Kit . . ." His voice was husky. "Why did you run away from me?"

Kit slowly turned to face him, despising herself for the hot, sweeping tremors that were moving through her body. "I did not run away from you," she protested.

"But you did," he said, a slightly mocking smile on his sensuous lips. "Because you're jealous of the young lady I brought with me."

Kit gasped, shocked not only because he had guessed the truth, but because he was bold enough to say so. "Oh, you flatter yourself, Kurt Tanner. I couldn't care less who you're with—tonight or any other night! I've told you before that we seem to bring out the worst in each other, and I see no reason for you to pursue me. Now, if you don't mind, I will excuse myself."

She started to move past him, her head held high, but he reached out and grabbed her. Spinning her about, he said, "Oh, but I do mind, Kit. You're the most incredibly desirable woman I've ever met, and I've been waiting to do this . . . again." He crushed her against him, his lips hot and demanding.

Kit resisted him, but only then she surrendered to the strange, driving hunger that seemed to possess her mind and body whenever he touched her. She trembled with delight as she felt his hand move to her breast, stroking softly. Time stood still in that magical, enchanting moment. Fantasy had become reality, and Kit realized that she was exactly where she had wanted to be for so very, very long.

Finally, reluctantly, he released her. For the first time his expression was not arrogant or mocking. Instead, he gazed at her with adoration, and she glowed with happiness. She did not want the moment to end—there was such an intimacy, an unspoken acknowledgment that something wonderful was growing between them. Then she heard a soft coughing sound and turned to see the young lady who'd been with him earlier. She stiffened defensively, but Kurt smiled confidently.

"This is my cousin, Rebecca Henley, from Georgetown. She was only too happy to be my date this evening." To Kit, he whispered, "Because I didn't know how to find you."

They exchanged pleasantries, and Kit was beside herself with joy. An inner peace filled her, because she was no longer running from her true feelings.

Rebecca said, "Kurt tells me you're a wonderful dancer, and that the two of you shocked a few folks at the embassy ball in Madrid."

"I don't think I'll ever hear the end of that." Kit laughed. "I'm just glad the orchestra isn't playing a tango tonight. I'm afraid we have a few friends here who'd insist on a command performance."

From within came the lilting strains of a waltz. "Well, perhaps they'll settle for an old-fashioned dance," Kurt murmured. Without taking his eyes off Kit, he politely asked his cousin, "Would you mind?"

Rebecca could not help teasing, "Of course not. I knew the minute we walked in that you were looking for someone, and I must say that I approve of your choice."

Kurt led Kit to the dance floor, and they began to move in smooth, gliding steps. They couldn't take their eyes from each other. Kit wondered if her excitement showed, if her face was aflame with the heat that his touch had ignited in her body. She felt almost light-headed, as if his arm around her waist was the only thing anchoring her to earth.

He shook his head slightly, as if to reassure himself that this was not a dream. "I want to kiss you again and again. Hold you and never let you go . . ." He looked deep into her eyes. "And you want it, too," he whispered. "You fought it, tried to hate me, but it was meant to be. It *will* be.'' His smile faded, and he seemed to consume her with his eyes as he held her even tighter.

Kit swayed dizzily. She lost her rhythm for a moment, and Kurt quickly, smoothly, covered her misstep.

She closed her eyes and felt the heavenly warmth of his body. No more pretense, no more hypocrisy. No more running from her destiny.

The waltz ended, but not the feelings soaring between them.

''When do you leave Washington?'' he asked as he led her back across the floor to where Rebecca patiently waited. ''I'd like to call on you.''

''Why?'' she asked impishly. ''To try and take Pegasus away from me, or the ranch you think I cheated you out of?''

He gave her a look of mock anger. ''Oh, you're going to pay for those little capers later, my dear. I've got special ways of punishing vixens like you.''

She squeezed his hand. ''I can hardly wait!'' She laughed. Then, becoming serious, she explained, ''I don't know when we'll be leaving. My grandmother is quite ill, and I'm sure we'll stay here till she's better.''

''I'm sorry to hear that. Tell me where you're staying, so I can call on you there.''

''Kit! I found them.'' Travis beckoned to her. ''I've arranged for a toast in the library. Marilee is bringing Mom and Dad.''

Kit felt uneasy. ''Did she tell them what this is all about?''

''No, she's not telling them anything.'' Travis snapped. *''I'm* making the announcement. Now do you want to be there or not?'' Noticing Kurt for the first time, he said cooly, "Will you excuse us, please?"

"Wait here," Kit said. She hated to leave him for even a moment. "This is a family matter, but it won't take long." Kurt nodded in understanding and Kit went to the library with Travis.

As they reached the library, Marilee appeared with Jade and Colt. Jade demanded to know what was going on, then she saw Valerie standing just inside the door. She stiffened, her expression a mask of instant hostility. She turned to leave, but Colt caught her arm and steered her inside.

"Valerie and I have something to say," Travis began nervously, "but we're waiting for her parents."

Growing pale, Jade held up a hand in protest. "Travis, if you've called us together for the reason I think, I must say that this isn't the time or place, and—" She stopped when a butler knocked discreetly on the door.

"Come in," Colt said, and the butler approached him, whispering urgently so that only Colt could hear.

"Kitty's very sick," Colt explained to the others. "We have to get to her as quickly as possible."

Jade was two steps outside the library when she suddenly froze. For an instant she seemed to be paralyzed, her face deathly white.

Kit watched, bewildered. Her mother's eyes grew wide with terror, and she raised trembling hands to her mouth. Turning to see what unknown horror had caused such a reaction, Kit saw a strange man and woman standing directly in her path. They, too, seemed petrified, rooted to the floor.

Jade felt herself fading away. The last thought she

had before she lost consciousness was that she was seeing a ghost—the ghost of Bryan Stevens.

And in that awful moment, her worst nightmare came to life.

Chapter Twenty-one

ANOTHER nightmare was taking place with Kitty. Dr. Talton removed his stethoscope, his face filled with deep concern. At the moment, Kitty appeared to be sleeping, and her breathing was slow and labored.

Tight-lipped and grim, Colt stood at the foot of the bed. Suddenly he exploded, "What are you waiting for? Dammit, she needs to be in a hospital!"

Beside him, Kit touched his arm gently. Oh, how she wished her mother were here! Something very strange, even terrible, had happened to Jade back at the White House. Colt had carried her to the car, and she'd awakened during the frenzied ride back to the Buchers'. She had said not a word, and her face was a mask of horror. What had caused such a reaction? When the car had stopped in front of the Buchers', she had leaped out and run up the walkway as though the devil was chasing her. There was no time to question her, however, because Kitty's critical condition was their overriding concern at the moment.

Colt jerked away from Kit's restraining hand. "Well, are you just going to let her lie there and die?" he shouted at the doctor.

Dr. Talton sighed and shook his head. In his many years of practice he'd witnessed this scene so often that he knew exactly what to expect of distraught family members. He folded his stethoscope carefully and put it in his worn leather bag, then motioned Colt to follow him outside, Kit right behind him.

Dr. Talton took a deep breath. "I'm sorry, Mr. Coltrane, but Kitty's so weak I don't want to move her now. I can't do any more for her in the hospital than I can here, anyway. It's just a matter of giving her medication, trying to bring down her fever, keeping her comfortable. But I've got to be honest and say that I don't think she's going to pull out of this."

"You're wrong," Colt said, his voice hoarse with desperation. "You can't give up! There's got to be something more you can do to save her." Kit watched her father anxiously as he took a threatening step toward the doctor.

"I'm sorry," Dr. Talton said quietly. "It's pneumonia, and it's bad. If she'd gone to the hospital earlier, it might have made a difference."

Colt stood there frozen, unable to remove his eyes from the doctor's face. Kit was determined not to go to pieces. Kitty would expect her to be strong. She drew in her breath and said quietly, "Tell me what to do for her."

"Cold cloths may help bring down the fever," the doctor said. "Someone should be with her all the time. When she's awake, she'll probably be delirious."

"How long . . . ?" Kit forced herself to ask.

"I don't know," Dr. Talton confessed. "I have a feeling that she's a strong-willed woman. She just might have some fight left in her. I've done all I can do though. It's up to the good Lord now. I'll be home if you need me for anything," he said wearily as he turned to go down the stairs.

Kit went back into Kitty's room and drew up a
chair next to her bed. Kitty had not moved, and the
ominous rattle in her chest was the only sound in the
quiet, shadowy room. Kit touched her cheek cautiously, gasping at how hot she felt. Dear God, she
prayed silently, help her . . . and help me . . . to be
strong.

She heard the door opening and looked around to
see her father. Never had she seen him look so sad
and forlorn. She sensed that he was hardly aware of
her presence as he leaned forward to take one of Kitty's hands and press it to his lips.

Carasia came in with a bowl of ice water and a
cloth, and Kit sponged Kitty's face. As she worked,
she listened, spellbound, as her father began talking,
not to her, but to Kitty. He told her of his deep and
abiding love for her and his father. Kit felt like an
intruder, listening to his intimate reflections, but she
was far too fascinated to leave. It was like being an
actual witness to his past life, and as he spoke of
things she'd never known, a fierce love for both her
father and Kitty seized her. When Colt finally stopped
speaking, he bowed his head and began to weep with
deep, choking sobs.

Only then did Kit tiptoe from the room.

Jade felt as if she were suffocating. Bryan was alive!
Oh, God, to have her worst fears confirmed was more
than she could bear. She tried to tell herself that it
did not matter, *could* not matter, because Bryan had
no claim on her. He was married to someone else,
and he had a daughter. But, she thought with a great,
wrenching shudder, what if the fear she'd tried to bury
within herself all these years proved true? What if
Bryan were Kit and Travis's father? There was no way

to know, no reason he should suspect, but what about Travis and Valerie? Travis could be in love with his own sister! Jade bit her lip to keep from crying out loud. She swayed dizzily and tried to gain control of herself as she heard the door open softly.

Turning about, she found herself facing Colt. His eyes ran over her coldly, and she knew she must look completely distraught. Swallowing hard, she asked, "How is Kitty?"

He threw himself into a chair by the window. "She's in and out of a coma. Her fever is still high, and she's delirious. She thinks I'm Dad. . . ." His voice broke, and he covered his face with his hands.

Jade's heart went out to him. "I'm so sorry," she whispered, momentarily forgetting her own misery. She dropped to her knees before him and took his hands in hers. "Oh, Colt, I'm so very, very sorry."

"She thinks I'm Travis . . ." Colt continued miserably. "She said to me, 'Travis, please take me with you, because I don't want to go on living here without you.'" A tear slid from the corner of his eye and rolled slowly down his cheek. Then he looked down at Jade. An invisible hand seemed to pass over his face, changing his expression of grief to one of anger. His eyes narrowed as, through clenched teeth, he asked, "Do you want to talk about Bryan Stevens?"

Jade stood and walked to the window. She stared out unseeingly and held her hands together to keep them from shaking. "I . . . I don't know what to say. It's such a shock to realize that he's alive, and married to Lita Tulane—the father of the girl Travis is in love with."

"That," Colt growled, his fists clenched, "will end immediately! I won't have my son bringing a member of that bastard's family into mine!"

Jade stifled a sigh of relief. She would be spared having to explain the real reason for her own opposition to the match. "You know we agreed never to tell Travis or Kit the details of that horrible time. They've never heard about Bryan Stevens, and Travis is not going to understand why we feel as we do about Valerie."

"Well, this is one time he's going to have to obey without questions." Colt went and put his arms around her. "Stevens is not going to bother you. I swear it."

Jade could not shake her terror. "To think that he's alive, after all these years! I don't understand how he could have survived."

"That isn't important, Jade. Forget about it. Forget him."

"I can't. . . ."

"You've got to, dammit!" Colt spun her around roughly, his fingers digging into her shoulders. He glared at her with burning eyes. "I can understand your shock, Jade, but why do you have to dwell on it? Bryan Stevens has nothing to do with us or our lives. If he's living in New York, so be it. We'll make sure our paths don't cross, and if they do, I'll let him know that he'd better leave us alone. There's just no reason for you to stay so upset about this. I need you. The whole family needs you. Now please, get hold of yourself."

Jade closed her eyes and breathed a silent prayer for strength. She knew that she would have to bear alone the unspeakable horror of having her worst fears come true. Taking a deep, ragged breath, she forced herself to look up at Colt. "You're right," she whispered. "I'm being foolish. He might as well be dead, because he has no place in our world. It's time I came back to ours . . . where I'm needed.''

"Kit, wake up!''

Startled to realize that she had fallen asleep during her night's vigil, Kit opened bleary eyes to find Marilee shaking her awake. "What is it? What's wrong?'' she asked, quickly checking on Kitty and sighing with relief that she was still alive.

"It's him,'' Marilee whispered, her face glowing with excitement.

Kit shook her head. "Him? Who are you talking about?''

"Kurt Tanner. He's downstairs—asking for you!''

And in that moment, despite the sadness that pervaded her world, Kit felt a rush of inexpressible joy.

Chapter Twenty-two

HE was waiting in the parlor. Kit had quickly changed into a silk dressing robe, but there was no time to put any finishing touches on her appearance. She entered the parlor, the mellow morning sunshine spilling through the long, cathedral windows, and was immediately struck by how handsome he looked despite the ruggedness of his dress—leather coat, denim trousers, scuffed boots. His hair was tousled, and her fingers ached to brush back the dark curls that tumbled onto his forehead. He was watching her intently as she approached. Suddenly, impulsively, she rushed across the room to fling herself into his strong arms.

Holding her tightly against his chest, he touched his lips to her forehead. "I hope I'm not intruding, but I had to come. It took some doing, but I managed to find out where you and your family were staying. I wanted see how your grandmother is . . . and how you are," he added tenderly. Kit drew back to smile at him gratefully, then took his hand and led him to a settee in front of the crackling fire.

Kurt listened quietly as she told him about Kitty. When she'd finished with the doctor's gloomy prognosis, he said, "I'll do anything I can. I've got to leave for New York today, and Spain next week, but if there's anything I can do, just tell me.''

Kit thanked him with her eyes. Then she said, ''If she makes it, she'll need a lot of rest before she can travel, so I don't know when I'll get back to New York, much less to Spain.''

He was silent for a moment, then he voiced the concern that had been bothering him. ''What about Pegasus? You can't leave him in a stable indefinitely, Kit. A horse like that needs open land, where he can run. You'll ruin him by keeping him confined without exercise.''

Kit was stung by the edge to his voice. ''He's taken for a ride every day,'' she said defensively.

Kurt knew that, just as he knew everything about the stable where she'd boarded the Hispano he still considered his property. He'd made it his business to find out. Knowingly risking Kit's anger, he said, ''I'll take him back to Spain with me. You've got enough to worry about here.''

''No,'' she said as she slowly pulled from his embrace.

He did not want to argue, but he felt compelled to speak his mind. ''I can't let that horse suffer simply because you're so stubborn, Kit. We both know that the only reason you brought him all the way over here was because you were afraid I'd claim him.''

''Isn't that what you're trying to do now?'' Kit was worn out to the point of exhaustion. ''You seem to forget that he's my horse, and his welfare is my concern. Not yours!''

''Oh, Kit,'' he groaned, getting up suddenly. Standing before the fireplace, he looked down at her reproachfully. ''Why does it always have to be this way? Especially now? I didn't come over here to argue with you.''

"Then why are you?'' she coldly challenged him.

''I'm just thinking of the horse's welfare. Besides, you know that he's rightfully mine. You tricked me into a wager that was nothing but a joke, and made me look like a fool. That doesn't even matter, though. The truth is, you've just got no business with an expensive animal like that. Do you have any idea what he's worth? Did you even look at the bill of sale? Ten thousand dollars!''

Kit stood, fighting to hold her temper in check. ''You signed the bill of sale over to *me*,'' she reminded him curtly. ''How dare you say I've got no business keeping him? Who are you to judge? I know plenty about horses, and—''

Kurt growled.

''I signed him over to you in the heat of the moment, and you know it. He's never been your horse, and he never will be!

Furious, Kit cried, ''Then why did you pretend he was? What were you trying to prove?''

''Prove?'' he echoed mockingly. ''What was I trying to prove? Think about it, Kit. Be honest and admit that you were attracted to me the same as I was to you, only fighting over the horse kept getting in the way.''

Kit was astonished. ''Do you mean that you only signed that bill of sale to . . . to patronize me?''

''Exactly.'' He smiled confidently. ''I was willing to do anything to make you realize that you wanted me.'' He pulled her roughly against him and kissed her passionately.

''Why can't you at least be honest with yourself?'' he whispered.

For a moment, she could only stare up at him in shocked silence, stunned by his audacity. Then she could stand it no longer. She reached back, preparing to swing at him, but he caught both her wrists and pinned them behind her back, rendering her helpless.

"You bastard!" she raged. "You'll never have me, and you'll never have that horse! Now get out of here—"

Suddenly the parlor doors banged open loudly, and Kit turned her head to see her father storm into the room. "What the hell is going on here?" he roared. Then he saw the way Kurt was holding her, and, with a muttered curse, he headed straight for him with mayhem in his eyes.

Kurt released her at once. "I'm sorry, Mr. Coltrane. We had a slight misunderstanding."

Kit rubbed her wrists, stifling her fury with difficulty. The last thing she wanted was for her father to get involved. "We had a disagreement," she explained. "It's nothing serious. I'm sorry I lost my temper."

"Well, you picked a fine time! Your grandmother is upstairs on her deathbed, and you can be heard all over the house screaming like a trollop. And you, Tanner . . ." He directed his fury at him. "Do you make a habit of manhandling women?"

"Only when they're trying to slap me," Kurt informed him coolly.

"Somebody had better tell me what's going on here, and be quick about it," Colt said menacingly, looking from one to the other.

Kit shrugged nervously. "I told you. We had a little argument. I lost my temper, that's all. I'm sorry."

"Do I have to remind you that we are guests in the

Buchers' home, and you're disgracing our family by acting like this?''

''It's about the horse,'' Kurt said wearily.

Kit glared at him. ''I'll handle this.''

Kurt shook his head. ''I'm sorry, but I think your father's got a right to know what provoked all this.'' He turned to Colt. ''The Hispano she brought from Spain is mine.''

Colt frowned. ''She told me that she won him in a race.''

''She did, but at the time, she didn't know the horse had been stolen from me by the man who made the wager.''

Colt stiffened with indignation. ''Well, I can sympathize with your position, Mr. Tanner, if what you say is true. You should have come to me, however, not my daughter—and not now. So I'll ask you to leave us. If you'll contact me when we return to New York, we can discuss it then.'' He walked to the doors to indicate that the matter was closed.

Kurt did not move. ''I'm not going anywhere until you hear me out, because I'll be damned if I'm going to be considered an insensitive clod who'd pick a time like this to claim a horse. The truth is, I care about your daughter, and I came here to let her know that. The horse has always been a sore subject with us, though, and I guess all the tension made us say some things we shouldn't have. Isn't that true, Kit?'' He looked at her intently.

Kit raised her chin defiantly. If he had not taunted her, made a mockery of the way she'd begun to feel about him, she would have stood by him. Now, however, she was angrier than she could ever remember being in her whole life, and she wasn't about to agree with him on anything.

"All right," he said quietly, ominously, when her silence continued. "You leave me no choice."

For an instant Kit was actually frightened, for his fury was palpable. Instinctively she moved farther away from him.

"I didn't come here to claim the horse tonight. Kit has known for months that the horse was stolen from me, but she wouldn't give him back. I kept hoping we could work things out. Then she made a wager of her own, and got me to agree that if she had the guts to play matador, she could keep him. I agreed, thinking she was bluffing. I never thought she'd do it, and I sure as hell had no way of knowing she'd been climbing in bullpens for years. In case you didn't know, your daughter is quite an accomplished bullfighter," he added with a wry grin.

Colt looked at Kit. "Is this true, Kit? Did he come to you after that race and tell you the horse had been stolen from him?"

Kit nodded mutely. Then she snapped at Kurt, "Are you satisfied? You agreed that the horse was mine, and now you're reneging on our deal. You're a scoundrel, and I hate you!"

To her surprise, Kurt shook his head and laughed. "No, you don't, Kit. You're just a spoiled brat, used to having your own way. Deep inside you care, and you know it."

"That's enough, Tanner!" Colt roared. "Get out! Now! Claim your damn horse in New York at the stable where Kit's got him boarded, and then get the hell out of our lives!"

Horrified, Kit cried, "You can't do that! It isn't fair!"

"Maybe not, but it's fair punishment for your tricking him into a wager you knew you could win. I'm disappointed in you, Kit. Your mother is right," he added tersely. "Maybe we should send you to Europe with Marilee for more schooling. I think you do need to learn how to act like a lady!"

Kit turned on Kurt, hot angry tears streaming down her cheeks. "I hope you're happy, damn you!"

"I didn't want it to be this way," Kurt said, shaking his head miserably.

Their eyes met and held—hers reflecting venomous hatred; his mirroring disappointment and regret.

Kit feared that he had not finished yet, that he'd even tell Colt about her buying the ranch. Her father would make sure she never returned to Spain! Dear God, that was the dream she clung to now, for it was the only one she had that wasn't being destroyed. "Won't you just go now?" she begged him. "You've done enough damage for one day, don't you think?"

Kurt knew what she was thinking. He wished he could assure her that he did not want to hurt her, but he knew she would not listen to anything he had to say. He went to the door, and looked Colt straight in the eye, not intimidated by the man's furious expression. "I don't even want the horse. Let her have it."

"Claim the goddamn horse," Cold growled. "Or so help me, I'll have him destroyed. My family wants no part of ill-gotten gains."

Seeing that he meant it, Kurt nodded, and walked out.

Kit started to leave the room, but Colt blocked her way. "You should be ashamed of yourself! I should have listened to your mother years ago when she said we needed to get you out of that environment—riding with vaqueros, fighting bulls!" he said contemptuously. "What else have you done that I don't know about?"

Despite her rage, Kit loved her father, so she bit back her anger and whispered tremulously, "I'm sorry."

Shaking his head, Colt walked back into the parlor and poured himself a drink, downing it in one gulp. He was about to speak when the sound of footsteps thundering down the stairs caused them both to look up in alarm.

"Travis, you come back here! Don't you dare run out when I'm trying to talk to you—" Jade's hysterical cry echoed through the house.

Bewildered, Colt and Kit rushed into the foyer in time to see Travis reach the bottom of the stairs. He glanced in their direction, red-faced and furious, then turned and headed for the back of the house.

Colt yelled, "Travis, come back here!"

Jade appeared at the landing above, pale and shaken. "He just won't listen," she sobbed. "Talk to him, Colt. Tell him that if he sees that girl again, you'll disown him!"

Travis spun around. "No, talk to *her!* Tell her she can't run my life, can't tell me who I can fall in love with and marry! For God's sake, she won't even give me a reason why she hates Valerie so much!"

Colt looked from his son to wife. Suddenly he felt a sharp pain in his chest. "Stop it, all of you!" he bellowed. "Have you gone crazy? My mother is dying, and this family has turned into a goddamn circus! I find out that my daughter kept stolen property, my wife has turned into a hysterical shrew, and my son is insolent and disobedient! I'm not going to have it, and—" The pain became worse, a knife of white-hot agony that made him grab at his chest and double over.

Jade screamed and started down the steps; Travis

and Kit rushed to his side. They helped get Colt into the parlor and lie down, and Kit ran to call Dr. Talton.

"I'm all right . . ." Colt tried to assure Jade, as she hovered over him.

Kit and Travis stood to one side in the room until Dr. Talton arrived. After examining Colt, he said that he'd had an anxiety attack. "Let it be a lesson," he warned, leaving a bottle of sedatives.

Jade stayed beside him, for the moment forgetting her argument with Travis. He slipped out of the house to escape, for the time being, further confrontation, and Kit went upstairs to be with Kitty.

Chapter Twenty-three

EPIPHANY had given in to the pleas of her Negro housekeeper, Sara, to try some old family remedies with Kitty. Dr. Talton scoffed at what he called black magic, sarcastically calling her a witch doctor. She had Colt's dubious approval, however, so she set out to concoct her favorite potions for colds and fevers.

Kit wondered whether it was just her imagination, but Kitty did seem slightly better after Sara's ministrations. She was breathing more easily and her fever seemed to have gone down.

Carasia had been tirelessly applying cold packs to Kitty's face, and Kit told her she would take over for a while. "Are you sure?" Carasia asked worriedly, scrutinizing her. "How long since you've slept? You look exhausted."

Kit shrugged and said that it didn't matter. The truth was, she felt driven to stay busy, afraid that if she did go to sleep, Kurt Tanner would find a way to steal into her dreams. She wanted only to try and forget that he ever existed, but, she acknowledged with a painful twinge in her heart, that was going to be very difficult.

Suddenly Kit felt a tiny sensation of pressure and realized with a start that Kitty was trying to squeeze her hand. Her eyes were open, and although they were glassy, there was a faint glint of lucidity within their soft lavender depths. Kitty tried to lift her head from the pillows, but the effort was too great. Her lips parted as she tried to speak. "Tell me," Kit urged her anxiously, leaning closer. "What is it? Is there something you want? Can I do anything?"

Her feeble whisper was barely audible. "Go on . . . to Spain. Don't . . . don't let your dream die with me."

Kit nervously dabbed at her face with a wet cloth. "Stop that," she scolded gently. "You're going back with me. You're not going to die."

Kitty managed a wan smile. "Everybody dies, child. It's living they . . . sometimes get cheated out of. Really living . . . like the love of a good man . . . being blessed with children . . . grandchildren . . . like you, my darling. I was one of the lucky ones . . . I had all that . . . Now I'm tired . . . so tired."

"I'm going to go get Daddy."

"No!" Kitty protested, her voice surprisingly strong. "Not now. My bag . . . Get it, please . . ."

Kit looked about the room uncertainly. "What bag are you talking about? Your purse?"

"There . . ." Kitty pointed weakly to the tapestry bag lying on the floor beneath the window. "There. In the lining. At the bottom. Look, please . . ."

Kit hurried to do her bidding. Pushing aside the lingerie packed within, she saw that the satin lining had been slit toward the back, then sewn shut with large stitches. She popped the thread, spread the cloth, then cried aloud. With trembling hands, she lifted out a large wad of bills. "What are you doing with so much money? I'll give it to Daddy, and he can keep it for you until you're better.'' She laid it on the bed.

"No!'' With great effort, she grasped Kit's wrist with clawlike fingers, straining to pull her closer. "No one must know. They'll stop you, Kit. They'll never let you go back after I'm gone. Take it. It will tide you over till—'' She coughed, unable to continue, then slumped back weakly against the pillows.

Kit shook her head, terror crawling up her spine. "No. I'm going to give it to Daddy to invest for you. You're going to get well, and we're going to our place together, and—''

"Take it. Do as I say. We both know I won't be going with you.'' She paused wearily. "I'm tired, child, tired of living without your grandfather. I'm ready to join him. I hate to leave you, but it's the way it has to be. So go on, live your life to its fullest and savor every moment of every day, because one morning you'll wake up old, and you'll realize you've got more yesterdays than tomorrows.''

"No, you can't die!'' Kit cried, hot tears spilling down her cheeks.

Kitty seemed not to hear her. Her face suddenly seemed to glow with joy, and she held her arms open wide. "Oh, Travis, hold me . . . love me . . . like yesterday . . . yesterday . . .''

And with a smile of supreme happiness on her lips, Kitty Wright Coltrane died, joining at last the spirit of the only man she had ever loved.

Chapter Twenty-four

THE day after Kitty's death, Jade came downstairs to begin receiving visitors. Kit could see that she was under great strain. She looked deathly pale, and her lips trembled as she responded mechanically to expressions of condolence.

The hours passed, and soon night fell. Kit wanted to collapse, but she was not about to give in to exhaustion—or the tears that constantly threatened.

Just before dark, Jade wearily called Kit into the kitchen to share tea and sandwiches that neither of them could eat. Staring moodily out the window, Jade said, "I'm really getting upset about Travis running off. He should be here with the rest of the family."

"No doubt he's with her!" Jade spat out, her green eyes filled with rage.

"Mother, just what do you have against Valerie?" Kit asked impulsively, watching her mother intently. "Why do you dislike her so? Frankly, I've never known you to be so . . . so venomous toward anyone. You don't even know her!"

"Travis has four hard years of study ahead of him. He has no business getting involved with anyone. Besides, young lady, I don't have to justify myself to you," she said frostily.

Kit sighed. "Well, I'm afraid that you'll have to

give Travis a reason. He and Valerie had worked everything out. They'll wait till he graduates from West Point to get married. He couldn't see that you'd have any objection to that, and frankly, Mother, neither do I," she added candidly.

Jade felt sick at heart. No one could ever know why she demanded such a sacrifice of her son. "I don't want to talk about it anymore." Suddenly she said, "Marilee told me that Kurt Tanner was here yesterday, and you two quarrelled. What happened?"

"It was nothing," Kit said. "Besides, it doesn't matter, because he won't be coming back."

"Not if he knows what's good for him," Colt said ominously, entering the kitchen. He went to the stove and poured himself a cup of coffee. His hair was disheveled and he looked awful.

Kit moved toward the door, but he told her to stay right where she was. "I want a few things settled right now, young lady."

"Daddy, please . . ." she protested. "Can't it wait?"

"Colt, what is going on?" Jade looked from him to Kit. "This isn't the time for arguing."

"Right!" he replied sarcastically. "Then why couldn't you wait to speak to Travis about that Stevens girl? Now he's run off God-knows-where, and the whole family is falling apart. As for Kit, it just so happens she lied about that horse. She won him in a race all right, but she was racing against a horse thief. The horse just happened to be stolen from Mr. Tanner, and although she knew that, she refused to turn him over."

Jade stared at Kit in disbelief. "Tell me this isn't true," she begged her. "Tell me you wouldn't do such a thing."

Kit turned away, knowing there was no point in trying to explain.

"Let's just get through this, and then we can talk," Jade suggested wearily. "We'll be canceling Kit's debut, of course, because of our mourning period, but I've been thinking of other plans."

"Well, let's hear them now," Colt said. "Maybe it'll get my mind off everything else that's been happening around here."

"It's still a few months until Travis enters the Point," Jade began hesitantly, "so I think it would be best for us to get away for a while, recover from all of this."

Kit grew tense with suspicion.

"Go on," Colt said, looking interested.

"You're going to take your mother back to France, aren't you?"

"She wanted to be buried beside my father, and I promised her I'd see that she was."

"Well, we can all go to ·Europe together. Travis, Kit, and I can see Marilee to Switzerland, and then go to Russia to spend a little time with my family. You can meet us, and we can return together later, just before Travis enters the Point."

"I'm not sure that's such a good idea," Colt said. "There's talk of political unrest all over Europe, and—"

"But not in Russia," Jade pointed out. "This summer is the celebration of the three hundredth anniversary of Romanov rule, and there will be official festivities and ceremonies. It's a wonderful time for the children to meet their Romanov kin, however distant the blood might be. One of my cousins wrote me about it just before we left Spain, but I gave it no thought. Now, with all that's happened, I think we should go.''

Colt nodded thoughtfully. ''All right. That's what we'll do. And it might be best to have Kit go to school with Marilee for a year or so, to learn a few social graces,'' he added sarcastically. He ran his fingers through his hair. ''God knows, I'd like to just get away and not worry about anything for a while. We're in no hurry to settle in New York, anyway.''

Jade felt as if the sun had just come out. Maybe there was a chance that they would never return to New York—that they'd settle somewhere far away from Bryan Stevens. Only then would she know true peace. She was suddenly filled with such relief and happiness that she had to hide her emotions. It would be unseem to appear so joyful at such an unhappy time.

Colt opened his arms, and she moved into his embrace, her head pressed against his chest. She would preserve her marriage and the future happiness of her family at all costs, she vowed.

They did not notice as Kit walked quietly out of the kitchen. Draping an old rain cape about her shoulders, she went outside. A half moon cast a soft glow, and the bare tree limbs clattered together in the breeze like dry bones. A whippoorwill called mournfully, as though sympathizing with her misery.

She had to return to Spain as soon as possible. She would not go to Europe with her parents, and she certainly had no intention of going to school with Marilee! But if her father ever found out what she was planning, he would do everything in his power to stop her. That meant she had to run away, which would not be easy.

The first thing her parents would do when they discovered she was missing would be to check the passenger lists of every ocean liner. If she booked passage they'd discover her destination, and she did not want anyone coming after her. She would have to stow away. Later, when she was settled, she would write and explain her reasons for leaving, and ask for their forgiveness and understanding. If they refused, well, it was her life. She had the right to live it the way she chose, where she chose.

Kit sighed, shivering with despair and cold. She gathered the cape more tightly around her and put her hands into the pockets of her dress. The money! Slowly, hesitantly, she pulled it out. She had forgotten all about it, absently stuffing it in her pocket when Kitty had taken a turn for the worse. Now she counted it, unable to stifle a gasp as she realized just how much was there. Kitty knew that she would have to go on alone, without her, and had thus provided the necessary funds to help her. Dear God! She stuffed the money back in her pocket.

Even in death, Kitty made her feel that she was not truly alone in life. Maybe, Kit reflected, that's what love was all about.

"Kit?"

She looked up to see Travis coming through the gate, and she ran to meet him. They embraced for a long moment, then he pulled back. His face looked haggard in the moonlight. "I'm sorry I ran off like I did, but I just had to be alone to try to accept that she's really gone."

"I know." Kit nodded toward the house. "I'm afraid you're in hot water, though. Mom thinks you've been with Valerie."

"I wish I had been," he admitted readily. "I've been to every hotel in Washington, but I couldn't find her. She and her family must be staying in a private home, too. Dammit, I just wish I knew what Mother has against her. Valerie is so sweet and kind. I can't imagine anybody disliking her."

Kit agreed. "It's a mystery, all right. I told her that you'd decided to wait until after the Point to marry, but it didn't make any difference. She's still determined not to let you see Valerie." Kit told him of the planned trip to Europe, and was surprised that he was not opposed to the idea.

"Maybe that's a good idea. It'll give us all time to get over Kitty's death, and I'll have a chance to convince Mother that she's wrong about Valerie. I'm going to talk to Dad, too, and—"

"Forget that," Kit said quickly. "He'd never side with you against her." She proceeded to tell him of her own difficulties with Colt, how he wanted to send her to school with Marilee.

"That might be perfect for you, Kit," Travis replied, to her surprise. "What else do you have to do? Maybe you'll meet a count or a prince, and get married and live happily ever after in a castle," he teased, putting his arm across her shoulder and walking her back inside.

Kit had wondered whether to confide her plans to Travis so someone would know where she was, and could assure everyone else that there was no need to worry. Now she threw that idea to the wind. There was just no one she could trust.

She had to make her way . . . alone.

Chapter Twenty-five

THE next afternoon, the Coltranes disembarked from their train at Grand Central Station and taxied to their three-bedroom suite at the Waldorf-Astoria Hotel. Kit immediately called the stable where Pegasus had been boarded and was told that a Mr. Kurt Tanner had picked up the horse that morning, claiming full authority to do so!

Enraged, she was about to speak when her mother exploded first.

In her usually efficient way, Jade had paused at the sideboard to leaf through the messages and calling cards the maid had left in the huge silver receiving bowl. Eyes widening, she stared at a cream-colored calling card. In a thin voice edged with fury, she hissed, "That girl! She's been here twice today, and there are telephone messages!"

Travis stormed over to his mother. "Give those to me! You have no right!"

"I have every right!" she snapped, slapping his hand away. "I told you, young man, it's over. You are forbidden to see that girl again, and I won't have her chasing after you this way. I'm putting a stop to it immediately!"

As Travis watched helplessly, Jade snatched up the telephone receiver and ordered the operator to put her through to the hotel manager. She then gave orders that no further communication from Miss Valerie Stevens was to be allowed, and that if she showed up again, she was to be escorted from the hotel by the security guards. The manager assured her that it would be done.

Kit's heart went out to her brother. She tried to catch his eye, let him know silently that she'd find Valerie for him, but he whirled around and went to his room, slamming and locking the door behind him.

"Maybe now we can get back to more important things—like getting ready to sail for Europe in two days," Jade stated, unmoved by her son's tantrum. "We'll need to make arrangements for the memorial service, and . . ."

Kit was no longer listening as she surreptitiously made her way out the door while her mother's attention was diverted. She rushed to the elevator and was downstairs quickly. Once in the lobby, she found a telephone and requested to be put through to the local number Travis had slipped to her in the taxi to the hotel.

After one ring, a masculine voice with a slightly British accent answered, "Mr. Stevens's residence."

"Miss Stevens," she requested breathlessly. "Miss Valerie Stevens."

"One moment."

Kit waited impatiently until she heard Valerie say hello. "It's Kit Coltrane," she announced. "My brother asked me to call you, and—"

"Oh, Kit! What's going on?" Valerie burst out. "I've been out of my mind! I couldn't find Travis in Washington. Why hasn't he called me? My father's been like a madman since the other night, and he won't talk to me about it. I just don't know what's going on!''

"Travis wanted me to call you, because he can't," Kit explained. "We don't know what's wrong with Mother, but something else has happened. Our grandmother passed away.''

"Oh, Kit, I'm so sorry. . . .''

Kit hurried to tell her of the plans, glancing over her shoulder, lest her father come through the lobby and see her on the phone.

Valerie started crying. "Oh, that's not fair. Why does that woman hate me so? What have I ever done to her? Kit, I love your brother with all my heart. I know it happened quickly, but I also know I could never love anybody the way I love him. That's why I'm willing to wait for him to finish four years at West Point, even longer, if I have to. How can she object to that?''

"I don't know," Kit repeated. "I wish I could help you, but I've tried to talk to her and it just doesn't do any good.''

"Travis has to meet me somewhere. I've got to talk to him.''

"I'll be glad to get a message to him. Just tell me where and when.''

"The library at Fifth and Forty-second," Valerie said immediately. "My mother has been after me to go there, so my father won't be suspicious when I do. Make it in an hour.''

Kit could not promise that Travis could be there that soon. "So much is going on, Valerie. Mother is watching him like a hawk. I'm going to have to find a way to tell him without her overhearing. Let me see what I can do and call you back.''

"No!" Valerie cried. "It has to be then. My father

will be home soon, and if I don't leave before he gets here, he'll ask a lot of questions. If he's the least bit suspicious, he won't let me go anywhere. Please have Travis meet me there in an hour! It may be our only chance to talk for months! Everybody is against us . . . ." Valerie started to cry as she hung up the phone.

Kit hurried back upstairs, expecting to face her mother's wrath. Instead she found only Carasia, who told her that the whole family, even Travis, had gone to be fitted for mourning clothes. They expected her to meet them, and Carasia handed her a slip of paper with the address.

Kit sighed with frustration. Valerie was going to be waiting at the library in vain. She decided that there was nothing to do but go there and let her know what had happened.

She reached the library half an hour early. Hurrying to a nearby restaurant, she asked to use their telephone. When the White Star Line offices answered, she was thrilled to discover that the ship she planned to hide on was the very one on which she'd sailed over. She knew where it was docked, and she knew her way around the vessel. Stowing away would not be so difficult after all!

Filled with relief, Kit headed back to the library. Valerie was standing there, her golden hair tumbling about her face, her blue eyes wide with excitement.

"Is he coming? This is our last chance! My father called just as I was leaving and told me that we're going to Bermuda first thing in the morning. There won't be another time for me to see Travis!"

"Valerie, calm down." Kit tried to explain why Travis could not be there. "Everything is turned upside down, Valerie," she finished apologetically. "My heart goes out to you, but I just don't know what I can do. If you'll give me your address in Bermuda, maybe he can write to you there.''

''My father would intercept any mail for me,'' Valerie wailed miserably. ''And I'm sure your mother will do the same if I try to get in touch with Travis.''

Kit agreed that was very likely. ''You'll just have to write to him at the Point. That's only a few months away.''

Valerie bit her lip. ''That's an eternity when you love someone.'' She was quiet for a few seconds. Then she cried excitedly, ''You can help us! Just give me a list of the countries you plan to visit in Europe. I can write to him in care of the American embassies there. Surely he can sneak away long enough to go and pick up his mail.''

''No.'' Kit shook her head. ''I told you—it's only for a few months, and mail would take nearly that long.''

''Then *you* write to me!'' Valerie said brightly. ''Just write me a few lines any chance you get and tell me how he is. Refer to him by another name, though, so if my father sees my mail, he won't know who you're talking about.''

Kit couldn't let Valerie harbor false hopes. ''I'm sorry,'' she said regretfully, ''I can't because—''

''I thought you liked me!'' Valerie cried. ''I thought you were my friend, that I could trust you to help me. I'm sorry I bothered you.'' Valerie turned and started to walk away, her head bowed in defeat.

Kit ran after her and spun her around. ''No! It's not like that at all! I do like you, Valerie. Believe me, I'd help you if I could, but I can't, because . . .'' Her voice trailed off as she bit her lip thoughtfully.

Valerie was looking at her intently. "Please," she begged, "tell me why you won't help me."

Kit hesitated for another moment, then she threw caution to the wind. It really made no difference— Valerie was not going to be in touch with her family, anyway. "I'm not going to Europe with them," she said boldly. "I'm running away. I'm going back to Spain—tonight."

Valerie gasped so loudly that several passersby turned to stare. Kit then told her everything. It was such a relief to have someone to confide in that she even told Valerie about Kurt Tanner and the Hispano. "So, you see," she finished breathlessly, "I have no choice but to run away. I refuse to let my parents dictate to me any longer."

Valerie clasped her hand. "I admire you, Kit, for being strong enough to go on alone. I wish I were like you. My parents have always dictated to me, too, especially my father. He's determined that I'm going to marry the son of a friend of his who lives in Bermuda, but he's wrong. I'll never marry anyone but your brother, and I'm going to wait for him, no matter how long it takes!"

Kit assured her that Travis would find a way to get in touch with her sooner or later. "He told me that he loves you, and he's miserable the way things are. Everything will work out, I know it will." Kit opened her purse and found pencil and paper. "Here's my address so you can write to me. When the time is right, I'll contact my family and let them know where I am, and I'll write to Travis as soon as he starts at the Point. The two of you can use me as a go-between if you like."

Valerie hugged her. "I always had a feeling we'd be good friends! You have to promise to write to me and let me know how you're doing. I'm going to be worried about you stowing away on that ship, so you be careful,'' she added with a frown.

"That's the least of my problems. All I have to do is make my way to the hold where they keep the animals and hide out in one of the empty stables.''

"Do you have enough money? I can give you what I have in my bag—''

"I'm fine,'' Kit assured her, wishing it were really true.

Chapter Twenty-six

I<small>T</small> was time.

Kit threw back the covers and quietly got out of bed. Padding silently to the door, she leaned against it to listen intently. She could hear nothing, everyone was asleep. She pulled out the bundle of clothing she had taken from Travis's trunk earlier. A woman would arouse attention at the docks as this late hour, so she had decided to disguise herself as a boy. She tucked in the too-big shirt and rolled up the cuffs of the pants. Pinning up her long, golden-red hair, she tucked every strand beneath the borrowed derby.

She wrote a hasty note, saying that she was going away to live her own life. No one was to worry—she had plans and money, and would be in touch later. Kit made a perfunctory request that she be forgiven, and left the folded paper lying on the coffee table in the parlor.

The need to stay hidden on the ship for five days was going to make it difficult to find food, so she took some bread and cookies, and a small jug of water from the little tea kitchen.

Finally, glancing about one last time, Kit took a deep breath . . . and the first step toward her destiny.

* * *

Her feet ached in the large, ill-fitting shoes, and she had a painful stitch in her side from walking quickly along the cobbled side streets.

As she neared the waterfront, she paused to rest. In the distance she could see a blaze of lights and frenzied activity. The pier was busy with men loading cargo onto the *Olympia*. She could see the mighty ship glowing in the dock lights, and her heart began to pound with excitement. Soon she would be free and independent. That idea was so exhilarating that it made her present tension and weariness bearable.

Kit moved cautiously among the crates. Some of the rows were so narrow that she had to inch her way along, praying that she wouldn't get wedged in and trapped. It seemed to take forever, but at last she faced a wide, empty space before the next stack of cargo. Not seeing anyone, she took a deep breath and ran as fast as she could for what looked like rows of large barrels. She had just reached them when she heard a man cry sharply, "Hey, what was that?"

"Giant rat!" another voice cackled gleefully. "Go on with ye, Jordie. Take yer swig and gimme back my bottle."

Kit froze. The two men were somewhere amid the barrels. They were either drunken bums who lived around the waterfront, or dock workers sneaking off to have a drink. It did not matter which, though, because both were a threat. Peering out, Kit decided to crawl around the barrels to the very edge of the dock, there go along the back. She could not stay where she was, because soon it would be light. There was no time to lose.

Crawling on her hands and knees, Kit began to make her way. Suddenly something big and warm brushed against her hand. A nearby postlamp bathed the world about her in a golden pool of light, and she found herself facing a huge gray wharf rat. Its narrow red eyes seemed filled with malicious glee, as if it sensed her terror. It opened its mouth and bared its teeth. Kit could not stifle a soft cry of terror.

"Eh? Ye hear that?" the drunk yelled. "Warn't no goddamn rat made that sound. Somebody's about here!"

Eyeing the rat, Kit scuttled backward on her hands and knees until she had several barrels between them.

"I tell ye, someone's about," she heard the drunk say. "I'm gettin' outta here!"

There were footsteps running . . . then silence.

Taking a deep breath, Kit continued on. Crawling past the barrels, she saw with relief that the next stacks of cargo were awaiting transport to the *Olympia*. The great ship stood proud and regal before her. The pier was ablaze with light, and Kit shrank back into the shadows. She had to wait for the perfect moment to run for the rope gangway leading into the hold.

A movement caught her eye, and she saw a boy of about fifteen pick up a small box. A burly man nearby yelled, "Hurry up and get them things to the galley. We got a load of potatoes comin' any minute now, and we gotta have room for 'em on the pier."

The boy scurried inside the hold as fast as his scrawny legs would carry him, and the impatient workman turned his attention to a huge boxcar. Kit decided to make her move. Dressed as she was, she could pass for one of the galley boys. It was her only chance.

Her heart pounding painfully, Kit strode purposefully toward the waiting galley supplies, telling herself repeatedly to be calm. Reaching the boxes, she selected what looked like the smallest. She gasped in surprise as she strained beneath the weight of what felt like a hundred pounds of rocks. Gritting her teeth, she started toward the gangway. She had gone only a few feet when someone yelled irritably, ''Get yer ass movin', laddie. We ain't got all day!''

With great effort, Kit moved more quickly, although her body cried in protest. Her spine was stretched to the breaking point, and her knees threatened to buckle.

''I don't know why they can't hire boys with some meat on 'em,'' the man roared. ''They hire you skinny asses, and then you ain't worth shit for nothin'. Hustle on in here, boy, or I'm gonna keelhaul your butt as soon as we set sail. What's your name, anyway, you little bastard. . . .''

Kit forced herself to make one last surge forward, almost falling as she entered the dimly lit hold. No one was about, thank God, and she attempted to lower the box as slowly and quietly as possible. The effort proved too great, however, and her stiff fingers gave way. The box fell to the floor with a loud thud, breaking open and shattering its contents—jars of golden honey.

''Did you drop that, boy? I'm gonna whup your ass good if you broke somethin'!'' her tormentor cried, running toward her.

Kit looked about wildly and saw a stack of lumpy burlap bags filled with smelly onions. Summoning her very last ounce of strength, she dove headfirst over the top of land on the other side. Then she lay frozen as she heard the man burst into the hold.

''Aw, goddamn! Look at this mess! You're fired, boy, but first I'm gonna give you a beatin' you ain't never gonna forget!''

Kit held her breath, her eyes squeezed shut. This couldn't be happening!

Another voice boomed, "What's goin' on here, McAdoe? What's all the yellin' about? A wagonload of taters just got here. We need to get 'em unloaded, but the dock's full."

Kit's enemy explained that an incompetent galley boy had dropped a crate of honey and was hiding. The other man angrily told him to get back to work and find the culprit later.

"You can bet yer ass I will, too," McAdoe grumbled, his words fading as they left the ship. "He shows hisself again, I'll get him. He was wearin' a derby hat, and I'll know him by that."

The activity outside seemed to be increasing as the time for sailing grew near. Kit could not stay where she was, as there was a chance the bags she hid behind would be moved elsewhere. Holding on to the lumpy sacks for support, she forced herself to stand. She peered over the top to check her surroundings and looked through the hatch to the pier. The world beyond was getting lighter by the moment, and time was running out.

Kit ducked down as a crewman came on board, his kit bag slung over his shoulder. Someone else passed by, and the two exchanged pleasantries. Then there was silence. She waited a few seconds longer before daring to move over the sacks and head for the kennels.

The main storage room was as dark and oppressive as she'd remembered, with animal cages bordering a pathway back to the stables.

Kit pushed open the big door to the stalls, hoping there would not be many horses. The fewer to be fed and cared for, the less her chance of discovery. She was relieved to see that the first two stalls on either side were empty. She walked farther back, away from the small light that was always kept burning by the door.

The next two stalls were also unoccupied. She dared to think she might have the entire section to herself. Then she heard the sound of agitated hooves pawing the floor of the very last stall.

Kit went to the gate and boosted herself on the bottom rung. She leaned over to reassure the animal it had nothing to fear. She nearly toppled over in shock as the mellow light revealed that the horse was Pegasus!

He whinnied softly in recognition, and Kit choked with emotion as she rubbed his soft velvet nose. She thought of how she'd looked forward to riding him on her ranch, making a special stall for him in the red barn. That dream would not come true now, thanks to Kurt Tanner. Kit stiffened instinctively. That Pegasus was on board meant that he was, too. Kit was suddenly glad to be a stowaway and not a passenger. Hiding in the hold with the animals was certainly preferable to his company.

The ship suddenly lurched with a loud, grinding noise, and Kit realized that they were starting to move away from the pier. She was on her way to a new life! She turned to the stall opposite, grateful to find it clean, the floor covered with fresh, sweet-smelling hay. Sitting down, she opened her bag and took a sip of water.

The ship made soft creaking sounds as it was guided slowly out of the harbor. Snuggling down in the pungent hay, Kit closed her eyes and was soon floating away on dreams of green Spanish valleys and wild Hispanos.

Kit woke up feeling queasy and hot. There was no way to tell how long she'd slept, for time stood still there in the shadowy stalls. She knew she should eat something, but she felt nauseated. She tried to sip water, and realized her throat was sore. Dear God, please don't let me get sick, she prayed. She felt weak and light-headed, and knew that it was not just from weariness. A hot fever seemed to be engulfing her, and she felt dizzier with each passing moment. Kit grew frightened. She knew she had to have help. Mustering her last shred of strength, she crawled through the straw to the gate. She then grasped the rungs and tried to pull herself up. The gate swung open, and she clung to it desperately as she felt herself slipping away. Her last conscious sight was Pegasus staring curiously down at her.

From somewhere far, far away, the voices came to her. She could not speak to them, for her throat seemed paralyzed with pain. She could not reach out, for there was no strength left within her to move. She could only lie there in the thick, gray fog that surrounded her, wondering where she was.

A disgruntled officer stared down at Kit. "This is where you found him?" he asked Norman Thatcher, the kennel boy.

"Yes, sir," Norman replied nervously. This was his area of responsibility, and a stowaway was a serious matter. "I just came here to feed Mr. Tanner's horse, and I saw somebody lying here and ran to get help. I haven't tried to move him, and—"

The officer gave him an impatient shove. "Oh, get out of my way! Bleedin' stowaways! We ought to just throw him overboard and be done with him, less trouble then." He rolled Kit over on her back and gasped, "I'll be goddamned. It's a woman!"

Norman peered over his shoulder, then pushed the

officer aside to kneel beside her. "It's Miss Kit Coltrane! She was a passenger last trip. She comes from a very wealthy family."

"So what's she doing here dressed up like a man?" The officer frowned. "Something funny is going on, but we'll worry about that later. She's awfully sick right now."

Norman thought for a moment. "Mr. Tanner—the man who checked the horse in—said it was his. I thought it odd at the time, being as he belonged to Miss Coltrane on the trip over. She sure was fond of that horse, too. I can't imagine her selling him to anybody. Let me go get Mr. Tanner and see if he knows what this is all about."

"You do that," the officer said grimly. "But my guess is she's a stowaway, for whatever reason. Why else would she be dressed like this? We'd better not move her until the doc looks her over. I'll get him while you fetch Tanner."

Kit did not try to speak to them. It was so much easier to sink into the quicksand of oblivion.

Chapter Twenty-seven

KIT opened her eyes with great effort. She felt utterly drained both physically and emotionally. Trying to focus despite a throbbing headache, her eyes were drawn to the only source of light in the dark room—a round window. Then she realized that it was a porthole, which meant she was on a ship. As she lifted her head from the pillow, her vision became clearer. She saw a small sofa, a chair, a table, and a desk. She was lying on a large bed. There were paintings on the walls, a rug on the floor. What was she doing in a suite! Kit tried unsuccessfully to sit up. The blanket fell away, and she saw that she was wearing an unfamiliar shirt. Whose shirt was it? Who had put it on her? And how had she gotten there?

Too weak to get up, Kit could only fall back and lie there overcome by a feeling of terror. The last thing she remembered was being in the stall and feeling sick. A wave of hysteria swept over her. Then she heard a scraping sound and saw the doorknob slowly turning, able only to await helplessly whatever fate had in store.

Kurt Tanner walked into the room.

"You!"

"Welcome back. You had me worried for a while there."

Her parched lips moved wordlessly, and Kurt poured her a cup of water from the pitcher on the table. Then he gently lifted her head so she could drink slowly. Kit loathed his touch, but she desperately wanted the water.

"Do you feel like eating? I can have the galley send up some soup. Your fever broke during the night. The doctor said the worst seemed to be over, but you'll be weak for a while." He gently lowered her head to the pillow once more, concern etched on his face.

Kit shook her head in amazement. "How . . ." she began in a tremulous voice. "How did you find me?"

Kurt laughed softly, sitting down on the side of the bed. "I didn't. The kennel boy did. Thatcher, I think his name is. He called an officer. They thought you were a stowaway."

"Then how—"

"How did I get involved?" he finished for her. "Well, after Thatcher got a good look at you, he recognized you from the last voyage. He also remembered that you were the one who brought Pegasus over, and wondered why I was the one who'd brought him on board this time. He came to ask me if I knew what was going on. I didn't, but I made up my own story to cover for you."

Kit frowned. He was obviously enjoying himself, trying to make her feel forever indebted to him. Well, he needn't waste his breath, she fumed inwardly, her resentment giving her strength. "You had no right to meddle. Why didn't you just mind your own business?"

Kurt raised an eyebrow and chuckled. "If I had, you'd be in a place I don't think you'd like very much—the ship's jail."

"That's ridiculous," Kit protested. "You just said Norman Thatcher recognized me, and—"

"Doesn't matter. He might be able to eventually confirm that you are a member of the prestigious Coltrane family, but as far as the captain was concerned, for the moment you were just a stowaway. It's obvious that you weren't merely out for a stroll and got lost in the kennels. Especially," he reminded her, "since you weren't listed on the passenger roster."

"So what am I doing here?" she asked weakly.

"Recovering from a fever that nearly did you in. You've been unconscious for nearly two days."

"Two days?" Kit echoed dizzily. "I don't believe it. I remember falling asleep because I was so tired, but that couldn't have been two days ago!"

"Thatcher found you when he went to take care of the animals. I had you brought here. That was the night before last."

Kit watched him silently. There was still one question he had not answered. Clenching her fists, she demanded, "I asked you why I am *here*, in your stateroom! And who's been dressing me?"

His dark eyes danced mischievously. "Why, your faithful and loving husband has been dressing you, Mrs. Tanner, and caring for you, and bathing you to bring down your fever. And, I might add," he said winking, "enjoying every minute of it." Unable to help himself, he threw back his head and laughed at her incredulous indignation.

"Bastard!" she cried, wishing she had the strength to slap his smug face. "How dare you? You had no right—"

"I had no choice," he replied with a shrug. "I knew what you were up to—running away, back to Spain, so I decided to help you out. I made up a quick story about how we had been married in New York, and were on our honeymoon. I played the role of the relieved husband—explained that we'd had a little argument, as newlyweds sometimes do. You were dressed in men's clothing because you happened to be naked when you lost your temper.'' He paused, flashing a teasing grin. ''You must have snatched up some of my things in the dark when you stormed out. When they asked why your name wasn't on the roster, I said we eloped, and I'd already booked in my name, planning to pay your passage later. I gave the money to the purser and they were satisfied. Frankly, I don't know if they believed me or not. They probably just figured it was the easy way out of a sticky situation for everybody concerned.

''So,'' he finished with a dramatic wave of his arms, ''I brought you here, to our honeymoon suite. It isn't the luxury you're accustomed to, I know, but I did book late, and this was all that was available. Now would you like that soup?''

''I won't stay here!'' Kit cried furiously.

''You don't have any choice.'' He laughed. ''You can't go back to the stalls.''

''I'd rather go to jail.''

''That's your privilege.''

''Do you honestly think I'm going to share this cabin with you for the rest of the trip?''

''It's *my* cabin,'' he reminded her. ''Do you expect *me* to move out? The ship is full, and I'll be damned if I'm going to sleep in a deck chair just to please you. It's been pretty uncomfortable sleeping on the floor the past two nights.

''And don't get any ideas about making a wager for this cabin,'' he warned her. ''I've learned my lesson about betting with you, little one.''

She stared up at him with hate in her eyes. "You think that if you can keep me here, you'll be able to seduce me and add me to your list of conquests, but you're wrong, Kurt Tanner!"

He grinned insolently, saying nothing.

"Well, it won't happen! You've got my horse, but you'll never have *me*. If you'll be good enough to ask the ship's purser to visit me, I'll make other lodging arrangements, and get out of your way."

Kit turned her face to the wall. Kurt continued to sit there and look down at her. Despite her pallor and shadows beneath her lavender eyes, she was still the most beautiful woman he'd ever seen. She was like a hunger in his blood, an addiction he could not give up. He had to admit that when he'd bathed her, touching her incredibly soft skin, tracing the sculptured perfection of her body, it had been only with great self-control that he'd not taken her then and there.

In a tight voice, he now said, "That won't be necessary. I'll make other arrangements."

Kit did not reply, but he could see the trace of a triumphant smile on her lips.

"I'll send someone with your soup. You need to start eating."

"Thank you."

Silence hung heavily between them as Kurt continued to stare at her thoughtfully. Then he felt compelled to ask, "Since I've stuck my neck out for you, paying your passage and giving you my room, I think I have a right to know what the hell you were doing down there."

"My grandmother died."

"I'm sorry," he said sincerely, "but that still doesn't tell me why you were running away."

"My life got turned upside down all of a sudden.

Thanks to your telling my father about how I got Pegasus, he decided I was totally incorrigible. He wanted to send me away to school in Switzerland, and my mother agreed with him.''

"Kit, I'm genuinely sorry," Kurt said again. "I never meant for things to turn out like that."

"I had no choice but to run away. It's what my grandmother would have wanted me to do. . . .''

Kurt's eyes narrowed thoughtfully. He knew that she wasn't going to like what he was about to say. "Well Kit, the thing for you to do when we get to Cherbourg is to rejoin your family. I'll be glad to buy the ranch from you, even give you a tidy profit.''

Kit bolted upright, despite her weakness. "Go back? Sell *you* my ranch? Are you out of your mind? I'll see you in hell first!'' Her face was red with rage.

"Kit, be reasonable." He stood up. "A woman hasn't got any business trying to run a ranch by herself. It's rugged land, and a rugged life. It would be dangerous. Besides, I'm sure Colt Coltrane is not going to be sending you an allowance every month, so how are you going to live? If you had the money, you wouldn't have been hiding in a horse stall, for God's sake!'' He looked down at her incredulously. "I think you're the one who's crazy, Kit, for doing something so dumb, and—''

Suddenly Kit began to look around the room frantically. "My bag! Where's my bag?''

Kurt shook his head, bewildered by her outburst. "What bag? You didn't have a purse.''

"Not a purse!'' She swung her legs over the side of the bed and tried to stand, but swayed dizzily. He caught her and tried to ease her back down, but she hit at him with weak, flailing fists. "No. I have to find my bag! There was a water jug, and food, and . . ." She paused as she saw the curious way he was looking at her. Forcing herself to be calm, she said, "Please, I need that bag."

Kurt thought for a minute. "Maybe it's with your clothes. I remember telling the cabin steward to bundle everything up and put it in my foot locker. Let me see." He opened his small trunk and began to rummage about.

Kit held her breath. The money Kitty had given her was in a drawstring pouch at the bottom of the bag. If it was lost, then so was she.

At last Kurt held up her bag. He took it to her. Kit grabbed it and clutched it to her chest, watching him fearfully.

"You've got money hidden in there, don't you? Well, don't worry, I'm not going to take it. I only want what's mine in life." He could not resist alluding to their past differences.

"My grandmother gave it to me, so I'd have some security until I get things going the way I want—not that it's any of your business."

Kurt nodded slowly, a smile of contempt on his face. "As conniving as you are, Kit Coltrane, I don't think you'll have any problem at all having things your way." He walked to the door. "I'll go see about having some soup sent up, and try to find a place to sleep for the rest of the voyage." With a last glance in her direction, he left the suite.

Kit did not have to look inside to know that the money was still there. Kurt wouldn't steal from her or anybody else. She wondered suddenly if maybe she *had* stolen something from him by "winning" Pegasus. At the time, she'd considered herself shrewd, but hadn't she done the same thing Galen Esmond had done when he tricked the vaqueros into racing him? She'd cheated him again when she'd hidden the ranch's "for-sale" sign.

Weakness was creeping over her like a thick, warm blanket, and Kit felt herself slipping away. She surrendered gratefully, eager to escape the unpleasant realization that she had wronged a man who had saved her from great embarrassment and harm.

The smell of warm vegetable soup made her stomach rumble. Kit opened her eyes and saw the cabin boy place a tray on the table beside her bed. There was also a plate of ham and cheese sandwiches, and a huge mug of steaming coffee. Never had food looked so good; never had she been so hungry.

The boy asked if she needed anything else, and Kit responded promptly, "Yes. A bath." He told her he'd send a maidservant to help her.

Kit had barely finished eating when the young girl arrived to draw her bath and help her wash her hair. Kit found Kurt's blue cashmere robe hanging on a wall hook and put it on. She could not help reveling in the lingering spicy scent of him. Wrapping herself in the soft robe, she returned to bed and immediately fell asleep again.

A metallic scraping sound woke her with a start, and she sat up to see Kurt rummaging in his trunk. Without looking at her, he said, "Sorry to wake you, but I need to get a few of my things."

She asked hesitantly, "Where are you going?"

He raised his head and looked at her with an expression of bitter amusement. "To the kennel. I told Thatcher it looked like we had an argument that wasn't going to be resolved, and we'd probably be getting a divorce. He said I could sleep with Pegasus. Even the crew is doubling up, the ship is so full."

Feeling a stab of guilt, Kit protested, "You can't sleep there—that's not fair. After all, it's your cabin."

"I've slept in worse places in my day," he informed her humorlessly. "Didn't bother me then, won't bother me now."

He rolled some things in a bundle and turned to go. Kit slid off the bed and walked shakily to the door, blocking his way. "Please don't go. I'll feel awful if you do."

"You will?" he asked, a sardonic glint in his eyes.

She folded her arms across her chest to hold his huge robe closed. She felt naked before him . . . then suddenly felt a warm rush at the thought that he had seen her naked, had touched her body. She hoped she was not blushing as she looked up at him and admitted sheepishly, "I'm very grateful for what you did. We've had our differences, and you didn't owe me that. You didn't owe me anything, and I certainly wouldn't be showing you much gratitude if I ran you out of your own stateroom to sleep with a horse."

Eyeing her warily, Kurt said nothing.

Sensing his distrust, Kit attempted to convince him. "After all, we *are* going to be neighbors. It might be nice if we could try to like each other, maybe even be friends."

Suddenly he was amused—and pleased. "Oh, I always liked you, little one, even when I wanted to turn you over my knee and spank your pretty bottom. So remember," he added in a husky whisper, "if I ever do just that, we're still friends."

Kit turned away so he wouldn't see how shaken she was by his nearness. She went back to the bed and sat down, and he watched her in silence. Kit nervously said, "I wonder what I'm going to do about clothes. I'd planned to sneak off the ship when we reached land and buy a few things, but now I've got nothing to wear when we walk off the gangplank as man and wife." Her attempt at a laugh came out as a silly schoolgirl giggle, and she felt very foolish.

"Kit."

She looked up to see him standing over her. He ran his hands gently over his warm brown eyes filled with desire. "You don't have to be afraid of me. I'll never do anything to you that you don't want me to."

Kit could not respond. She met his gaze silently, her own hunger reflected on her face.

"Yes," he admitted huskily, with a little crooked smile, "I've had a few women, but the truth is, I've never given a woman anything she didn't want. I angered a few along the way, because they had notions about marriage, but I never made any promises in the heat of the moment. I've never been dishonest with any woman, if I could help it. And you're wrong if you think that I've been waiting for a chance to seduce you.

"What I *have* been waiting for," he said as he gently laid her back on the bed, stretching himself out beside her, "is the chance to show you how much I've wanted you since the first day I saw you. I want to show you how good I can make you feel . . . how good we can be together."

He drew her close, and Kit could not resist as his lips claimed hers hungrily. The robe fell open, and his hands moved inside, his fingertips dancing gently over her naked skin, igniting a fire of desire that would not be denied. Kit felt as if she was floating on a cloud of supreme happiness. His touch was as warm as the sun, bringing joy to the darkest recesses of her soul. She had no doubts or fears—in fact she had no thoughts at all as she surrendered wholly to the all-consuming passion that was sweeping over her body like wildfire.

His knee slipped between hers to gently part her thighs. Kit moaned softly as he touched where no man had ever touched her before . . . He raised his head ever so slightly and whispered, "You're ready for me, Kit . . . and I've been ready for you for a long, long time. . . ."

He moved on top of her and lowered his mouth to her breast, sucking gently. She arched her back in exquisite ecstasy as his lips burned a trail of kisses between her breasts down to her stomach. He traced the curve of her hips with his tongue as she clutched his hair in her fingers. Then, suddenly, he was kissing her lips again, his tongue hungrily searching her mouth. Pausing for a moment to look deep into her eyes, he said, "I want you, Kit, more than I've wanted any woman. I don't want to hurt you."

"Please," Kit moaned, "take me. . . ." Gently parting her, Kurt entered her with one thrust, covering her cry with his mouth. Then he began to move, lifting her hips with his hands. Kit was lost in ecstasy, clinging to him fiercely as together they reached new heights of passion. Finally, crying her name, Kurt fell upon her, his head on her shoulder. Basking in a warm glow of happiness, Kit lay there spent, her fingers absently twirling his thick curls. Kurt rolled off her and sat against the headboard, pulling her into his arms. Cradling her gently, he traced her cheekbone with his fingers.

"It's just beginning," he said solemnly, his eyes burning into hers. "Now that I've found you, I'm never going to let you go."

His voice broke the spell, and Kit felt a cool wave of apprehension sweep over her. Could she really trust him with her heart? Kit didn't know, but something told her to move slowly. She would not give up her dream for him until she could be totally certain that she was not just another conquest.

His lips claimed hers again, igniting the flames of desire once more. Helpless, Kit yielded to the passionate hunger she knew he could fill . . . again and again and again.

Chapter Twenty-eight

KIT and Kurt disembarked in Cherbourg, looking for all the world like newlyweds who were madly in love with each other.

They had not ventured from the stateroom during the remainder of the voyage. Kit laughed that she'd be the center of attention in Kurt's robe and Kurt nodded, saying that she needed to regain her strength—a lascivious glint in his eyes.

So they had laughed together and fallen back into each other's arms. The long hours they shared resulted in a new awareness of each other, a better understanding . . . and the beginning of a warm and tender relationship that made Kit dizzy to contemplate. They made love as if possessed, their appetite for each other seemingly insatiable. Yet at times Kit wondered whether Kurt felt more for her than simply passion. She knew that there were other women in his life and she didn't know how she would handle that when they were back in Spain. She'd then get angry at herself. After all, Kurt owed her nothing. He had made no promises, and neither had she. They were enjoying each other now with no commitments. She told herself that she was a fool to attach any importance to the past few days. Love and lovemaking did not guarantee a tomorrow—only a pleasurable today.

After buying Kit some clothes so she could leave the ship, Kurt checked them into one of the finer hotels. While they enjoyed a brunch of champagne and fruit, he announced that they were going on a shopping spree. "Can't have my wife looking dowdy," he said with a wink.

Kit laughed with him. "I don't need very much. Just a couple of traveling suits for the train ride home. Once I get there I won't need anything but dungarees and boots for a long, long time!"

Smiling to himself, Kurt said, "Well, dowdy little traveling suits with big feathered hats are not what I had in mind. Why don't you let me try my hand at choosing female clothes?"

Intrigued, Kit allowed him to take the lead. Bypassing staid dress shops, Kurt led her up a flight of crooked stone steps to an unusual shop. Kit was stunned to see a mannequin dressed in a provocative lace nightgown. She stopped short. "Kurt, what kind of place is this?"

"A place for fun clothes," he said matter-of-factly. "The lady who runs it is an old friend of mine, and she sells only the most avant-garde fashions. She does quite a business."

Kit did not want to offend him, but she was determined not to waste her money. "Really, Kurt, all I need are a few things to wear home. I'm not destitute, but I do need to budget what I have."

"This is my treat," he said, squeezing her hand. "And as I said, you need more than one or two dresses."

"Not for just a train ride," Kit protested.

"We aren't going by train," he announced.

"What?" She yanked her hand away and stared at

him in bewilderment. "You mean you've hired a car?"

Kurt shook his head, a secret smile playing around his mouth. "No, I didn't hire a car. Now, let's go buy you some pretty things to wear in the moonlight, sipping champagne under the stars, or sunning yourself on deck—"

"On deck?" Kit echoed.

"I have a yacht," he said nonchalantly.

Kit clapped her hands and squealed with delight. "How wonderful that will be," she cried, her eyes shining.

"I've got a small crew," he explained, his voice low and intimate as he slipped his arm about her waist and pulled her close. "We'll still have a lot of privacy though . . . for our honeymoon."

Kit laughed with him, but something suddenly began to nag at her . . . something she could not quite define.

Inside the store, Kit met Madame Voncina LaVoures. Madame clapped her hands in approval as she appraised Kit's slim, curvaceous figure. Then she disappeared into the rear of the shop, ordering the models to get ready for a command showing.

Kit wandered aimlessly around the room, wondering why she suddenly felt so uneasy. Then the reason came to her, although she really didn't want to admit it. The truth was that all the joking and bantering about their being married disturbed her. Somehow it made a mockery of what she'd dared to dream might be growing between them. And this place looked like a bordello! Did Kurt bring all his new conquests here? she wondered angrily. By the time Madame LaVoures returned, Kit had worked herself up into quite a rage. She was about to storm out of the shop and head for the train depot by herself.

Kurt sensed that something was wrong and was at her side as Madame clapped her hands for the first model to make her entrance.

"What you're thinking isn't true, Kit," he said quietly.

He tried to put his arm around her but she jerked away. "Are you a mind reader?" she snapped angrily.

"It doesn't take a mind reader to see that you're letting your imagination run away with you and that you're about to lose that peppery little temper of yours."

"Am I?" she said frostily, stepping away from him.

His smile faded. "Yes, you are, and one of these days that bratty little disposition is going to earn you a spanking."

"Don't you threaten me!" Kit hissed. "I have a right to be angry with you for bringing me to a . . . a harlot's designer!"

Kurt threw back his head and laughed. "Why don't you just watch the fashion show, Kit? If you don't see anything you like, then we'll go find your dowager dresses and be on our way."

Kit joined him stiffly, quite expecting to see red lace corsets and black negligees. Instead she was surprised and pleased to see very elegant designs—nightgowns and bathrobes, ball gowns and tea dresses, even bathing suits.

"Pick anything you want," Kurt told her. "We'll be stopping in different ports along the way to sightsee and dine. I brought you here because I knew you'd enjoy it more if you were dressed for every occasion."

She looked up at him in wonder. "How could you have crossed on the same ship with us if you took such a long cruise to get to Cherbourg?"

"I didn't," Kurt explained. "I went by train, motor car, and carriage, the same as you did."

"Then. . . ."

Again, Kurt knew exactly what she was thinking, and nodded with a grin. "I rented a yacht and crew this morning, Kit. I thought you'd want a few days to rest up here before we start out."

Filled with gratitude, Kit wanted to throw herself into his arms, but Madame was standing to one side watching her expectantly. Mindless of propriety, Kurt leaned over to grab her and pull her close against him. "I know what else you were thinking, *princesa,*" he told her huskily, his coffee-brown eyes glowing with the sheen of passion she had come to know so well the past few days. "You think that I've bought other women clothes, but you're wrong. I bought them presents, yes, but don't think you're like the others, Kit. You never could be. You're rare and special and beautiful, and . . ."

Kurt caught himself and fell silent, his gaze locked with hers. Then he suddenly kissed her, long and hard, leaving them both shaken.

Madame coughed discreetly to remind them that they were not alone. Kit's heart was pounding. She wondered if he'd been about to say that he loved her, and whether she would have believed him if he had.

Although Kit had been raised in luxury and wealth, she was visibly awed by the yacht Kurt had leased for their trip home. It was like a mansion afloat, with the same sumptuous accommodations.

The master bedroom suite was ornately decorated in rose and mauve, with a huge round bed and velvet headboard. Glass doors leading onto the deck commanded a sweeping view of the sea beyond.

Pegasus was safely ensconced below deck. The weather was ideal—smooth seas, blue skies, balmy breezes. Kit was so happy she felt as if she were in heaven.

One night as they stood on deck, the moonlight bathing them in silver, Kurt gazed down at her adoringly. "This is so perfect," he said huskily. "It almost makes me wish it *were* our honeymoon."

Kit shivered in delight at his words, not daring to admit that she'd had the same wistful thought more than once.

They stopped in Oporto, which, Kit learned, was the oldest and second-largest city in Portugal. Kurt explained that it was also the home of port wine, aged in caves along the river, where they visited to taste the precious vintage. They strolled hand in hand through the gorgeous Crystal Palace there, and the magnificent gardens near the Douro River.

Kit was enthralled by Lisbon, with its Moorish castles, Renaissance monasteries, and cathedrals. They spent delightful hours exploring the Estufa Fria, a huge, shady hothouse full of grottoes, streams, and bridges.

Next they entered the Strait of Gibraltar, passing the huge rock guarding the entrance to the Mediterranean. In the distance lay the coast of Morocco, and Kurt gave her a mock frown. "When I tire of you, wench, that's where I'm taking you—to the slave market in Tangiers. A sultan would pay a handsome price for an ivory-skinned harlot like you!"

Kit raised her chin haughtily. "You must first own something, sir, before you can sell it, and you will never own me!"

Kurt laughed and scooped her into his arms, taking her to their suite. Once there, he lay her gently on the bed. Cradling her in his arms, he stroked her coppery hair. Then, with infinite tenderness, he began to take off her clothes, piece by piece. When she lay there naked, her smooth porcelain skin glowing in the semidarkness, he slid over her, stretching his long, muscular length along her body. He traced her cheek with his finger and gazed deep into her eyes.

"You have no idea how much you've come to mean to me," he said in a husky voice. Kit's lavender eyes filled with sudden tears as her heart thrilled to his words. Then the cold voice of reason warned her to be wary—Kurt might have spoken these few words to countless other women. The next moment she forgot her fears and surrendered to his passionate touch. Kurt's lips trailed kisses between her breasts, making her clutch his dark curls in her fists. When he rose up and entered her, she moaned with pleasure. They began to move together, and Kit arched her back to take him deeper and deeper as they grew lost in the wonder of each other.

They soon passed M'alaga, where sparkling beaches lay beneath the picturesque old town of narrow, winding streets, whitewashed Moorish houses, and colorful African flowers.

The yacht sailed on, hugging the coastline of Spain. One morning as they stood at the bow, the sunshine warming their faces, Kurt said solemnly, "It's been said that to be a young sailor in the Mediterranean Sea is to feel like the gods on Olympus." Kit smiled up at him.

They would soon reach Valencia. She tried not to think about what lay ahead, wanting only to savor every golden, precious moment alone on the yacht with Kurt. "I hate for it to end. It's been a wonderful trip," she whispered tremulously. "Whatever the future holds, I'll never forget this time with you!"

Kurt brushed back a copper tendril, and gently kissed her forehead. "It's not ending, sweetheart. It's just beginning." He paused, searching for the right words to express what was on his mind, in his heart. "I know you've got to follow your dream. Even though I don't approve, I want you to know that I'll be there for you when you need me, but I won't interfere. Remember that."

Their gazes locked, and they sealed a silent promise of love and devotion with a kiss that left them both breathless.

When they arrived in Valencia, Kurt invited her to stay at his ranch until she could get settled at her own. "I don't think so," Kit said. "People gossip." She found it difficult to sound convincing because all she really wanted to do was sleep in his arms every night, and awaken to his kisses every morning. "It's important that I be respected in the community," she told him seriously.

Kurt shook his head in amusement. "You don't give a damn what people think, any more than I do, but play a little game, sweetheart. You know where to find me."

He left her at a hotel, where she lodged while the little house on her ranch was renovated. The days passed quickly, as she sat up at dawn with the workmen, falling into bed exhausted when darkness fell. She dreamed of Kurt, and the magical times they'd shared, trying not to worry because he hadn't been in touch. She knew that he was determined not to interfere, but she missed him terribly. She vowed that once she moved into her house, she'd ask him to come to her.

Finally, only two weeks after her return, Kit was ready to move into her house. She checked out of the hotel feeling more than a little disappointed that Kurt was not there to share her excitement. Suddenly she found herself wondering just how much he'd meant of what he'd said. Did he really intend to stay away until she sent for him? Kurt was used to women running after him, and Kit knew it was important to proceed with caution, lest she wind up getting hurt. Perhaps their time on the cruise had been as much a fantasy as their masquerading as newlyweds. Maybe Kurt was bowing out—and giving her a chance to save face.

Kit tried to forget Kurt and enjoy her new home. The little ranch house had been completely redone, with a new roof and floor, and a fresh coat of paint. The barn glistened red in the sunlight, just waiting for the horses she would buy as soon as she had a chance.

Kit walked through each room, savoring the feeling of absolute freedom. Now she would write to her parents and tell them how happy she was, ask them to understand and forgive her. But first she wanted to visit the barn and think about what kind of horses she would buy.

Kit walked the short distance up the hill, whistling happily in the warm spring sunshine. It was the middle of May, and the hills were covered with a riotous profusion of wildflowers. Birds were singing, and in the distance she could see the river flowing sleepily. She was supremely happy, and wished only that Kitty had lived to share this with her.

Suddenly Kit heard a strange sound coming from

inside the barn. Then she heard a soft whinny, and she began to run. She rushed into the barn to find Pegasus prancing around inside. He was wearing a beautiful leather saddle trimmed in silver, and his harness was pure sterling. There was a piece of paper tied to one of the reins, and Kit read with misty eyes: "My housewarming gift to you, *princesa.*"

With a sob of sheer joy, Kit swung into the saddle. She'd never ridden to Kurt's ranch, but somehow she knew that Pegasus would find the way.

Chaper Twenty-nine

JADE slept until noon, when finally the sounds of traffic on Fifth Avenue nudged her awake. She climbed out of bed wearily and padded to the window, looking down on the activity below with bored detachment.

For the past few months, life had been terribly dull. She had loved Kitty Wright Coltrane to a fault, but she was tired of the reclusive life led since her death nearly four moths ago.

Jade's misery was magnified by Kit's running away. Jade knew that she'd returned to Spain. Colt had wanted desperately to go after her and drag her back, but Jade had managed to persuade him that that wasn't the answer. Kit would, she predicted, find out soon enough that being independent was not as easy as she'd thought, and she'd return on her own. If they forced her to come back, she'd only run away again the first chance she got.

The had buried Kitty in Nice, beside her husband. Then, because of the unrest in Russia, they had gone directly to Switzerland to get Marilee settled. It had been an extremely tense time—Marilee did not want to be left in Switzerland, and Travis just withdrew further within himself, speaking to no one.

And, during the whole trip, Jade had to endure her

secret pain. She told herself repeatedly that it didn't matter that Bryan was alive—he was married to someone else and he had a family, but she could not forget his obsession with her, and she worried he might try to find her. He had been truly mad then . . . and perhaps he still was! What if it occurred to him that he might be the father of her children? Jade shuddered at the very thought.

They had arrived back in New York with no plans beyond seeing Travis enrolled in West Point. He had left yesterday, and Jade suddenly realized that her life seemed to have skidded to a halt. They had no plans, because Colt had become as withdrawn as Travis. They just didn't talk to each other anymore. He was still distraught about Kit, she knew, and only time was going to resolve his bitter feeling of betrayal.

Jade looked at the new gown Carasia had laid out for her with a sigh. She was sick to death of wearing nothing but black crepe, black stockings, and black veils!

She rang for Carasia to bring some tea and was surprised to see Colt carrying the tray, dressed in a blue serge business suit, instead of black, his black armband conspicuously absent.

Setting the tray down on the bed, he said simply, "It's time we got on with our own lives, Jade."

She nodded and smiled, reaching out to caress his cheek.

Colt then poured them each a cup of tea while he recounted the morning's business. "Our attorney said that Kitty's assets are being liquidated, and the proceeds transferred to our bank here. The land in North Carolina is going to be left to Travis and . . ." He hesitated, his face darkening. ". . . Kit."

Jade squeezed his hand. "She'll be back one day, Colt. We know that Kitty withdrew a large amount of cash from the bank before we left for Washington. Since it wasn't found, we can be sure she gave it to Kit."

Colt held her hand tightly. "There's more," he said slowly. "She bought Kit a ranch in Spain before we left."

Jade sat up straight, staring at him. "I don't believe it!"

Colt began to pace restlessly around the room. "The lawyer said he has a copy of all the papers. She bought the ranch for Kit, putting it in her name. I think they had planned to go back and live there together. That's probably where Kit is now."

"Are you going to try to talk her into coming back?" Jade asked.

"No. But I'll tell you what I am going to do." His gray eyes were cold with angry determination. "The management of Dad's trust fund for Kit and Travis is under my control. I'm having her share deposited in the bank in Valencia. She's entitled to it. No matter how badly she's hurt me, I still love her, and I want to know that she's safe. But I'm giving her a time limit to get this foolishness out of her system and come home, where she belongs."

An icy finger of dread suddenly ran down Jade's spine. "And if she doesn't?" she asked slowly.

"Then," Colt said bitterly, "I have no daughter."

Jade fought back her tears. She could only pray that Kit would come to her senses.

Watching her intently, Colt then said, "How soon can you be ready to go around the world?"

Jade tried to decide if he was serious. The gleam

in his eyes and the smile on his lips convinced her that he was, and she threw her arms around him.

"Make the arrangements!" she cried. "I can be ready as soon as you want me to be!"

"There's nothing to keep us here now," Colt declared. "We'll take a year, maybe two, and travel all over. Maybe we'll find our paradise, a place to build a home, far away from here. Oh Jade, I love you so much!" He kissed her until she was breathless. Then, glowing with enthusiasm, Colt hurried out to start making arrangements.

Jade lay in bed for a few moments, basking in happiness. She felt peace and contentment for the first time since the horror of discovering that Bryan was alive. Then she dared to reach beneath the mattress to withdraw the report from the Pinkerton Agency. It was so ironic! Nearly twenty years ago Bryan had hired the detectives to find Colt. Now she had hired them to find him.

She read once more that Bryan Stevens owned two mansions, one in the city and one in the Catskills. His business was "shipping investments" and he was quite wealthy. He and his wife, Lita, had a daughter named Valerie, and they were presently living on Mr. Stevens's private island near Bermuda. Other than that, there was not much information. The agency reported that Mr. Stevens was a very private person, leading an almost reclusive life.

Jade folded the papers and returned them to their hiding place, to be destroyed later. For the time being, everything seemed to be under control.

For that much, she was grateful.

He came to her in the still of the night, as quiet as a stalking panther. Only when she felt his warm body

cover hers was she aware of his presence. She did not
cry out in fear, instead she opened her mouth eagerly
to receive his kiss.

He came most nights—sometimes early, sometimes
very late. This time it was near dawn when he
wrapped his arms about her. It had been almost a
week since she'd seen him, and she delighted in his
warm caress.

His hands moved over her body slowly, his fingertips gently teasing and touching her as if her body
were a delicate piece of china. She thrilled beneath
him, trembling with anticipation. In the moonlight
she could see the smiling play on his full, sensuous
lips as he gazed down at her, delighting in her pleasure. His dark hair tumbled onto his forehead, and
she reached out lovingly to brush back the tendrils
trailing one finger to the tiny scar she found so in-
triguing. His dark eyes were hooded, moist with longing. Only when he knew he had aroused her to a fever
pitch did he take her, and she arched against him,
moaning deep in her throat, succumbing once more
to an ecstasy unlike anything she had ever dreamed
possible.

Afterward she lay with her head on his shoulder,
and asked him about his week in Madrid. He was
tired, and spoke vaguely of business and boredom.
Once more she teased him for not taking her with
him, only to be reminded that she had a ranch to
run. There was a familiar hint of bitterness in his
voice, which she allowed to pass. Only once had
they quarrelled since returning to Valencia, and that
had been over her insistence to run the ranch—and
her life—her way. He had tried to send one of his
foremen over to hire her some wranglers, and had

offered to advance her prime stock. She had adamantly refused, and he had said angrily that with her attitude she would wind up a sun-wrinkled old maid. She had retorted that that was better than being subservient to a man. Later they'd laughed about their argument, and he never offered to help again, although his resentment was revealed sometimes in his voice.

Kit lay there watching the silver fingers of moonlight play about the room as the soft summer breeze rustled the leaves of the sycamore outside. She could tell by Kurt's even breathing that he had fallen asleep. The last thing she remembered was turning to lay her head on his broad shoulder, slipping her arm across his strong chest . . . and feeling blissfully happy, if only for a little while.

Kit awoke to bright sunshine and the sound of bluebirds singing. It was a glorious day, and she was disappointed to find that Kurt had left, although usually he rode away before dawn to avoid gossip.

She dressed quickly and saddled Pegasus for her ride to Valencia. Arriving there, she went first to the general store for supplies, then walked down the street to the post office. Domingo, the clerk, grinned when he saw her. "It came, *señorita*. The package you have been waiting for."

Kit snatched up the large box he held out to her, tears of happiness springing to her eyes. "I can't believe it," she breathed in wonder. "All the way from North Carolina."

Domingo asked curiously, "What's in it?"

"A grape vine!" Kit explained how she had written to the people leasing the Wright land, asking for a grafting of one of the scuppernong grape vines Kitty had planted long ago. "And this is it!" she exclaimed triumphantly. "I'm going to start my own vineyard, and one day I'll produce the best wine in the region. You'll see."

"Ah, *señorita.*" Domingo shook his head doubtfully. "Do not be too excited. The plants, they are probably dead by now. It is a long way to ship them. You can see by the mark on the box that it took nearly two months to get here."

"Well, we'll see. I'm going home right now to set them out. It takes three years for a vine to produce, so I'd better get started!" As she turned to leave, she smacked right into Anaya Esteban.

Anaya drew back as if she'd been scalded. "Watch where you're going, you piece of trash!" She hissed furiously.

Kit ground her teeth together, gripping the box tightly as she fought to hold her temper in check. She had managed thus far to avoid an encounter with the insufferable Esteban girl. Now she wanted only to leave, but Anaya stood in the doorway, blocking her way.

"Did you hear me?" Anaya screeched, waving her parasol menacingly. "Back away so I may pass. Do not come near me with your horse fleas and stench of manure. I have heard how you are living on that wretched little farm, and it is disgraceful! Even a *puta* does not dress like a man, live like a man! You are a disgrace to our community, and should be made to leave!"

Kit drew in her breath and let it out slowly. She closed her eyes momentarily before flashing a venomous glare of warning. "You're in my way, Anaya."

Anaya did not move. "I pay no heed to trash." She jabbed the package Kit was holding with the tip of her parasol. "Back out of my way, and keep your distance."

That did it. Kit swung the box and shoved Anaya to one side, taking her by surprise. Anaya stumbled and hit the floor, landing soundly on her bottom. Domingo burst into laughter, delighted to see the spoiled Anaya get what was coming to her.

Kit stepped over her and continued on her way.

Behind her, she could hear Anaya railing, "You will pay for this, *puta!* I will see that you are run out of this town. We do not want trash here! *Puta* trash!"

Kit was aware that people were stopping to listen, several coming out of stores to see what the commotion was about. She crossed the street and was putting the box into the back of her wagon when Kurt walked out of the cantina at the same moment that Anaya charged hysterically out of the post office.

"She assaulted me!" Anaya screamed. "I want the sheriff to arrest her for assaulting me!"

Kurt looked from Kit to Anaya, bewildered. Anaya hurried to his side as though seeking his protection. Glaring hatefully at Kit, she continued her tirade. "She hit me and knocked me down. I'm going to be bruised, I know it! I may even have permanent injuries." She rubbed her hip. "She must be arrested and punished!"

Kurt just stood there, looking baffled. Anaya finally stamped her foot in frustration. "Well, are you just going to stand there and do nothing?"

Kit looked at him warily. He winked at her, then,

with exaggerated patience, said to Anaya, "I think we'd better have the doctor check you over first. You seem all right to me though!"

"I tell you she assaulted me," Anaya cried, indignant. "I need the sheriff, not the doctor!"

Kurt sighed. "Do you mind telling me what happened?"

Kit shrugged. "She wouldn't move, so I moved her."

Kurt couldn't help laughing, and that made Anaya even more furious.

"How dare you laugh?" she raged. "How dare you take her side!"

She raised her parasol as if to strike him. He caught it and wrestled it away from her, throwing it into a nearby watering trough. "Calm down, Anaya. Enough is enough!" he said sternly, beginning to lose his temper. Turning to Kit, he ordered, "Go on home. I'll take care of her, and come out to talk to you later."

Kit wanted to do just that. She was swinging up into the saddle when Anaya suddenly began to cry loudly.

"*Mi amante!* After our beautiful nights of love in Madrid this week, how can you treat me this way?" she sobbed brokenly. "I tell you that *puta* assaulted me, and you do not believe me. . . ."

Kit felt suddenly paralyzed. Turning slowly, she saw that Anaya was clinging to Kurt, who was trying to disentangle himself from her clutching embrace.

Kurt's eyes met Kit's, and he looked away quickly, misery etched on his face. He knew she was not going to believe anything he said. At that moment, he wanted to strangle Anaya. Instead, he could only stand there as she hung on to him and screamed for the whole town to hear that he'd broken her heart. He watched helplessly as Kit snapped the reins over Pegasus and began to gallop down the street.

She did not look back.

Chapter Thirty

KIT was watering the scuppernong graftings she had set out the day before, when she heard hoofbeats approaching. She did not have to guess who it was. She stayed right where she was, gently patting the soft dirt around each plant.

He reined in perhaps twenty feet away. From the corner of her eye Kit could see the strong golden legs of his fine palomino stallion. Even when she saw his boots planted firmly before her, she did not look up.

"Will you listen to what I have to say?"

Kit did not speak. She'd done a lot of thinking since returning home yesterday. Home! She savored the sound of that word, the taste of it. Her ranch. Her barn. Her land. All of it was hers. No one made decisions for her. She was truly in control of her life now, and, yes by God, she was in control of her heart as well. She had known all along what kind of man Kurt Tanner was, that he would never be satisfied with the love of just one woman. Well, that was his privilege and his right, just as it was hers to maintain her pride and dignity.

"Kit, I think you owe me that much."

Her laugh was bitter. "I think you've been amply rewarded. A *puta* would have considered you repaid by the time the ship reached Cherbourg."

He could not resist a barb of his own. "With a *puta,* maybe I would have been."

At that, Kit leaped to her feet, her lavender eyes blazing. "So that's all it was? You thought I was just paying you back for saving me from being arrested? Well, I can assure you it was the hardest debt that any woman could honor, because you're a terrible lover, and I hate you!"

"You're lying, and you know it!" Kurt flashed a lopsided grin. He pushed his hat back and his dark curls tumbled boyishly onto his forehead, belying the throbbing ache he felt at her very nearness. Growing impatient, he said, "Stop acting like a brat and hear me out."

"Why did you come here today?" Kit asked angrily. "Did you try to come through the window last night and realize you were locked out?"

"No, but if I had, a closed window wouldn't have stopped me. Now, dammit"—his dark brown eyes narrowed ominously—"you're going to listen."

"Go to hell!" Kit spat out. She turned to stalk away, but he caught her arm and spun her around roughly. "Anaya was just trying to make trouble. Can't you see that?"

"She did a good job," Kit shot back.

"Only if you let her," Kurt replied.

"Was she in Madrid?" she asked bluntly.

"Yes, but—"

"That explains why you didn't want me to go along!" Kit interrupted harshly.

His eyebrows shot up. "Dammit, Kit, you're the one who was so determined that no one find out about us. I didn't think you were serious about wanting to go to Madrid, because that would have definitely made tongues wag."

"So you took someone who doesn't mind being fodder for gossip."

"Who said anyone went with me?"

"You admitted that she was there. It really makes no difference *how* she got there. Now, if you don't mind, I have other things to do, Mr. Tanner. Nothing you can say will interest me, I'm sure."

He looked at her thoughtfully for a moment. "Maybe I've just gotten tired of sneaking around, Kit. Maybe I'd like to walk right up to your front door and call on you properly, court you, if you'll permit me to sound so . . . conventional." He smiled despite himself.

"You want to be proper?" she scoffed. "Do you honestly think I could ever take you seriously after you kept joking about us being newlyweds? The beginning of our relationship should have been a tender, special time, but you made me feel like a fool!"

Kit blinked back scalding tears, determined not to let him see her cry. "For the first time in my life I knew what it meant to feel loved and desired. Then you snatched all that away and brought me back to reality by making it nothing but a joke."

Kurt shook his head, stunned at her revelation. "Kit, you silly little fool," he whispered tenderly, "I only teased you about it because that's the way I thought you wanted it. I didn't want to scare you away. I knew you had your doubts, because I do have a reputation with women. Maybe some of the things you've heard about me are justified, but that doesn't mean I've got to carry my mistakes on my back like a cross for the rest of my life."

"It seems to me," Kit said evenly, "that after your little tryst with Anaya in Madrid, there's no doubt about your reputation being justified."

Kurt had reached the end of his patience. He released his hold on her and stepped back. "I'm wasting my breath. Maybe you're the one who never took our relationship seriously, Kit, and *I'm* the one who should feel like a fool."

"Get off my land, Tanner," Kit said, her gaze steely. "Next time I'll blow you away." She nodded to the rifle she'd propped against a nearby tree.

Kurt stood there a moment, stunned, looking into the lavender eyes that had once burned with desire for him, and were now filled with fiery hatred. Then he turned and walked away.

Kit watched him go. Her heart ached, but she knew it was for the best. She had her destiny, and he had his. It was just not meant for them to be together.

July melted into August. The days were long and hot, and Kit worked from dawn to dusk, loving every minute. Her money began to run low, but Doc Frazier had leased her a small herd that would bring a nice profit in the future. She also began an egg business, selling to markets in the village. It would be slow going, but she'd been prepared for that. She had a peaceful contented existence, and asked for no more than that.

There were times, however, when memories crept over her without warning. She would be riding the range or cleaning the barn, and, suddenly, she'd remember Kurt's arms around her, his kisses, the way they'd laughed and loved together. A great warmth would overtake her body, and she would fight against it with all her might. Finally, it would pass. She could get on with her life . . . though still haunted by a love that could never be.

One day, while repairing a section of fence, she

saw a man approaching on horseback. Since she wasn't expecting anyone, she dropped her tools and grabbed her rifle. Holding it at her side, she shaded her eyes against the glaring sun. As the man drew closer, she groaned, laying the rifle aside. She supposed it was inevitable that sooner or later Esteban Yubero would hear she was back and pay a visit.

"Señorita! What is this?" He stared, startled at her appearance. He swung off his horse and dropped to the ground, carrying a bouquet of roses that seemed foolish and out of place.

"This is nothing you should be doing! I heard you had bought this place"—he waved his arm—"but never did I think you were actually working the land."

"It's my land," Kit said coldly. "Why shouldn't I work it?"

He thrust the flowers at her. "Because you are too beautiful for such drudgery. You should be the mistress of a fine hacienda, with many servants, and do nothing all day but sip sangria and plan delicious dinner parties."

"And wind up a fat, drunken cow," she retorted. "I'm sorry, but that kind of life isn't to my liking. Maybe you should court Delhy Esteban's daughter, Anaya. She seems more suited to you."

"All the valley knows she is in love with the rich Americano, Kurt Tanner. Don Esteban hangs his head in shame, and they say his wife refuses to go out in public, because Anaya makes no secret that she sometimes stays all night at his ranch."

Kit froze at his words. Realizing that he had her complete attention, Yubero rushed on to confide more, in hopes of gaining favor.

"She tells everyone that it is just a matter of time until they marry. Her father, it is said, went to Señor

Tanner on behalf of Anaya's honor, to ask him his
intentions. Señor Tanner said he owed her nothing,
for she had come to him of her own free will—
uninvited. Everyone says she is no better than a *puta,*
and the Americano, he is like a dog chasing a bitch
in heat!''

He suppressed a smile of satisfaction at the anger
in Kit's eyes, so he was not prepared for her next
words.

"Get off my land, Yubero! I've got no time for
gossip about trash."

He sucked in his breath. "And I've got no time for
a *campesino!''* He threw the bouquet on the ground,
and swung up into his saddle shooting her a con-
temptuous look before riding away.

Kit didn't care. Let him call her a peasant. She
didn't care what anyone said. All she wanted was to
be left alone.

As for Anaya and Kurt—they deserved each other!

Yet her heart still ached to think of what they had
shared in the past, what they'd hoped to share in the
future. And she cursed herself for her weakness,
swearing once again that she would forget him, forget
that he had ever touched her life.

Kit went back to her work, staying out in the sear-
ing August sun longer than she had planned. She
wanted to be so tired that when night came, she would
sleep too deeply for dreams to haunt her.

In the distance, she could hear the creak and rumble of the postman's mail cart.

"Señorita Coltrane," the postman called excitedly,
"I have a surprise for you!"

She turned with a sigh.

"Kit, oh, Kit, I found you!" called a familiar voice.

"I . . . I don't believe it," Kit cried, stumbling forward, her arms outstretched. "How—"

Valerie threw her arms around Kit and nearly knocked her off her feet. They hugged each other tearfully.

Finally they pulled away from each other. Kit's questions tumbled forth breathlessly. "How did you get here? And how did you find me? I still can't believe you're here."

"Neither can I!"

Taking her arm, Kit led Valerie toward her little house. "Just start at the beginning, tell me everything," she said.

"Did you get my letter?" Kit asked. "I'm afraid there wasn't time for me to tell Travis about our meeting, but I did write him at West Point. I haven't got an answer from him yet."

"You probably won't, because he probably didn't get your letter," Valerie said flatly. "I wrote him, too, but his mail is obviously being intercepted."

"Did he have your address in Bermuda?"

She shook her head. "No, but it wouldn't matter if he did. My mail is being intercepted, too. I never even got *your* letter."

Kit's mind was whirling. "Valerie, why did you come here?" she asked bluntly.

"I had nowhere else to go. The entire way to the island, my father railed that he'd rather see me dead than married to a no-good Coltrane."

"He has no right to say that!" Kit burst out. "He doesn't even know my family."

"I know that. Mother says that he has bad headaches sometimes that make him mean and crazy. Anyway, I told you that he wants to marry me off to the son of his friend. The minute we got to the island,

he started making plans. His name is George Burn-
baum, and I hate him. He's fat and lazy, and every
time we're alone together he starts grabbing at me and
telling me how good it's going to feel when he does
'it.' I won't marry him! I'd rather die!'' She curled
her hands into fists.

"So you ran away?" Kit asked incredulously.

"That's right—just like you. Except that I didn't
stow away on a ship. I took some money from Poppa's safe and bribed one of the servant boys to take
me to the mainland. Then I started making my way
here.''

Kit was properly impressed. "How long did it take
you?''

Valerie thought for a moment. "About three
months.'' Kit looked at her in awe, and Valerie
laughed. "It wasn't so bad, really.'' She held up her
callused hands. "I worked as a cook in the galleys
when I ran low on money. Fortunately the head cook
made sure I was properly protected from the sailors!''

Kit felt like crying, But now what do I do with you?
Instead she said, ''Well, let's get you inside and fed.
I imagine you're starved. Then I'll show you around
my little paradise.'' She glanced around. ''Where's
your luggage?''

"Back in town, at the hotel.''

Kit started inside, but Valerie hesitated. "Is it all
right?''

Kit turned to stare at her, not quite sure what she
meant.

"My being here, I mean.'' Valerie twisted her
hands together nervously. "I didn't know where to go
that my father wouldn't find me and make me marry
George. I couldn't go to Travis, and I couldn't think
of anywhere else,'' she repeated, her voice cracking.

Her dress was tattered and dirty, and her hair hung limply about her face. There was only a shadow of the delicate beauty Kit remembered, yet there was a lovely glow about her. Kit's heart went out to Valerie as she waited anxiously for Kit's response, her blue eyes filled with hope. Impulsively Kit walked over to give her a warm hug. "I'm glad you're here," she assured her. "Don't you worry about a thing. My home is your home."

When she had gotten Valerie comfortably bedded down, Kit went into town and picked up her two small trunks. She went to the post office to mail a new letter to Travis, and Domingo greeted her excitedly, waving an envelope. "It just came, *señorita,* on the afternoon train. All the way from America." Kit took the letter with trembling fingers. Recognizing her father's handwriting, she felt her heart constrict with an undefinable emotion.

She forced herself to wait until she was on the outskirts of town before dismounting Pegasus under a shady tree. She then opened the envelope with shaking fingers. Unfolding the letter, she read her father's ultimatum. He was giving her one year to come home, otherwise she would be disowned. Kit knew that it was just his anger talking. She cried with joy when she read that he was having her trust fund sent to the Valencia bank. No doubt he thought she'd spend it foolishly and soon run home in shame. What he didn't know was that she was mature enough to handle that money so that it would provide her with all the security she would ever need.

Swept by conflicting emotions, Kit mounted Pegasus and headed for home. Lost in thought, she was unaware of the men watching from the rock ridge above.

Galen Esmond pointed at Kit with his knife. Grinning, he told his men, "There, *amigos,* is the señorita who has my Hispano. We must follow her and steal him back, because he is worth *mucho dinero.*"

"You steal the horse," one of the men cried, "and we will steal the *señorita!*"

They all laughed. Then Galen waved them to silence as they began to follow him along the ridge.

Chapter Thirty-one

VALERIE was awake when Kit got back to the ranch, and she apologized for sleeping so long. She was so pale and thin that Kit worried she might get sick after her ordeal. Then what would she do? In fact, Kit stewed, what was she going to do with Valerie, anyway?

Later, after supper, Kit bluntly asked, "What are your plans now, Valerie?"

Valerie stiffened. "If I could just get in touch with Travis, I'm sure he'd know what I should do. I even thought about going to West Point, but I was afraid that Poppa might hire detectives to find me in New York. This is the only place I felt was really safe."

Kit knew she could not turn Valerie away. "Well, we'll just have to make the best of things. You can stay here and help me around the place. We'll eventually get through to Travis, even if we have to hire someone to get past Mother's interceptors, whoever they are." Kit told Valerie about the small fortune that was being deposited to the bank in her name. "So at least we don't have to worry about money," she said with a smile.

Valerie then began to tell of some of her experiences, and Kit was amazed at her ingenuity and cunning.

"You amaze me!" Kit cried, astonished. "To be honest, Valerie, I never thought you had any grit. I mean, I liked you, but I took you for a dainty little doll, groomed to marry a rich man, and do nothing but plan tea parties and have babies. Now I discover you're as big a daredevil as I am!"

They laughed, then Valerie urged, "Tell me about your trip. It must've been rough hiding out all the way."

Kit's expression became somber.

"What's wrong?" Valerie asked. "Is there something you don't want to talk about?"

"Why shouldn't I want to talk about it?" Kit replied airily. "It's like a toothache. Pull the tooth, and the pain is gone."

"What are you talking about?" Valerie asked, mystified.

"Kurt Tanner."

"Kurt Tanner?" Valerie sputtered. "What's he got to do with anything?"

"He was on the ship, too," Kit replied flatly.

"Tell me what happened!"

Kit told Valerie the entire story. When she described the scene with Anaya, Valerie surprised her by cursing like a sailor.

"The conniving bitch!" She squeezed Kit's hand. "But you're crazy to let her take your man away."

Kit stared at her. "He wasn't my man, Valerie. Not ever."

Galen struck a match inside the barn. He found a lantern and lit it, and he and his men looked around curiously. Galen pointed proudly at Pegasus. "See? I told you he was a fine animal!"

"So is the red-headed *señorita!*"

Galen looked at the man who had spoken. Chico Dupez had only recently joined his gang, and Galen was not sure he liked him. Only a week ago, he'd gotten into a fight over a woman, and killed a man by slitting his throat. Galen did not like such trouble. He dealt in horse stealing and petty robbery. Murder was not to his taste.

Chico licked his lips. In the lantern's flickering light, his dark eyes glowed with lust. "I could see from the ridge she is prime meat!"

The other men laughed nastily, and Galen stiffened.

"I also know she is alone—except for yet *more* delicious meat!"

"Ah, *sí!*" Mendez Puertos agreed. "The golden-haired beauty we saw walking with her is my kind of woman. You take the flaming hair, Chico. I take the gold!"

"*Sí!* I want to have some fun before we move on. I am sick of paying cantina *putas!*"

The others hooted in agreement while Galen scratched his chin thoughtfully. He himself had watched the one called Kit Coltrane with desire, wondering how it would feel to touch such fine white skin. But he was not stupid. Women like that came from good families—families that would pay much money to make sure they were not ravished by *bandidos*.

Chico flashed his broken teeth. "I am going there to have some fun. The rest of you can decide who goes second, and third. . . ."

He threw back his head and laughed, starting out the door. Suddenly a knife crashed into the wall right beside his head.

"You go nowhere until I say so!" Galen snarled.

''I give the orders, and I say the women are worth nothing to us once you have dirtied them with your lust.''

Chico turned slowly, rage showing on his face. ''Then what do you have in mind?'' he asked tightly.

Galen's grin was slow and triumphant. He looked at each of his men in turn before smugly declaring, ''Ransom. We take them and hold them for ransom.''

''Pah!'' Chico spat. ''What makes you think anyone would pay for them?''

''I know about the red-headed beauty with the light purple eyes. Her father is Colt Coltrane, a very rich Americano. He'll pay much to buy his daughter back.''

Chico sneered. ''If her family is so rich, why does she live here alone, working a ranch?''

''Who knows?'' Galen replied. ''It makes no difference. She is still a Coltrane.''

''And what about the other one? Who will pay for her?''

Galen shrugged. ''She's a stranger to me, but we offer them both for one price. We share the ransom evenly, but I keep the horse,'' he said, nodding toward Pegasus.

The men agreed that Galen's plan sounded good—except Chico. ''And where are we going to hide out till the ransom is paid?'' he asked warily. ''It's dangerous to hang around here.''

Galen described a secret cave in the rocks along the beach, not too far away. ''It won't take long, I tell you. As soon as Coltrane finds out his daughter has been kidnapped, he will pay any price to get her back.''

Chico nodded slowly. ''Very well. But this I promise you—I will have my taste of her honey before we give her back.''

With a lightning-quick lunge, Galen yanked his knife from the door frame and held it against Chico's throat. ''And I promise you that if you so much as touch her, the only thing you will taste will be your own blood! Understand me, *bastardo?*''

Chico's eyes bulged in horror. He blinked rapidly in agreement, not daring to shake his head for fear of cutting his own throat.

Galen released him, and he staggered away, clutching his neck. Looking at no one, he melted sullenly into the shadows of the barn.

Galen slipped his knife inside his boot. ''Now''— he glanced about smiling—''we take care of the rest of our business.''

Kit slept so soundly, that she was unaware that anyone was in the house until a big, dirty hand clamped over her face. Instinctively she began to swing her fists and kick wildly.

Beside her, Valerie managed to twist her face from beneath the hand holding her down and scream.

''Stop fighting, or you will make us hurt you! Be still!'' a harsh voice cried.

Kit knew that she had no choice but to obey. Valerie whimpered as a rag was stuffed into her mouth.

Slowly the hand over Kit's face lifted. In the dim light she saw that the man grinning down at her was somehow familiar.

''Ah, the *señorita* will cooperate,'' he said, pulling her up into a sitting position.

''Who are you?'' Kit hissed, glancing to where she'd left her rifle.

He laughed and motioned to one of the other men

to take the gun. "No, no, Señorita Coltrane. That is not a good idea."

He knew who she was! *But who the hell was he?* Kit shook her head in confusion.

"Take them into the kitchen. I am hungry. They can cook for us while we see if there is anything here of value. We have time."

Kit was jerked to her feet. She saw that Valerie was also being pulled along, her eyes wide with terror. The six men had bandoleers across their chests, double holsters at their waists, and rifles slung across their backs.

In the kitchen, Kit suddenly realized that the band's leader was Galen Esmond.

Kit heard Valerie whimpering and overcame her shock. "Take that gag out of her mouth," she said as firmly as possible. "She won't cry out, I promise."

Galen nodded to Mendez. "Do it. If she does not keep still, we'll gag them both." He said to Kit, "Cook for us, and be quick about it. We must leave before first light."

Kit reached for a bowl of eggs on the counter. "What do you want from us? We have no money. We are just poor ranchers, and—"

"You waste your breath," he taunted her. "I know that you are a Coltrane, and your family is rich. They'll pay plenty to get you back."

Kit froze in panic. "What do you mean? Where are you taking us?"

"Don't ask so many questions. Do as you are told, and you won't be hurt. We are going to hold you for ransom. That is all you need to know. If your father acts quickly, this will all be over soon."

Valerie gasped. "But her father isn't here! He's in America!"

Kit turned on her angrily. "Don't tell them anything!"

Galen's face darkened. He stepped closer to Kit and demanded, "Is that true? Your parents no longer live south of Valencia?"

"Go to hell!" Kit spat out.

He grabbed her hair and gave it a vicious tug, yanking her head back painfully. "I'm not telling you anything, you son of a bitch!" she ground out.

Galen flung her away from him. "Tear the place apart!" he roared. "Take anything of value. We leave for the cave as soon as we've eaten. I've got ways to make the bitch tell me what we need to know. Her family will pay much for raising such a stubborn child! The price on her head just doubled."

Kit drew in her breath, commanding herself to hold her temper. Valerie was staring at her anxiously. Galen walked out of the room for a second, and Kit whispered, "It's okay. I'll think of something. Just be quiet and—"

"No talking!" Galen rushed back in. "Make the food so we can be on our way. It's dangerous to hang around here."

Kit and Valerie watched them eat like pigs, and then they made ready to leave. They were dragged out of the house, and gagged, their wrists and ankles bound together. As they were slung over the back of a horse, the sky was just starting to lighten in the east.

The ride was bumpy and rough, and Kit felt sick to her stomach. The run rose, and she knew the heat was soon going to be unbearable. Just when it seemed she could stand it no longer, she realized they were on the beach. The Mediterranean breeze was mercifully cooling.

They stopped suddenly, and Kit was pulled roughly

from the horse. One of the men slung her over his shoulders and headed inside a yawning cave set in the rocks. After he walked for what seemed like hours, he dumped her onto the ground. She hoped they would remove her gag and untie her, but all the men disappeared outside.

Valerie moaned and cried, while Kit struggled uselessly to undo the ropes binding her wrists.

She finally heard footsteps, and looked up to see Galen Esmond's evil face in the semidarkness. He bent down and yanked off her gag. She saw that he was furious. "Now what do I do with you?" he cried, pulling off Valerie's gag as well. "I find you tell the truth—your family *has* moved away. I can't wait to send word to America. It's too dangerous."

Kit felt a flicker of hope. "Let us go, Galen," she said quickly. "I told you, I'm just a poor rancher. I don't have any money. My family moved back to America, and I ran away. The ranch is worth nothing to anyone except me."

"I don't know. I could leave you here and be on my way. By the time you walked back to town, no one would find me. But my men won't be happy. They want something for their troubles. . . ." His eyes flicked over Kit hungrily. "I have my Hispano back, but they have only a gnawing hunger for the luscious fruits of two beautiful *señoritas.*"

Kit cried furiously, "The Hispano was never yours, you horse thief! You stole him from Kurt Tanner!"

"That's right!" Valerie came alive again. "Stealing his horse is one thing, but stealing his woman is another. If you touch her, he'll kill you!"

"Oh, Valerie, be quiet!" Kit cried, seeing the sudden change of expression on Galen's face.

"So! You are his woman!"

"No!" Kit shook her head. "I used to be, but no more!"

Galen slammed his fist into his hand. "That is all I need—to have kidnapped Tanner's woman! He will kill me for sure!"

He turned and ran out of the cave. Kit hissed furiously, "I told you to keep your mouth shut! He was about to let us go. Now he's run away and left us here to die!"

Valerie squeezed her eyes shut and began to tremble from head to toe. "I'm so sorry, Kit. I just thought I was helping. I—"

"Oh, don't cry again!" Kit rolled over onto her back and stared up at the roof of the cave. She tried desperately to think of a way out. Her hands and feet were tightly bound, and although the gag was gone, no one would hear her if she screamed until her throat was raw. Her hands were behind her back, but maybe she could try to free Valerie. "Turn your back to me," she said. "Maybe there's a way out of this after all."

"There is!"

Galen returned, sounding jubilant. Chico and Mendez were behind him. At the snap of his fingers, they picked up the girls and threw them over their shoulders. As they were being carried out of the cave, he bragged, "By the time Tanner finds out you are gone, we will be in Morocco."

"Morocco?" Kit echoed in horror. "Why are you taking us there?"

"Because I am not a fool, *muchacha*. I will not flirt with death twice. When I stole that horse, I didn't know Tanner was a dangerous hombre, just as I didn't know you were his woman. If he catches me now, he will kill me for sure. I'm not waiting around for that to happen."

"Then go!" Kit begged him. "Just leave us here. Taking us along will only slow you down."

"My men demand something for their trouble, so I am taking you to Tangiers to sell you. Sheiks pay much money for Americana women. You should thank me. If I let my men have their way with you, no man would ever want you again. That would make me feel very bad."

Valerie looked as if she was going to faint, but Kit lost her temper. "You think being sold into slavery is a better alternative?"

Galen shrugged. "You will live like a *princesa* in a harem. You lie around a spa or pool all day, looking *delicioso*, waiting for the sheik to take his pleasure. It is not so bad." He grinned and winked.

"Oh, pardon me," Kit said sarcastically. "Now why didn't I see it that way?"

He shook his fist at her. "You have a sharp tongue. Watch yourself, or a sheik will cut it out."

Hearing that, Valerie fainted.

Chapter Thirty-two

KIT was grateful to ride upright behind Galen on Pegasus, although she'd never admit it. Anything was better than bouncing along on her stomach, tied on the back of a horse.

At first she was worried about Valerie, riding behind the ugly Mendez. The first few days she'd seemed to be in a state of shock. Then, almost overnight, a kind of metamorphosis had taken place. Gone was the complaisant, genteel young lady. In her place had emerged a woman doggedly bent on survival. Kit was glad to see the change. It would only help their chances of escaping.

The weather was good, and they rode hard, stopping only to give the horses a rest. Late on the second day, they reached the small town of Lorca. Galen said they would make camp just outside. "We need fresh horses. We still have a long way to go, and they are exhausted."

"Well, so are we!" Kit reminded him tartly. "We haven't had any real food since we left. What are you trying to do? Starve us to death?"

Galen ordered two of his men, Armillito and Carlos, to ride into Lorca and bring back supplies. "But no whiskey!" he yelled, seeing the sudden gleam in

291

their eyes. "We've got a long journey ahead. There is no time for revelry."

The men brought back food as instructed, but they also hid several bottles of whiskey in the rocks near the campsite. Exchanging sly smiles among themselves, all of the men slipped away to take a drink when Galen was not looking.

Kit and Valerie sat close together, as far away from the campfire as Galen would allow them. Kit made a face at the big plate of beans and sausage he handed them and demanded to know what was in it. "Red beans and *chorizo*," he growled. "Eat it."

"What is *chorizo?*" she persisted.

Mendez guffawed. "Blood sausage, *señorita*, made from pig's blood."

Repulsed, Kit flung the plate of food into the bushes. Galen drew back his arm and slapped her across the face, sending her sprawling into the dirt. Valerie screamed and scrambled after Kit, but Galen roughly shoved her away. "I'm sick of both of you! Starve if you wish! But don't be throwing away food that others can eat."

He whirled around and commanded Carlos to take them to the edge of the campsite, gag them, and tie them to trees. "Let the wolves and coyotes get them. I'm tired of their whining. I'm going to get some rest. We leave at first light. I am anxious to get to Morocco and be rid of them."

He picked up his blanket and saddle and strode angrily away from the campsite, calling over his shoulder, "And keep your hands off the women! I'll be watching."

Carlos went to pull Valerie to her feet when suddenly Mendez appeared beside him. "I take care of this one," he growled menacingly.

Carlos shrugged and turned to get Kit, but she sprang up like a shot and went crashing through the brush—straight into the waiting arms of Chico. "Ah, you should not be so eager, *muchacha.*" He laughed, running his hands over her breasts as he twisted her around to hold her tight against him. Pressing his ear against her cheek, he whispered, "Tonight you will be mine, wild one, so save your fire for when I show you what it is like to have a *real* man!"

He slammed a beefy hand over her mouth and held her while Carlos tied and gagged her.

Kit was swept with terror. She didn't know where they had taken Valerie, because she couldn't see or hear her. Darkness fell, and she lay where they had left her, propped against a huge rock just over a ridge and out of sight of the camp. In the distance she could hear the men laughing softly among themselves as they sneaked over to their hidden whiskey cache.

The hours passed with agonizing slowness as Kit lay there in cold dread. While she was confident that Galen wouldn't let anything happen to them, there was always the chance he might sleep too soundly to hear their cries if trouble came.

Suddenly Kit heard a crashing sound in the brush behind her. At first she was terrified it might be a wolf, then she saw Chico step into the pale moonlight. He chuckled drunkenly as he stumbled over to her. Straddling her frantically twisting body, he growled, "I have waited a long time for this." He began to unzip his pants. "You will love it, *muchacha.* You will beg for more." He dropped to his knees, and Kit tried to scream against the choking gag. She thrashed from side to side, but he held her tightly in his grip.

Enjoying her torment, he slowly unbuttoned her

shirt. Finally yanking it open, he gasped aloud at the sight of her naked breasts bathed in the silver moonglow. *"Caramba!* Never have I seen such perfection—"

Suddenly, out of nowhere, Galen leaped at him, wrestling him to the ground. "Son of a whore!" he roared. "I have been waiting for you to show your colors, you *canalla!"*

The two rolled over and over on the ground, groaning and cursing, and the others came running to watch.

Mendez cried, "I am glad I did not touch the golden Americana. Jesus! They will kill each other!"

Suddenly Chico's searching fingers found a sharpedged rock. Galen was on top of him, slamming his head against the ground, when gasping, Chico mustered his last bit of strength and brought the rock down on the back of Galen's head.

Galen crumpled immediately.

A knife appeared in Chico's hand but before he could act, a bullet struck a rock next to him. Chico found himself staring up into the smoking barrel of Armillito's six-shooter. Lips curled in an ominous snarl, Armillito growled between clenched teeth, "There will be no killing this night!"

Chico scrambled to his feet, swiping blood from his broken nose with the back of his hand. Forgetting his saddle, he mounted his horse bareback and quickly disappeared into the night.

When he realized that no one was coming after him, Chico slowed his horse. He was disgusted with himself. Now he had no saddle and no money. Well, he would go back to Valencia. After all, no one knew that he, Chico Dupez, had been involved in kidnapping the Americana women.

But, he mused with a sinister smile, someone might be willing to pay many pesos to learn who *had* been.

Travis Coltrane walked across the parade grounds of the United States Military Academy at West Point, headed doggedly for the post exchange to see if, by some miracle, there might be a letter from Valerie.

The postmaster looked down at the envelope in his hand. The return address was somewhere in Spain, from a Coltrane. The order had come only a month ago that Travis Coltrane wasn't to get any mail from there, either. The postmaster again felt guilty that he had agreed to intercept the boy's mail for pay. What harm would it do for him to get a letter from his sister? If the party paying him ever found out, he could say it slipped by on a day when he was out sick. Still, he hesitated. Then, throwing caution to the wind, he yelled, "Hey, cadet. For you!"

The grin on Coltrane's face as he reached for the envelope was worth more than all the bribe money the postmaster had received.

He'd worry about the consequences later.

Chapter Thirty-three

KIT lost all track of time as they plodded onward. As best she could tell, they had been traveling for over two weeks. When they finally reached Tangiers, with its turreted towers and mosques and narrow, winding *medinas,* she could not help being relieved. Escaping from Galen had been impossible. He had kept her hands tied almost constantly, except when she and Valerie were allowed to bathe and take care of their personal needs. Even while the men were out of sight, they were within hearing distance.

They had traveled the side roads to avoid being discovered. Galen paid the owner of a small boat to take them from Gibraltar, and only when they reached Morocco did he relax.

They arrived late in the day, and Galen found refuge just outside town with a skinny, bearded man named Hashim.

Kit and Valerie were glad finally to be untied, even though they were locked in a small room.

Hashim brought food. "Roast mutton and a mixed pie of vegetables," he explained in answer to their doubtful looks. "My wife, she makes the very best in all of Tangiers."

"Is she a slave trader like you?" Valerie snapped.

His smile faded. "I am an innkeeper, not a slave

trader. Now, you eat, or go hungry. It matters not to me.'' He walked out stiffly, locking the door behind him.

''Our only chance to escape now is by persuading somebody to help us,'' Kit said. ''But we aren't going to get it if you make enemies of everybody we meet.''

''All right. If that's what it takes to find a way out, I'll be friendlier.''

''Good.'' Kit smiled. ''Now let's eat. We need to keep up our strength. It's been a long trip, but at least we'll soon be rid of Galen and his *bandoleros.*''

The next morning Hashim brought more food. Valerie managed to be pleasant, but Kit was unable to wheedle any information from him.

Finally Galen returned in midafternoon, looking very pleased with himself. ''I was right!'' he exclaimed triumphantly. ''Americana women are worth much. An agent for a high caliph who lives in Marrakesh is coming to look at you. But I warn you''—his eyes suddenly darkened—''you do anything to ruin this sale, and you will go on the auction block at the market, where *pervertidos* and *manicomios* buy what the rich do not want. What they do is too ugly to put into words. And remember, that will happen *after* my men have tired of you!''

When he left them, Valerie fearfully asked what those strange names meant.

''Perverts and lunatics,'' Kit told her. ''That isn't going to happen, though, so don't even think about it,'' Kit reassured her. ''Remember we're going to make everyone think our spirit is broken, that we've lost all our fight. Pretend to be docile. That's the key to catching our next captor off-guard.''

The door swung open, and Galen ushered in a huge, fat man dressed in a flowing robe and a turban.

He had a long black beard, and little black eyes. Kit loathed him on sight. With him was another fat man, but this one had kind eyes and looked almost as if he felt sorry for them.

"You see?" Galen gestured. "I told you they are rare pearls. See the beauty of their faces? The smoothness of their skin? They are *magnifico*, no? Go ahead, touch them, feel them. They will not resist." He shot them a warning glare.

The snake-eyed man circled them slowly, as though he were inspecting food for his table. A slow smile spread over his thick, wet lips. "Perhaps you are right. They are ripe." He stopped in front of Kit, his eyes devouring her. "Her breasts are firm and plump. The caliph requires this. She also has cheeks like roses. I'll be able to tell more about her when she is naked."

Kit stiffened.

The man then went to Valerie, and she forced herself to remain perfectly still as he pushed her hair back from her face. "She has skin as fair as the moon in the night sky, and a neck like a gazelle. That is good. But the golden hair!" he exulted. "The caliph will like that very much. I do not believe he has ever had a golden woman in his harem. Has he, Abjar?" He looked at the bald-headed man.

"No, sire." Abjar bowed his head respectfully.

He turned his attention to Kit once more and began to walk around her. "Abjar is one of the high caliph's most trusted eunuchs," he remarked. "He has served the family since he was a child." He suddenly grabbed Kit's face with his fat, stubby fingers and yanked her mouth open. "Teeth like pearls, lush, red lips. I believe he will like her, but I still wish to see her naked before we talk price."

He went to yank open her shirt, but Kit could stand no more. With a swift move, she brought her knee up between his legs. "Keep your goddamn dirty paws off me, you . . . you camel eater!"

Doubling over in pain, he stumbled backward, his eyes bulging. As Galen went to help him, Kit thought she saw Abjar smile.

Galen and Abjar helped the huge man out the door. Just before they disappeared down the hall, Galen yelled that he was going to make Kit wish she were dead.

Kit sank glumly to the floor, sitting with her chin on her hands.

Valerie stood over her, hands on hips. "Docile!" she cried. "You call that acting docile, Kit?"

They looked at each other, and despite their desperate situation, they suddenly broke into hysterical gales of laughter—but only to escape momentarily from the terror they felt.

The cantina was filled with the usual Saturday night crowd, playing poker and gathering at the bar.

One man sat alone at a table in a rear corner. He drank from the bottle of whiskey in front of him, and a cigarette hung from the corner of his mouth. A flickering candle cast his stubbled face in shadows, and the scar at the corner of one eye seemed to twitch ominously. No one dared to bother him, for he looked like an angry panther, ready to spring at first provocation.

Chico Dupez stomped down the rear stairs and glanced curiously at the Americano sitting alone in the shadows. He made his way on to the bar, adjusting his gun holster as he walked. Ordering a drink, he heard the barmaid mention a Mr. Tanner as she slipped around the bar with a cold beer on her tray and headed toward the silent stranger.

Chico went to the far side of the room and leaned back against the wall, looking at the Americano out of the corner of his eye. So that was Kurt Tanner. When he had first returned to Valencia he'd heard that Tanner was searching like a madman for the missing Coltrane girl.

He began to inch his way slowly toward Tanner as he tried to decide whether to betray Galen. He didn't like to betray him to a *gringo,* but without a single peso to his name, honor suddenly didn't seem to matter so much.

Chico stepped away from the wall—and found himself staring into a gun barrel. The Americano's hawkbrown eyes burned with rage. "Who are you, and what the hell do you want?" he demanded.

Chico held his arms up. "Please, *señor,* I only wish to speak with you. I think you will be interested in what I have to tell you."

Kurt nodded to the empty chair. "Sit, and keep your hands on the table. Start talking."

Leaning back in his chair, Chico became smug. "I can help you find what you have been looking for."

Kurt sipped his drink slowly. "I'm listening," he said in a low voice.

Chico leaned across the table. "Do you think it's worth ten thousand dollars in Americano gold to know what became of the red-headed *señorita?*"

Like a shot, Kurt's hand closed around his throat. With one arm he lifted Chico straight up and out of the chair, so high that his boots barely touched the floor. His eyes bulged, and he kicked wildly. "Do *you* think it's worth your life?" Kurt hissed. "Because that's all I intend to give you in exchange."

He held Chico up for a few seconds longer, then let him drop back to the chair. He poured another drink while Chico clutched his throat, coughing and gasping. "Talk," he commanded. "And convince me that you know what you're talking about—or you die."

His voice hoarse and raw, Chico told him everything. When Kurt was sure there was nothing more, he shot him one last look of hatred, then got up and walked out of the cantina.

After galloping straight to his ranch, he threw a few supplies into his saddle bags and collected his best rifle, a shotgun, plenty of ammunition, and several canteens of water. It was a long way to Morocco and, by God, he would be going full speed all the way. He would find Kit no matter how long it took. He felt confident that the *bandido* was telling the truth. All he had to do now was follow the trail and hope he could get to Morocco in time to keep Kit from being sold into slavery.

God help Galen Esmond when he found him, Kurt vowed, the taste of vengeance like blood on his tongue.

He passed Kit's ranch on his way to the main road and looked down on the quiet buildings. Someone was down there, moving around. Kurt saw a lone figure walking from the barn to the house. The figure went inside, and light spilled from a window. Damn, whoever he was, he was making himself right at home!

Slowly Kurt rode down the ridge, then dismounted. Creeping stealthily towards the lighted window, he drew his gun before looking inside.

He saw a man sitting at the kitchen table, his back to the window. His head was resting on his arms.

Kurt crept around to the front door and found it

standing open. He walked into the kitchen. Startled, the man looked up, his eyes swollen and red-rimmed.

"Tanner . . ." he whispered hoarsely. "Thank God! I was going to ride over to your place in the morning," Travis said.

Kurt holstered his gun. "How the hell did you hear about Kit's disappearance? I didn't think she was in touch with her family."

"I didn't know until I got here this morning. I went to the sheriff's office to ask directions to her ranch, and he told me."

Travis stood up. "Will somebody tell me what the hell happened to my sister and my fiancée?"

"Fiancée?" Kurt repeated. Then it dawned on him—the blond girl. He remembered her from the crossing and the inaugural ball.

Travis told him about Kit's letter saying that Valerie was now living with her. He had left for Spain at once. "And this is what I find," he finished despondently. "Both of them gone. Do you know anything at all?" he asked desperately.

Kurt nodded. "As of tonight I do. If you've got a horse, let's ride."

Chapter Thirty-four

GALEN could not remember ever being so angry. There was a great roaring in his head, and he was shaking. "I am so sorry," he said to Jaewal, as he and the eunuch, Abjar, helped him along.

They met Hashim, who opened the door to an empty room. "Lay him on the bed. I will get him whiskey," Hashim said.

Jaewal looked up at Galen. "I will buy her," he declared. "I want to watch the caliph's whip cut into her when he tames her. He will reward me for bringing such a spirited filly to his harem."

"Of course, of course." Galen nodded, greatly relieved. Jaewal called to Abjar, "She deserves the caliph's special punishment, does she not?"

Abjar said nothing. He despised Jaewal. It had been all he could do to keep from exploding in laughter when the one with flaming hair gave him what he deserved.

Offended that Abjar was ignoring him, Jaewal snapped contemptuously, "Pah! What do you know? If it had been you she kicked, you would not have felt it."

Abjar's blank expression did not change, but inside the volcano of hatred grew ever closer to eruption.

"My men and I would like to be on our way, so can we talk about money?" Galen asked.

A few moments later he triumphantly informed Kit and Valerie that he had been right—Americana women did bring top price in the slave market. Then he shook his fist at Kit. "You are lucky. That temper of yours could have ruined everything, but Jaewal says the caliph will enjoy breaking your spirit. I only wish I could be there to hear you scream when the rawhide cuts your arrogant flesh."

Kit shrugged, but Valerie fired back, "And we only wish we could be there to hear you beg for mercy when Kurt Tanner takes his revenge!"

"That will not happen, because I won't be going back to Valencia," he said smugly. "After a few days, I am heading for Portugal to spend my fortune there. So even if Señor Tanner finds out I was responsible for his whore's disappearance, he will never find me!"

Galen tipped his sombrero and flashed them a satisfied grin. *"Adios, muchachas,"* he said, leaving them.

"Where are they going to take us?" Valerie wailed. "Oh, Kit, no one will ever know what became of us!"

They sat in silence, each lost in thought, until Jaewal arrived. He carried a whip, and he snapped it over Kit's head. She glared at him with unflinching, venomous eyes. "I should cut your head off," he growled.

"You just paid for it, I hear," she said with a shrug. "I guess that's your privilege, but if you think I'm going to fall on my knees and beg for mercy, you're wrong."

Jaewal's face reddened. "Hear me, *infidel!*" he screamed. "I will beat you myself till your skin hangs in shreds if you ever try anything like that again! You will obey me, and you will obey Abjar. Now get up. We are leaving.''

He snapped his fingers at Abjar, who walked over woodenly to pull them to their feet. Then he led them downstairs, where Hashim stood watching fearfully. Kit gave him an imploring look, but he only stared at them silently.

"I am not going to tie you," Jaewal said as Abjar lifted them onto the backs of waiting horses, "because if you try to escape, I will just leave you to be auctioned here. And that, I promise you, is a fate worse than death for a woman. The men who bid on slaves know they are getting what the caliphs and sheiks will not have, so they buy them for reasons too ugly to describe. Is that not so, Abjar?''

Abjar grunted.

Hashim dared to whisper, "What he says is true. I have seen women kill themselves before being sold on the block. Obey him. I have heard of the caliph he serves. It is said he is not a bad man. You will fare well in his house if you do as you are told.''

They rode on toward Tangiers. Kit wished she could tell Valerie her idea—that Abjar might be persuaded to help them escape, if only to annoy Jaewal. Maybe she was wrong, but it was their only hope at the moment.

In Tangiers, they were taken to the second floor of a building on a narrow back street. Kit had never been inside a bordello, but she immediately knew that's what it was. Scantily clothed women lounged around smoking cigarettes and sipping whiskey, watching them with mild curiosity as they were shoved down a dimly lit hallway.

At the end of the hall, a plump woman with ratlike eyes motioned them into a big room.

"I leave them with you and Abjar," Jaewal said, sounding relieved. "I have to buy other women, but I return tomorrow morning. Have them ready."

She stared at Valerie and Kit, then nodded at Abjar. "Why is he here?" she asked Jaewal.

"The red-haired bitch is crazy. She needs watching. You might not be able to handle her, and she has cost me many dinar. I take no chance."

"Ha! I wish she would try something with me," the woman said as Jaewal left. She began to circle them, her hands on her hips.

Kit stiffened with resentment, as once again, she was being inspected like a piece of beef. Maybe she was in for a lot of pain, but, by God, she would not give up without a fight. In Spanish, she asked the woman, "Who are you?"

"No habla," was her curt response.

Kit smiled to herself. The woman did not understand Spanish. She asked again in English, and got another negative answer. Kit and Valerie would be able to communicate without Rat Eyes understanding them!

Speaking in fluent French, which the woman understood, Kit learned that her name was Anna Lebance. It was her job, she said, to make slaves ready for presentation to the caliph or sheik who bought them.

She crossed to a small table to get a cigarette, taking a deep gulp from a glass of wine she'd left there. She did not offer them or Abjar anything. "What is done is done," she said. "You would be wise to make things easy on yourself and accept your fate. You are slaves now. If you do as you are told, you will live a good life, much like royalty. You will never lack for anything, except freedom." She shrugged. "But perhaps you will not even miss that. When the newness wears off, you will relax with the other concubines to wait your turn in the sheik's bed. Depending on how many he has, you may not be called to please him too often."

She sighed, pausing to finish her wine. "Let's get busy."

"Doing what? You still haven't told us why we're here, and we have a right to know!"

Kit turned to stare at Valerie, surprised that she could speak French.

"Listen, bitch . . ." Anna Lebance took a menacing step toward Valerie. "I don't have to tell you anything, but you were brought here to get cleaned up for the rich son of a bitch who bought you. I'm not taking any crap from you, understand? I keep those sluts out there in line, and I can handle you little prima donnas, even without help from the big monkey." She nodded to Abjar. He merely stared straight ahead as though he had not heard a word.

"Now strip!" Anna growled.

Kit began to unbutton her shirt. "Do as she says," she whispered in English to Valerie. "Act as if you're scared to death, so they'll think we're beaten. The first chance we get, we'll run."

Valerie began to remove her clothes with shaking fingers. "I don't have to act scared—I am. The thought of some fat, slimy old man pawing me any time he feels like it . . ." She shuddered.

"Shut your mouths, or I will have you gagged," Anna shrieked. "If you think there's a way out of here, you're wasting your time."

When they were naked, Anna circled them again,

boldly patting their bottoms and squeezing their breasts. "Yes, the sheik who bought you will be delighted," she mused aloud. "Seldom do I see such fair skin. Are you virgins? That would have brought an even higher price."

Anna poured herself another glass of wine before going to the door and calling for someone to fill the bathtub with hot water.

Kit noticed that while they stood there naked, Abjar continued to stare straight ahead like a zombie. When Anna left the room to find out what was keeping the girl with the bathwater, Kit covered herself with an afghan and walked over to him. "Abjar," she said gently in French. "You seem like a kind man, with a good heart. You can't condone what is happening to us."

After a long moment, he declared, "One must accept one's fate. It is easier that way."

"Abjar, please . . ." Kit clutched his arm in desperation. He looked at her sharply, and for an instant she thought he was going to push her away. When he did not, she dared to press on. "You're the only chance we have! You must help us escape."

Hearing a sudden commotion, Kit leaped away from Abjar. Anna returned with two prostitutes who were to help with Valerie and Kit's preparations. The girls laughed and joked as they sprayed Kit and Valerie's hair purple. Valerie suppressed a scream when she saw herself in the mirror, and was told that this was an effect the sheiks and caliphs liked very much.

Kit sat perfectly still as her eyebrows and eyelashes were tinted with bluish-gray crystals of galena, her eyelids powdered with lapus lazuli shadow. She and Valerie were pretending complete submission. It was their only hope.

They were given loose-flowing trousers of transparent pink silk, fitted at the ankles with gold cuffs. Their bellies were bare above the sequined waistbands, and golden cups held their breasts. Veils were attached to their hair, but their faces were left exposed.

Valerie watched as one of the girls put rings on her toes, shook her head dismally, sadly. Kit chanced that no one around understood English and urged, "Don't give up. He may help us yet." She cut her eyes toward Abjar, who maintained his zombie pose.

"Even if he doesn't, I still feel sorry for him. I like to think we'll at least have a friend in that zoo."

When they were finally dressed and ready, Anna Lebance brought them hot mint tea and lamb pie. She told them to eat and try to rest, because Jaewal would be coming for them soon.

She started out of the room, pausing before Abjar. "I'm sure I don't have to worry about you spoiling the ladies—in the time they have left." She laughed cruelly as she closed the door.

Abjar's expression changed as soon as she was gone. No longer was he cold and impassive. An angry fire lit his eyes, and he got to his feet with steely determination. Coming over to them, he said, "I will help you. I'll lower you out the window, but before I drop you to the ground, you must knock me out. Jaewal will cut my throat if he discovers that I let you escape."

"You speak English!" Kit gasped.

"Yes," he told her proudly. "There was once an English lady in the caliph's harem, and she taught me to speak her language."

"And you heard everything we said?" Valerie cried.

He nodded. "That is why I decided to risk my life to help you. I knew you truly felt compassion for me. Now go," he ordered suddenly, "before Jaewal comes back."

They ran to the window and stared at the dark silent alley. It was not a terribly long distance down.

"Make your way back to the innkeeper, Hashim. Tell him that if he does not help you make your way back to Gibraltar, I will kill him the next time I see him. He will believe you."

Kit believed him, too. She helped Valerie to go first. Then, when she was about to make her own escape, Abjar solemnly handed her a large brass candlestick. "Hit me with this. Hit me hard. Do not worry, I have a hard head." He almost smiled.

Kit hated to hit him, but she knew it would save him from worse. He turned around, and she brought the candlestick down as hard as she could. With a soft grunt he crumpled to the floor.

Kit turned quickly and jumped out of the window . . . straight into Jaewal's waiting arms.

Struggling furiously, Kit peered through the milky darkness, to see someone holding Valerie, his hand over her mouth. "One of Anna's *kehbehs* heard the eunuch help you escape. She wisely sold her information to me," Jaewal said, an evil smile on his face.

"You can't blame Abjar—he refused to help us. I had to hit him when his back was turned. He may be dead," Kit said.

Her pleas were stifled by a gag. "It doesn't matter whether he helped you or not." Jaewal laughed. "If he lives, I will have something to hold over his head. I have always resented that he is held in high favor with my caliph. Now he will use his influence under my guidance, for his life is now in my hands. As for you two,'' he continued ominously, ''I made a promise, and Jaewal always keeps his promises. At the next auction on the common block, you will be sold!''

He snapped his fingers at the men holding them. ''Take them away. Whatever they bring, hold it for me until I return. I have to see to the stupid eunuch, and start back for the casbah before I have yet more trouble.''

Kit had thought that things could get no worse, but she now knew that the misery was only beginning.

Chapter Thirty-five

THEY were taken through a maze of narrow, crowded streets in a district where the sight of two struggling women, bound and gagged, attracted little attention.

At the end of a long, littered alley, the man dragging Kit suddenly twisted her about to hold her beneath one arm while he unlocked a door. She stared in terror at the gaping black hole beyond, wondering if they were just going to be thrown into some pit to die. Then he reached inside for a lantern, fumbled to light it, and began to pull her down a narrow, stone stairway.

The air was cool and sour-smelling, like rotting garbage, and the farther they descended, the colder and more unpleasant it became. Behind her, in the arms of the other man, Valerie whimpered with each step.

Rounding a sharp curve, they suddenly found themselves in a large chamber, bathed in a sickly mellow light from small hanging lanterns. Kit reeled at the horrible sight before her. Women, sick and dirty, were sprawled on the stone floor. Some wore rags, others were naked. They all had blank expressions on their haggard faces, and their eyes were dull and unseeing.

A huge rawboned woman dressed in black came out of a rear chamber. "American?" she asked the men as they dumped Kit and Valerie on the floor. "Rich blood, too. I can tell. Why are they dressed so fine?" she asked, pointing to their clothes. She yanked away Kit's gag and asked whether she spoke French.

With a furious glare, Kit nodded silently.

"Then hear this!" the woman snapped, not liking the look in Kit's eyes. "I will tolerate no trouble here. My chamber is crowded, as you can see. There has not been an auction recently, but we will have one soon. Till then, find a place to sit, and keep your mouth shut. Some of these women are crazy. If you anger them, they might try to claw your eyes out, and I will not stop them. Understood?"

Kit just continued to glare at her and said nothing. With her golden hair streaked purple, and her eyelids a shimmering blue color, Valerie looked grotesque in the sickly light. She nodded like a puppet, and the woman seemed to see her for the first time. Taking a step closer, she observed, "You are a fragile little thing, aren't you? Perhaps I will take pity on you as I have some of the others, and give you some opium to make it easier."

"No!" Kit cried sharply. "Don't give her any drugs. She'll be fine. Just untie us, and we won't make any trouble. I promise."

The woman shrugged. "Very well. Most of them beg for my favors." She winked suggestively. "Some are willing to do anything to get them."

"Well, I don't want anything from you," Valerie said firmly. "Just leave us alone."

The woman laughed—a horrible, toothless sight. "Oh, I want to be there when you two are sold. Maybe the sheik who buys you will have your teeth pulled, as mine were, to make his pleasure even greater!''

Kit felt sick with fear. When their hands were untied, they quickly picked their way past the women sprawled on the floor to the farthest corner, and sat down.

Valerie clutched Kit's hand and whispered anxiously. ''What are we going to do now? How long are we going to have to stay in this place? What's going to happen to us? Kit, I think I'd rather die!'' She stifled a sob.

Kit squeezed her hand. It was her responsibility to be the braver one, she felt, because it was her fault that Valerie was involved in this nightmare. ''No,'' she told her firmly, ''you wouldn't rather die. Neither would I. We're going to keep our chins up, and no matter what happens, we're going to keep looking for a way out of this madness. We're going to be strong so we'll be ready for our chance when it comes. Abjar helped us. Maybe someone else will, too.''

''If they pull out all my teeth, I'll kill myself!''

''Nobody is going to pull your teeth out. She just said that to scare you.'' Kit wished she could believe her own words.

After a while they slept, hugging each other for comfort. It was cold and damp, and they heard sounds in the shadows like rats scurrying about. Now and then someone would begin crying hysterically, and the toothless woman would administer opium, bringing silence for a while.

They assumed it was morning when some kind of gruel was poured into a wooden trough in the middle of the room. They didn't feel like eating, after they had passed but another hellish day, their hunger drove them to fight for a place at the trough.

Several more women were brought into the chamber the next day, and one of them approached Kit and Valerie. "I heard on the streets that there are two beautiful American women to be auctioned. A crowd is gathering, demanding to see you. The slave master is helping to spread the word, for it is said you will bring high prices," she said, appearing almost envious.

"Thank you for the information," Kit replied dryly.

The girl gave her a strange look and backed away.

"How much longer?" Valerie wailed. "How many days are they going to keep us in this hellhole?"

"Not many," Kit assured. "They don't have that much room left."

Finally, after what Kit calculated had been four days, there was a commotion as a dozen men stomped down the steps and started dragging several women back up. Some screamed in protest, other went docilely, no longer caring what happened to them. The toothless woman supervised with a big whip. Walking over to Kit and Valerie, she taunted, "You two will be the last to go. I hear that never before has such a crowd of bidders assembled at the block, because word has spread that ivory skins are to be auctioned. *I* am even going to be there!"

"How nice," Kit forced a yawn, pretending unconcern.

The women shook her whip menacingly, but did not dare to mar the flesh of her most prized merchandise. "You will get what's coming to you—that I promise."

She walked away, and Valerie huddled yet closer to Kit, unable to hold back her tears any longer. "Please," she wept, "please, God, get us out of this or just let me die."

Kit felt like crying, too, but she refused to give in
to tears. She ground her teeth so tightly that her jaw
ached. It looked as if there was no way out for them.
They were going to be taken up to the auction block
and sold to the highest bidder, and there was nothing
she could do about it. It seemed a lifetime ago that
she had walked in freedom, confident of a happy future. And oh, how she wished she hadn't been so
stubborn, hadn't let Anaya get the best of her. She
now knew beyond all doubt that she loved Kurt. Had
she only fought for him, he would have been with her
that night when Galen came, and—

Kit shook her head, determined she would not
spend the rest of her life mourning what might have
been. Kurt had been right when he said she was
spoiled, but that was a long time ago. She now knew
that she was truly strong, and was determined to survive, no matter what lay in store.

Finally Kit and Valerie were the only ones left.
Two men in turbans and white robes roughly yanked
them to their feet, throwing them over their shoulders
and carrying them up the steps. The toothless woman
pranced along behind them, laughing and taunting.

The sudden glare of daylight was blinding. Blinking, they saw a horde of cheering, turbaned men
reaching out to touch them. Kit saw that Valerie
seemed to have gone into a trance. She was standing
perfectly still, her arms at her sides, her eyes tightly
closed, swaying ever so slightly from side to side.

They stood in the middle of a raised platform. The
auctioneer pulled Kit's arms up high above her head
and forced her to twirl around and around, much to
the delight of the prospective bidders. He announced
happily that she was the diamond, the pearl, of all
womanhood, a beautiful American woman of gentle

birth who would be the crown jewel of any man's
harem.

A booming voice came from the crowd, demanding that she be shown naked. Kit cringed in terror.
Dear God, not that, she prayed furiously. Don't let
them strip me naked in front of all these savages!

Her prayer was answered when the auctioneer declared that such a feast would be offered only to the
one paying the highest price. Amid the cries of protest, he commanded that the bidding begin.

Figures were shouted loudly, but a hush fell suddenly over the crowd as someone in the back roared
that he wished to make an opening bid for the women
as a pair. The amount he offered, Kit realized, was
so high that some of the men actually backed away
from the block, not willing to match it. The auctioneer happily agreed, and the bidding quickly became
frenzied. But no matter how high the offer, the first
bidder raised it.

Again and again the auctioneer forced Kit to parade
around the platform. He thought that Valerie was
drugged, so he allowed her to stand there with her
eyes closed. Kit was so furious that she didn't even
mind stomping around with her hands on her hips,
withering all those hungry eyes with a glare so cold
and vicious that many of the men turned away, decid-
ing that she was a demon from hell. "Buy me!" she
shouted, shaking her fists. "But always be on guard,
lest I cut your throats the first chance I get!"

The crowd grew thinner in the relentless sun. Many
stood under awnings to wait and see what the final
bid would be.

The man who kept raising the price had moved
closer. Kit stared at him in wonder and fright. A man
willing to pay so much for her body must have all

sorts of perverted ideas in mind. He was dressed completely in black, and his eyes could barely be seen through the black cloth that swathed his face. There was another man with him, also mysteriously dressed in black. So they were together, and they would probably take turns with her and Valerie, Kit thought dazedly.

"Sold!" the auctioneer shouted suddenly.

The two men in black walked over to the table beside the block where money was collected.

"Valerie!" Kit nudged her sharply with her elbow. "Come back to life, Dammit! I need you." A desperate plan was forming in her mind.

Valerie looked at her in hopeless silence.

As the auctioneer had strutted around the platform, Kit had noticed that he carried a knife strapped to his ankle. "When I tell you to, pretend to faint." Valerie nodded, willing to try anything.

The auctioneer was at the edge of the platform, watching the men count out their money. Finally he turned and started toward them. Kit whispered, "Now!"

Valerie crumpled to the floor.

Kit screamed and dropped to her knees. Just as she had hoped, the auctioneer came running and knelt beside her. With a lightning-quick movement, Kit slipped the knife from his ankle sheath and concealed it inside her ankle band.

"Get up!" he commanded, shaking Valerie. When she did not respond, he signaled to one of his helpers. "Put her on the back of that horse over there. This one, too. The one who bought her commanded they be tied on their bellies across the horses."

Kit clenched her teeth again. Once more she was going to be tied like a sack of potatoes, and there would be no chance to get to the knife. Still she was comforted by the knowledge that at least she had a weapon now.

They were tied in place and led through the streets of Tangiers once more. Kit wondered where they were going and how long it would take, all the while itching to plunge her knife into the flesh of the arrogant bastard who thought he'd bought her body and soul.

The day wore on, and then shadows began to fall. The two men leading them did not speak as they continued to plod on relentlessly.

Finally they stopped. Kit tensed. She would have one chance, and one chance only. She would stab the man who untied her, then take the other by surprise and stab him, too. What happened then, where they would run to, Kit did now know, for she had no idea where they were. But it did not matter. They would be free.

She felt her ankles being untied. Then her captor walked around to the other side of the horse to free her wrists. She got ready to drop to her feet and grab the knife from its hiding place, to cut him the instant he came back around.

Just as she was freed, strong hands suddenly caught her waist from behind. The other man was holding her! Kit knew that it was now or never. She threw herself forward, taking him by surprise. Grabbing the knife, she brought it up and around to plunge the blade into his throat . . . and froze!

"Dammit, Kit, you're dangerous!"

Kurt's hand locked around her wrist, holding it firmly as he gathered her in his arms for a kiss that seemed to last forever. She felt faint, sure that it had to be a dream. Her mind must have finally snapped in the wake of all the horror and madness.

Then she heard Valerie scream with joy and call Travis's name. She knew that it was real—Kurt was actually holding her, and, dear God, it was wonderful!

Kurt kissed her until she was breathless, then they were both laughing at the same time as he tried to explain how it had all happened—how they had ridden like the very devil to get to Tangiers only to lose their trail until they heard of the innkeeper, Hashim. It had not taken much persuasion for him to confide that he had seen the American women, one with hair like sunshine, the other like sunrise. Finally, once they heard about the auction of two American beauties, they knew they'd found them.

"We just decided to buy you," Kurt said matter-of-factly. "Rather than get in a fight."

Stunned by the wonder of it all, Kit stammered, "But . . . but how did you happen to have so much money?"

He and Travis looked at each other and laughed. Then Kurt said, "Well, we ran into a certain Spanish outlaw who tried to buy his way out of a real bad situation, and he just happened to have sold a couple of American women."

Epilogue

THEY stood together on a knoll overlooking the river in front of Kit's ranch, beneath the protective arms of a cottonwood tree. The groom was strikingly handsome in a gray suit, and he gazed down adoringly at his bride, an ethereal vision of loveliness in white lace.

The priest heard their vows and spoke the words that declared them man and wife.

Kit and Kurt kissed each other with such passion that they drew sighs from several of those in the small crowd. Then they moved away to share a moment of intimacy before receiving congratulations and good wishes.

Jade had stood with Colt, watching in silence. She was happy for Kit, but was preoccupied with another matter.

She watched as Travis held Valerie's hand and gazed down at her, both of them oblivious to everyone around them. Jade sighed with resignation. The time had come for her to tell the truth. She had to share her nightmare to prevent another one occurring—there was no other way.

She and Colt had been about to leave for their cruise around the world when West Point officials notified them that Travis had abruptly left the Academy. It did

not take long to learn that he'd booked immediate
passage for Europe; neither did it take long to learn
his ultimate destination. So they had followed, arriving only the day before to learn what had happened.
It would be impossible, Jade knew, to separate Valerie and Travis again. She had no choice but to tell
Valerie why they could never marry, and hope that
the girl would do the honorable thing and never reveal
the reason.

Just then someone announced that champagne and
wedding cake were being served on the porch, and
everyone began to move in that direction. Jade waited
until she saw Travis leave Valerie's side to get her
refreshments, then Jade approached her.

Valerie paled when she saw Jade.

"We must talk," Jade said tightly.

Valerie stiffened and shook her head firmly. "No,
Mrs. Coltrane, I won't let you intimidate me again.
I've been through hell and back, and I've grown up.
No one is going to stand in our way now."

"Hear me out, please."

Valerie saw the tears in her emerald eyes and sensed
her desperation. "All right," she said quietly. "But
I warn you, there's nothing you can do to change my
mind."

Jade began to talk hurriedly and Valerie's blue eyes
seemed to grow wider and wider. When Jade had finished explaining that she could never marry Travis
because he might be her half brother, Valerie did not
know whether to laugh or cry. "So that's why you
hated me?" she cried, incredulous. "Oh, Mrs. Coltrane, how I wish you had told me all of this sooner!"

Jade blinked, unnerved by her reaction. "You must
never tell a soul—"

"No, no, you don't have to worry about that,"

Valerie assured her. "Bryan Stevens is not my real father!"

Jade swayed in sudden shock. "Child, don't lie to me," she begged hoarsely. "Please don't lie. I know that you love my son, but it just can never be. The risk is too great!"

"No!" Valerie shook her head violently. "You're wrong. Listen to me, please. I can't do anything about your fear that Bryan Stevens may have fathered Travis and Kit. God knows, I hope it's not so, but you can stop worrying about me being Travis's half sister, because Bryan Stevens in *not* my real father."

"What are you saying?" Jade gasped.

"I never knew anything about your being involved with him. No one ever told me anything. All I knew was that a long time ago, my mother thought he was dead, and she was so heartbroken that she started drinking and hanging out in waterfront bars. She took up with men and eventually got pregnant . . . with me. My real father was a sailor, and quite frankly . . ." Valerie swallowed with difficulty. "I'm not sure she even knew which one he was. But when Bryan Stevens showed up again, he took pity on her and married her. He gave me his name and promised her he'd raise me as his own daughter, which he did. I never wanted for anything—except love, which he didn't seem to be able to give. In fact, I might never have known the truth if he hadn't gotten drunk one night and told me everything."

Jade's heart went out to Valerie, and she felt terrible to have caused her so much pain. "Valerie, can you ever forgive me?" she choked out.

"Oh, yes," the girl fervently assured her, "and your secret will be safe with me forever."

They hugged each other, laughing and crying at

once. Colt saw them and hurried over, and Jade quickly told him that Valerie was adopted. A great weight seemed to lift from his shoulders, as he, too, embraced Valerie and welcomed her into his family and his heart.

Travis began to run toward them, not knowing what was going on. When he heard that Jade had made peace with Valerie, his gray eyes glistened with tears of joy, and he pulled Valerie close.

Jade felt blessed relief for her son and her daughter. Their pain and misery were ending, and their lives of joy just beginning.

But what of her own?

What of the doubts she had harbored all these years?

Colt put his arm around her, and her heart warmed as always at his nearness. She loved him more with each beat of her heart, had never doubted his devotion to her.

Suddenly the years ahead loomed bright and promising. She looked at her children again. Grown though they were, they were forever children in her heart.

They were Coltranes, if not by blood then surely by spirit.

And love.

And honor.

That was all that would ever matter.

The Timeless Romances
of *New York Times* Bestselling Author

JOHANNA LINDSEY

*If you enjoyed this book, take advantage
of this special offer. Subscribe now and . . .*

GET A *FREE*
HISTORICAL ROMANCE
—— NO OBLIGATION(a $3.95 value) ——

Each month the editors of True Value will select the four best historical
romance novels from America's leading publishers. Preview them in
your home Free for 10 days. And we'll send you a FREE book as our
introductory gift. No obligation. If for any reason you decide not to keep
them, just return them and owe nothing. But if you like them you'll pay
just $3.50 each and save at least $.45 each off the cover price. (Your
savings are a minimum of $1.80 a month.) There is no shipping and
handling or other hidden charges. There are no minimum number of
books to buy and you may cancel at any time.

send in the coupon below

Mail to:
True Value Home Subscription Services, Inc.
P.O. Box 5235
120 Brighton Road
Clifton, New Jersey 07015-1234

YES! I want to start previewing the very best historical romances being published today. Send
me my FREE book along with the first month's selections. I understand that I may look them
over FREE for 10 days. If I'm not absolutely delighted I may return them and owe nothing.
Otherwise I will pay the low price of just $3.50 each; a total of $14.00 (at least a $15.80 value)
and save at least $1.80. Then each month I will receive four brand new novels to preview as
soon as they are published for the same low price. I can always return a shipment and I may
cancel this subscription at any time with no obligation to buy even a single book. In any event
the FREE book is mine to keep regardless.

Name _____

Address _____ Apt. _____

City _____ State _____ Zip _____

Signature _____
   (if under 18 parent or guardian must sign)
Terms and prices subject to change.
                                              75557-2A

THE MAGNIFICENT NOVELS BY
NEW YORK TIMES BESTSELLING AUTHOR
KATHLEEN E. WOODIWISS

Her Newest Bestseller
SO WORTHY MY LOVE   89817-8/$10.95 US/$12.95 Can
An Avon Books Trade Paperback

COME LOVE A STRANGER   89936-1/$4.95 US/$6.50 Can
To Ashton, she was Lierin, the enchanting bride he had carried
home to the family plantation. But to another man, she was
Lenore, the bride he dragged through a nightmare of dark
passions and murder. Confused and afraid, she remembered
nothing. Who she was, nor the horrors she had suffered—or the
two men who now fought to claim her.

A ROSE IN WINTER   84400-1/$4.95 US/$6.50 Can
This passionate, haunting story of love and vengeance set in
18th-century northern England tells of Erienne Fleming, a
raven-haired beauty torn between loyalty to her deformed but
loving husband and the handsome, witty Yankee who has
captured her heart.

ASHES IN THE WIND   76984-0/$4.95 US/$5.95 Can
Dark-haired Alaina MacGaren, orphaned by the Civil War is
forced to flee her family's plantation. Masking her beauty under
the disguise of a ruffian youth, she stows away aboard a
riverboat bound for New Orleans, where she finds passion and
love in the arms of a handsome Yankee surgeon.

SHANNA   38588-0/$4.50 US/$5.95 Can
THE WOLF AND THE DOVE   00778-9/$4.50 US/$5.50 Can
THE FLAME AND THE FLOWER 00525-5/$4.95 US/$5.95 Can

AVON Books